THE SERIES IN ORDER:

For St. Patrick, who turned the superstitious into the faithful; and for all others like him.

CHAPTER 1

The Husband must not be made aware. This, above all.

*D*etective Sergeant Kathleen Doyle listened-in as Detective Sergeant Isabella Munoz spoke to their Senior Investigating Officer over her mobile phone. The two detectives were driving out to Lambeth to investigate a possible homicide, and Officer Gabriel was giving them what few details he could.

"Dispatch says female in her late twenties; no obvious cause of death. I wish I knew more, but I was just assigned as SIO and so I'm not up-to-speed."

"What have you done to DI Williams?" Doyle joked. Inspector Thomas Williams was her usual SIO, and so it was a surprise that they were hearing from Gabriel, instead.

"The estimable DI Williams has been pulled onto another case, and so I'm afraid you are left to deal with my own lesser endeavors."

"Williams never talks fancy to us," Doyle protested. "We're simple creatures, Gabriel."

"Right. Well—someone's been killed; please solve the case so that I look good."

Doyle smiled. "Got it."

"We'll make a preliminary report as soon as we've done the initial assessment, sir," Munoz offered in a more formal tone. Munoz was in no mood to joke-about with Gabriel.

"Thank you, Sergeant. I'll send a back-up unit for additional support. The officers on the scene say there are spectators gathering, and I'm not a big fan of Lambeth spectators."

"Thank you, sir," said Munoz. "No information on cause-of-death?"

"No. The field-unit says no wounds, no weapons—but for whatever reason, they're worried enough to call-in Homicide. The Coroner's team should meet you there."

As Munoz signed off, Doyle offered, "Drugs, I bet." The victim had been found in a London neighborhood that was somewhat notorious for drug-trafficking. The initial call reported that a vagrant—who'd been looking for bottles in the rubbish bins— discovered the body, and had gone to ask a nearby shopkeeper to phone the police, since he didn't own a mobile phone. The field-unit was holding the vagrant on the scene for questioning.

"Probably drugs," Munoz agreed. "If there's no obvious cause-of-death she may have overdosed."

Doyle nodded. She was easing back into work after taking maternity leave, and she'd been assigned to be Munoz's "assist" today, which was no easy task, since the other detective didn't want to hear about other people's babies, just now. Munoz had been trying to get pregnant, and—even though she was young, and there was still plenty of time for it—Munoz was not used to not having her way. As a result, Doyle found they'd precious little to talk about, since wrangling babies was all she'd been doing lately—her second son was just a few months old.

But it seemed that Munoz had found another likely topic, as she glanced over at Doyle. "Are you going to Savoie's wedding?"

In all wonder, Doyle replied, "How can I *not* go to Savoie's weddin'? It's the eighth wonder of the world—it's like bein' invited to the partin' of the Red Sea."

"Definitely didn't see that one coming," Munoz agreed with a small smile.

Philippe Savoie was one of London's more notorious criminal kingpins, and—in a completely unexpected turn of events—the lifelong bachelor was going to marry Mary Howard, Doyle's former nanny. Munoz had dated Savoie herself for a short time before she fell for her husband—an Irish Inspector who'd come to work at the CID on loan. And because she was very content with her own husband, the Spanish beauty harbored no ill feelings on the subject, and wished the couple well.

Munoz glanced at Doyle again. "I wish I'd been invited—although I suppose that would have been awkward."

"Mary said they're keepin' it very small," Doyle explained. "And I think she's a bit embarrassed that she's marryin' again so fast." The nanny had been already twice-widowed—unfortunately—with her second husband dying less than a year ago, and under tragic circumstances.

With a thoughtful air, Munoz observed, "You know, Doyle, I think Savoie's liked Mary for a long time. When I was with him, he used to talk about her a lot."

"Faith, is that so?" Thoroughly bemused, Doyle shook her head. "It's amazin', truly; Mary's not even tryin', but she's had no trouble attractin' men—and from all walks o' life, I might add."

"She's got that 'Madonna' thing going on," Munoz offered. "It's a shame we can't bottle it up and sell it."

But Doyle only smiled. "There's no controllin' love, Munoz, and I might point out that no one knows this better than your fair self."

"Point taken. Although I wish Gabriel would take that point, too."

Officer Gabriel—their SIO, on this case—had been another one of Munoz's conquests before she'd met her husband, and from what Doyle could discern, Gabriel still seemed to be pining after what might-have-been, even though he was careful never to make it obvious. But Doyle's "discernments" were usually spot-on; she was what the Irish would call "fey," which—in her case, at least—meant she'd a perceptive ability that allowed her to read the emotions of the people around her. And as a result of this ability, she could usually tell when someone was lying, which was a useful sort of talent to have when one was a homicide detective who dealt with lying liars on a daily basis.

Her perceptive ability was a well-guarded secret, though; Doyle's husband, Chief Inspector Acton, knew of it, and tended to be very protective of her. Small blame to him, as one could only imagine the repercussions if the public-at-large became aware that Doyle was a walking truth-detector. Indeed, in the past, Acton had gone to great lengths—some of them a bit questionable—to make sure that any rumors about Doyle's remarkable "hunches" were thoroughly quashed. And it was a good thing that he was vigilant on her behalf—they'd weathered a few close calls, and Doyle wasn't one to be quick on her feet; it was lucky that she'd a doting husband who was.

The only other person who was aware of Doyle's perceptive abilities was Doyle's good friend Thomas Williams, and because of this, Acton tended to assign Williams as her Senior Investigating Officer so that he could handle any problems that might arise—which happened sometimes, due to the aforementioned unquickness-on-her-feet. But—in this instance, at least—Acton must have needed Williams elsewhere, and so she'd best watch herself and be extra-careful; Officer Gabriel—for all his joking-about—was a mighty shrewd boyo.

Doyle was recalled to the conversation when Munoz continued, "Gabriel never says anything—he always keeps it professional. But you can just tell—you know? And I can't avoid him, especially when he's my SIO."

"Aye," Doyle agreed. "You'd think that torch would be well-and-thoroughly doused, by now. Faith, I'm amazed that he still hangs about and festers that wound; if Acton had married someone else, I'd be well-away by now. No sense in yearnin' after someone you can't have—it seems like a recipe for perpetual misery."

Munoz made a derisive sound. "That's easy for you to say—Acton's not going to dump you any time soon."

This was true, in that Doyle was rather famously married to her husband. Chief Inspector Acton was something of a legend at Scotland Yard, and—as part-and-parcel of his mystique—he'd been reclusive and anti-social, until—to everyone's astonishment—he'd suddenly married his young support officer. Truth to tell, Doyle had been just as astonished as everyone else, and now—as a result of this epic case of marrying-in-haste—Doyle now held an English title or two, and lived rather uneasily in the lap of luxury.

"Gabriel just needs to meet someone new, and get over it. Everyone's had to, at one time or another."

"Aye," Doyle agreed, even though she couldn't relate—her husband was her one and only foray into romance, being as she'd been shy by nature before Acton bundled her off to the altar. "I suppose it's a shame we can't bottle-up an antidote for love, too."

"We'd make a fortune," the other agreed in a dry tone, as she parked the unit at the taped-off perimeter, and set the gear-shift. "Instead, it's our job to sort-out the fallout."

"Not in this case, at least," Doyle replied. "Doesn't sound like there was a jealous lover—sounds like an overdose, instead."

"Interesting that they called-in Homicide," Munoz agreed. "I guess we'll see why; will you do the video-record?"

"Yes, ma'am," said Doyle, with a touch of irony. Since she was the assist, she'd be the dogsbody in the case and at Munoz's beck-and-call. Such things used to rankle, but Doyle was less and less interested in climbing the career ladder, nowadays. It was a strange turn of events, that Munoz was now envying Doyle's path when it used to be the other way 'round.

Despite the fact that the weather was questionable—they were lucky to have a break in the rain—when they approached the PCs who'd been stationed to guard the crime scene, Doyle noted that there was indeed a small crowd that had gathered to silently look over the crime scene. This particular neighborhood tended to be low-income minority, with a full measure of immigrants amongst them—mainly from West African or Caribbean areas. Which made it doubly-interesting that a young Caucasian woman would be found dead in an alley; the initial report said there was no indication it was a body-dump, which would be the first assumption—that she'd been killed elsewhere, and dumped here.

Doyle followed Munoz as they threaded through the gathering, and realized—to her surprise—that many of the citizens that stood and watched the proceedings were wary—wary and rather silent. So mayhap this wasn't an ordinary overdose, after all; in the usual course of things, the onlookers would be speculating amongst themselves as to what had happened. Mayhap they already knew.

Prompted by this possibility, she suggested to Munoz in a low voice, "We should do a canvass."

"We will; let's see what we can find out, first."

This, of course, only made sense, and Doyle reminded herself to button her lip instead of blurting out whatever happened to cross her mind.

The PC who'd called for Homicide approached—a blond Caucasian man, which was rather interesting because Dispatch usually tried to match ethnicities, when they sent the Yard's finest out to the various neighborhoods in London.

"What do we have, Constable?" Munoz asked him, as she gazed beyond him at the crime scene.

"A female in her late twenties, ma'am. Time-of-death not clear. No blood, no sign of a wound, no signs of a struggle; possible overdose."

Munoz frowned slightly. "If she was here looking for drugs, it seems odd that she'd overdose on the spot."

"Yes, ma'am," the officer conceded.

With some surprise, Doyle noted that the PC was nervous, but was making a mighty effort to disguise this fact.

Munoz pulled on her gloves, as she thoughtfully looked over the immediate area. "Robbery?"

"No; she still has her handbag and her wallet—cash and credit cards inside."

Munoz raised her brows, as this was unexpected; even if the killer hadn't robbed the victim, it would be far too tempting for the other locals to resist. "Well, that's interesting. Do we have an ID?"

The officer paused. "As a matter of fact, ma'am, she has a Met ID."

Both Doyle and Munoz turned to stare at him. "She's a *Met* employee?"

"Yes. ID says Mallory Flynn."

After a surprised moment, Doyle surreptitiously touched Munoz's elbow.

Munoz said to the PC, "All right; let's have a look."

Doyle followed her with the video tablet running, both detectives stepping carefully so as to disturb the scene as little as possible. They then crouched down to look over the decedent. Mallory Flynn was an attractive brunette, peacefully lying on her back as though she'd decided to take a nap, here in this dodgy alley, save that her eyes were open, the pupils fixed as she stared sightlessly at the sky. The state of her rigor mortis indicated she hadn't been dead for more than a couple of hours, and around her neck hung the security card that was required whenever anyone was on-premises at Scotland Yard.

"What is it?" Munoz asked Doyle in an undertone.

"I think we need to call-in Acton," Doyle advised, in the same quiet tone. "This victim worked the tip-line at the Met, and she was implicated in the Public Accounts case." They'd just weathered a major scandal, where various government bureaucrats had been engaged in a wide-ranging embezzlement scheme.

But Munoz was skeptical. "This doesn't seem related to that, Doyle."

Since Doyle couldn't very well speak of the silent, wary crowd —or of the flutterings of fear that she could sense in the PC, she added lamely, "It just seems a huge coincidence."

Munoz glanced at her, sidelong. "Was a case-file ever opened on her with respect to the Public Accounts case?"

Doyle confessed, "I don't know."

Munoz continued to scrutinize the body. "It seems likely that she was cleared of any wrongdoing. Why would she still be working at headquarters, if they thought she was bent?"

Again, Doyle confessed, "I don't know."

Munoz rose, and Doyle followed suit as Munoz directed the PC, "The Coroner's team should be here soon. Since she's one of our own, let's call for SOCOs, although I'm not sure there's much they can do."

The Scene of Crime Officers were the ones who collected forensic evidence, but in this case—a cluttered and dirty alleyway, with no blood or weapons evidence to collect—they'd have precious little to do. And it would be impossible to meaningfully process the general area around the victim, since there would be no way to segregate evidence that might be useful from evidence that was not.

Munoz continued, "In the meantime, I'd like the second unit to start a canvass, to weed-out potential witnesses for questioning." This preliminary sift-through was often necessary because anyone who'd been even tangentially involved in such a shocking event tended to overstate their own importance, or regale the officers with speculation which wasn't at all helpful. Field officers were adept at sorting through the witnesses so as to separate the wheat from the chaff.

"Yes, ma'am."

Munoz glanced around. "The reporting witness is being held where?"

"I moved him into the back of my unit, ma'am."

"Good. We'll get to him in a minute."

The two detectives then retreated away from the others so as to confer in private. "Did you notice that he buried the lede?" Munoz immediately asked Doyle.

"I'm not sure what that means," Doyle confessed.

"You'd think the first thing he'd report when he called it in, was that she worked for the Met."

"Oh," said Doyle, and resisted a mighty urge to glance over at the aforesaid PC. "You're right."

"And she shouldn't be wearing her security lanyard when she's off-premises."

"Oh," said Doyle again. Then, to show she wasn't wholly oblivious, she added, "I thought it was a little odd that Dispatch would send him here in the first place—he's not a match for this area."

"True," Munoz agreed. "Although it may just be that he was out in the field, and was the closest unit." She then drew-down her brows. "I'd hate to call-in Acton if this is just an overdose in an alley. I'm up for a promotion, and I don't want him to think that I lack confidence."

"There's not a soul alive who thinks you lack confidence, Munoz," Doyle pointed out a bit dryly. "And I truly think Acton should have a look—we can say we called him in because the decedent is one of our own."

Munoz nodded. "Right—that's a good point. Do you want to call?"

"You should," Doyle deferred. "It's protocol."

Munoz duly phoned Acton, and was put through. "Hallo, sir; I am at a potential homicide scene in Lambeth with DS Doyle, and it appears the decedent is an employee at the Met—Mallory Flynn." She waited a beat, listening, and then said, "Very good, sir."

She rang off, and said to Doyle, "He'll be here soon. He agrees that we should handle it with the highest priority." She blew out a breath. "I'm relieved; he sounded like he meant it."

Doyle didn't mention that it was far more likely that Acton wanted to take a gander so as to see if anything needed to be whitewashed for the press, and instead assured the other girl, "He thinks you're very competent, Munoz, and I'm not just sayin' it."

The other girl slid her gaze Doyle's way. "Any news on the next round of promotions?"

"He doesn't tell me that sort of thing," Doyle confessed. "He knows I'm a weak link."

Munoz nodded as though this was completely understandable, and moved toward the field unit's vehicle. "Right. Let's go interview the reporting witness."

CHAPTER 2

He'd never seen The Red-Haired Policewoman before, but he recognized her immediately. Careful.

A s they approached the field vehicle, the PC came over to advise, "The Coroner's team is delayed a little; they said the original team was preempted, and so another one is being dispatched."

Munoz nodded—there was no rush, after all, now that the scene had been secured—and then she and Doyle climbed into the field unit so they could interview the reporting witness in private. He was a thin little Hispanic man, wearing a worn coat that was too large for him, and sporting a shabby watchman's cap perched atop his balding head. He also smelled a bit ripe, which prompted Doyle to casually crack-open the vehicle's window.

Munoz introduced them, and then asked, "Your name is Alfonso?"

The man nodded. "*Si.*"

Munoz asked him something in Spanish, and he replied in a soft tone, "No; I can speak English, good enough."

"I believe you are the person who found the victim, this morning."

"*Si*," the man said, and then self-consciously corrected, "Yes."

"Tell us what happened."

"I look in this alley for bottles—it is the day before the rubbish is collected, which is the best day." He nodded at her, in a savvy manner. "I take them to the recycling center on Gipsy Hill. They know me there."

"And what time did you find her?" Munoz asked, because the witness was going a bit off-course.

"Close to five o' clock this morning. I come early, because Ronaldo, he will collect them too, and so I must come early to beat him." He smiled in triumph, which revealed that a fair number of his teeth were missing. "I saw this *gringa*, lying there. I went over to the grocer and I asked him to call the police."

"Did you see anyone else in the area?"

He shook his head. "No, no."

"No one at all?" Munoz persisted.

The little man cocked his head, and admitted, "I saw some— some—" he searched for the word, and then said to Munoz, "*fantasmas*."

There was a pause, and then Munoz explained to Doyle. "Ghosts."

"Yes," the man nodded. "Ghosts."

And here we go, thought Doyle. It wasn't surprising, perhaps, that this poor fellow wasn't necessarily in full possession of his faculties.

"What were the ghosts doing?" Munoz asked, as though this was a routine question.

The man shrugged his thin shoulders. "They were sorry that she was dead, but she was—" he gestured with his hands, searching for the words "—*en busca de problemas*."

"She was looking for trouble," Munoz translated for Doyle. "Have you ever seen her before?"

"No, no."

"Then how do you know she was looking for trouble?"

He seemed surprised. "The ghosts told me."

Munoz decided that she may as well ask. "Did the ghosts mention who killed her?"

"No, no." He shook his head with regret.

"Thank you," Munoz said. "How can we contact you, if we need to speak with you again? Where do you sleep?"

The little man lowered his gaze and shrugged. "Here-and-there."

Doesn't want to let the police know too much, thought Doyle, and felt a stab of pity, thinking of him wandering about in the cold weather . She offered, "There's a church over in Chelsea—St. Michael's. If you need anythin', just ask for Father John, and say Officer Doyle sent you."

"Thank you," he said courteously. "The Red-Haired Policewoman." He smiled, and showed his questionable teeth again.

Doyle smiled in response. "Aye—that's right. He'll see to you."

They released the man, and as they watched him gather up his bags of bottles, Munoz remarked, "I wish we could interview the ghosts."

"I doubt they'd tell us much," said Doyle, who knew of which she spoke. "Should we see if any of the bystanders knows anythin'?"

"Yes—although it seems unlikely. She's not from this neighborhood, and people wouldn't have been around that early."

Doyle looked over toward the back entrance of the grocer's—a cramped little shop that was typical in these neighborhoods. "The shopkeeper may have seen something, if the shop opens early."

"Or heard something; let's go see."

The shopkeeper was another Hispanic man, who greeted the

police officers with great interest. "Do you know what happened to the *gringa*?"

"We're investigating just that," Munoz explained. "Tell me how you found out about her."

"Alfonso, he came in to tell me to call the police." The man made a face. "Sometimes the *gringos* come around here to buy drugs."

"Do you sell drugs?" Munoz asked in a polite tone.

"Oh—oh no, no," the man replied, waving his hands, so as to emphasize this fact.

"Did you go look at the girl?" asked Munoz.

"I did—I didn't come too close, just enough to see that there was a dead *gringa*, like he said. So, I phoned the police."

"Did you hear anything this morning? Or see anything unusual?"

"No—Alfonso came along just after I opened, at five."

"Did you notice any vehicles, driving away? Or hear anything in the back alley?"

He shrugged. "I did not notice—I had not gone into the back of the shop, as yet. I come in by the front door when I open."

The two detectives then walked outside, so as to interview the bystanders that the PCs had weeded out. The first witness—an African man, who sported a Kingsmen football cap—offered the information that the dead woman may have been a drug dealer, because he'd seen her in the alley before. "She sells bottles," he added, indicating their size with his fingers.

"Right, then," Munoz said to the fellow. "I'm not here to go after you, right? I investigate homicides. Can you tell me if you've bought drugs from her in the past?"

"No," the man said, shaking his head. "She does not sell to me. She only sells to the *cholos*."

This was interesting to Doyle, since his pronouncement rang true even though drug dealers were not known to discriminate based on ethnicity—not to mention the victim was Caucasian, and therefore it wouldn't make much sense.

Munoz continued, "Who would kill her? Was she fighting with anyone?"

The witness shook his head. "I do not know enough; the *cholos*, they are the ones who would know.""

But no other witnesses—Hispanic or otherwise—proved to be helpful, and the two detectives were met with disclaimers and denials that anyone had personally interacted with the decedent.

Once again, they stepped aside to confer, and Munoz said, "I think that first witness must have been mistaken; I think it's unlikely she was selling drugs in this neighborhood—much more likely she was buying."

"Aye," Doyle agreed, since what the bystanders had said was true—no one had interacted with the decedent. Of course, anyone who knew anything might be lying low, but again, it seemed unlikely that this sort of victim would be frequenting this sort of neighborhood.

Thoughtfully, Munoz offered, "I think there's more to this than everyone's letting on. I get the sense everyone knows something, but they're not saying."

"Wary, they are," Doyle agreed. "Seems as though there's a code of silence in place."

The other girl blew out a breath. "Let's get a timeline started, at least. Once the Coroner narrows down time-of-death, we'll take a look at the CCTV film." She lifted her head to review the city's closed-circuit cameras, which were mounted atop the nearby streetlamps. "We should have a pretty good view of what happened from that one—make a note."

"Yes, ma'am," Doyle replied, like a dutiful support officer. She was reconciled to having to review the CCTV film—usually a tedious slog, but in this case it should be somewhat interesting, since they'd no idea what had happened and it should be easy to narrow down the field-of-search.

"Here's the Coroner's team," Munoz noted. "Let's check-in."

As they watched the team personnel alight from their van, Doyle realized that one of them was a familiar figure who she'd met twice before. Yandra Corso was the Coroner's Assistant who'd been stationed at the central London morgue when Doyle had visited on two very memorable occasions; she'd come in each time hoping to ID a Jane Doe, only to find out that the unidentified decedent was someone she'd known personally.

From a distance, the young woman greeted Doyle with a nod of recognition, and Doyle thought—well, that's interesting; I think she's nervous, too, and she's not one who gets nervous easily.

"Let's get them briefed," Munoz said, and Doyle duly followed her over, wondering—a bit uneasily—why it seemed that the law enforcement personnel were more rattled by this death than the onlookers were.

CHAPTER 3

He shuffled away, before The Husband or The Foolish Child could catch sight of him.

"*H*allo again, Ms. Corso," Doyle greeted the Coroner's Assistant in a friendly tone, hoping to ease her nerves. "Are you workin' in the field, now?"

The young woman answered, "Not usually; I was called-in for this one."

This seemed a reference to the fact she was of Hispanic heritage —apparently Dispatch tried to match Coroner's teams, too—and Doyle offered, "Well, I'm glad you've come down from your castle, because I'm that reluctant to go anywhere near your morgue again, bein' as I'm always trippin' over acquaintances." Doyle then explained to Munoz, "I've wandered in twice to Ms. Corso's morgue, only to find out that the Jane Doe was someone I knew."

"You're bad luck, Doyle," Munoz pronounced. "I always knew it."

"Or good luck, since we wound-up solvin' the cases," Doyle defended herself.

"Tell that to the dead people," Munoz countered.

Corso interrupted, "I should get started—I understand the Chief Inspector will be on-site, soon."

Oh—small wonder she's nervous, Doyle realized. The last time they'd met, Acton had interrogated the worthy Ms. Corso something fierce, and she was no doubt hoping to avoid a similar experience today by having her answers already in hand. Therefore, in a reassuring manner Doyle advised, "He will, indeed. This poor victim is one of our own, from the Met. We don't know much, and we're waitin' for a time-of-death so as to get the ball rollin'."

Corso nodded. "I will get started straightaway, Officer Doyle."

"Officer Munoz is the lead," Doyle corrected gently. "Sorry, I should have made it clear."

"Not a problem," said Munoz; "but if you would proceed."

As the young woman returned to the van to instruct the others, Doyle thought with some sympathy that she wouldn't have pegged Corso as the nervous type—she'd been competent and self-assured, in the morgue. She was probably a laboratory-bee, so to speak, and wasn't comfortable out in the wild.

The Coroner's team had just begun their work when Acton's Range Rover pulled up, and—as was his habit—he spent a few minutes speaking to the PCs who were posted on the perimeter; not necessarily because he was trying to boost morale, but because they often had helpful insights about the crime scene, or the witnesses.

After he finished his conversation, he approached Munoz. "Sergeant," he said, and then nodded to his wedded wife. "Sergeant."

"Sir," said Doyle, and thought her police-officer voice sounded very professional, considering they'd had a very satisfying bout of early-morning sex a few short hours ago. Acton was very much a sex-to-start-the-day sort of husband.

Acton turned to Munoz. "Report, please."

"As I mentioned, sir, the victim is Mallory Flynn from the Met, who is wearing her security lanyard for all to see."

Acton immediately raised his head to look in the victim's direction. "That is of interest."

"Yes, we thought so, too, but there is no indication that this was a body-dump."

"Cause of death?"

"Unknown, sir. No visible signs of violence, no weapons, no drug paraphernalia. Pupils are dilated."

"Let's have a look."

The two detectives followed Acton as he stepped-in to crouch over the body, and the Coroner's team withdrew for a moment so as to allow him to do so.

Oh, thought Doyle; that's interesting—he's hiding his extreme annoyance, for some reason. Mayhap it's because the Coroner's Office has sent their second-best team, and he's not used to dealing with second-best teams.

"Do we have a time-of-death?" Acton asked.

"Yes, sir," said Corso. "Liver temperature indicates no more than four hours."

Acton nodded, and then said to Munoz, "Let's turn her over."

Munoz crouched to assist him, as they carefully rolled the victim onto her side and briefly reviewed her back. Doyle watched from her standing position, but could see no wounds or other indications for cause-of-death.

Acton and Munoz returned the victim to her original position, and Munoz reported, "She wasn't robbed—she still has her handbag, with cash and credit cards in her wallet. We've one witness who thought that she'd sold drugs here before, but no one was willing to corroborate this."

Acton asked, "There were no drugs found on her?"

"No, sir. Only the handbag. I imagine the CCTV tape will give us some answers."

He nodded in the direction of the grocer's back entrance. "There is a private security camera above the rear door of that building. If you could secure the video, it may be useful."

"Yes, sir," said Munoz, and Doyle could feel her chagrin at not having spotted this, herself. "Would you like to follow-up with the witness who mentioned drugs?"

But Acton replied in an even tone, "I am reluctant to pursue that aspect until there is some indication it was related to her death."

Doyle and Munoz nodded in understanding; no need to rake the decedent's reputation over the coals if her misdeeds had no connection to her death. It was one of the sad by-products of being murdered; all your private, personal matters were exposed for public consumption through no fault of your own.

"If you will excuse me, I will speak to the Coroner's team leader."

He stepped away, and Munoz immediately said, "Let's see if there's video from the grocer."

"Right," Doyle replied, and they ducked under the police tape to approach the shopkeeper yet again.

As Munoz knocked on the back door, Doyle glanced behind her to see that Acton was speaking quietly to Corso—not a surprise, actually; he was probably asking her to give him the head's up if they discovered anything dicey about the decedent, so that he could try to contain any fallout. Corso was a sharp one, though, and any such warnings hardly seemed necessary. In fact, when they'd last spoken to the young woman at the morgue, Doyle had wondered if Acton would try to recruit her onto his shadowy team of shadowy minions—she seemed just the type.

Soon after her rather abrupt marriage, Doyle had discovered that her wedded husband was not at all what he appeared to be; the general public thought him a dedicated and selfless solver-of-crimes, but the stark truth was that he took advantage of his larger-than-life persona to manipulate the justice system, if he felt the correct result might not come about on its own. He was an aristocrat to the bone, and came from a long line of people who wielded power as they saw fit, with little regard for the rule of law.

She'd been horrified by this discovery—being as she was a newly-sworn law enforcement officer—and had earnestly tried to convince him to change his vigilante ways. Despite her best efforts, however, she knew he continued to manipulate the system even as he tried to hide his questionable activities from his disapproving wife.

And to achieve his aims, Acton tended to recruit people within the system who were similarly inclined; Doyle's friend Thomas Williams was one of his henchmen, as was Williams' wife, Lizzie, who worked in the forensics lab at the CID. Come to think of it, Yandra Corso rather reminded Doyle of Lizzie Williams; she was competent and even-keeled, even as she was not much in the way of a social creature—the perfect recruit for team-Acton.

Faith, she wouldn't be surprised if Acton had already recruited Corso; Doyle had the sense they were familiar with each another, and it would explain why her husband wanted to speak with the young woman privately, without the wife of his bosom listening in —he may be asking her to manipulate the autopsy report, if it seemed necessary.

With a mental sigh, Doyle returned her attention back to the task at hand. She roundly disapproved of Acton's machinations, but she'd learned—from long experience—that Acton tended to protect the Met as an institution even at the cost of justice, and here they seemed to have a dicey situation involving a Met employee who'd already been front-and-center in another dicey situation— the Public Accounts scandal. Therefore, it wouldn't be much of a surprise if Acton was trying to manage the fallout in a way that would hide the fact that the Met should have shown Ms. Flynn the door, long ago.

Doyle and Munoz greeted the grocer once again, and as Munoz explained the need for the video tape—which existed, thank God fastin'; oftentimes such cameras were strictly for show—Doyle was compelled to glance though the store's back window at her husband and Ms. Corso, as they continued their conversation. With some surprise, she realized—as she watched their interaction—that

Acton was scolding the Coroner's Assistant about something, although it was being done discreetly, of course. This was something of a wrinkle—that someone like Corso would be in need of a rebuke from the illustrious Chief Inspector. Mayhap the young woman hadn't been recruited for team-Acton, after all.

As the shopkeeper scrolled though the video feed, Doyle dragged her attention back to the images on the screen, even as she thought over this rather surprising turn of events. Corso was not used to being in the field, so she may have put a foot wrong, somehow, which would explain Acton's attitude. Crime scenes were tricky, and if you weren't careful you could muck-up the evidence for trial—which was the whole point of any investigation; to marshal enough evidence so as to hold a trial. The last needful thing would be to give defense counsel an opportunity to argue that the whole case was compromised because a Coroner's Assistant didn't follow the protocols. It was rather like what was happening in that dry-labbing scandal—there'd been rumors that the forensics lab at the CID had been "dry-labbing"—making up results, rather than doing the actual work—and if such a thing became general knowledge, every defense attorney worth his salt would immediately claim that the evidence against his client had been cooked-up.

And—speaking of manipulating the evidence—Doyle said to Munoz in a low voice, "You know, it's interestin' that this fellow didn't tell us about this tape when we first spoke to him."

Munoz nodded as though this had already occurred to her. "Maybe everyone's involved in the drug trade, and he's worried about getting caught-up."

"Everybody's wary about somethin'," Doyle agreed. "And that's as good a workin'-theory as any."

Suddenly, the dim outline of a figure could be seen walking across the camera-field, and Munoz leaned forward. "There," she said. "There's the victim; if you could slow it down, please."

CHAPTER 4

The Harlot did not merit a moment of his pity—she interfered in things she did not understand.

The shopkeeper's video was low-resolution and a bit grainy, but it was easy to identify Mallory Flynn as she walked through the frame.

"So; definitely not a body-dump," said Doyle, and Munoz nodded.

"She doesn't look worried," Munoz commented.

"No—even though she should be, in this neighborhood, and at that hour."

"Nobody's up, that early," Munoz countered. "If it was midnight, it would be a different story."

"Aye; I suppose. And it looks like she's got somethin' bundled inside her coat—see how her arms are cradlin' it?"

"Her handbag, maybe? She didn't want it to show?"

"No—you can see the handbag strap over her shoulder. She's

carryin' somethin' else—mayhap that first witness was right about her sellin' drugs, after all."

"If she was, I guess it's not a surprise that they've since disappeared." Munoz suddenly leaned closer. "Here's someone else —freeze it, please."

The shopkeeper duly stopped the video as both Doyle and Munoz leaned in to scrutinize a figure—head down with arms crossed against the chill, and bundled in a hooded sweatshirt—as it followed the victim a few minutes after she'd walked by.

"Female, I think?" said Munoz, since this was not clear.

"Doesn't much look like a killer," Doyle offered. It was true; the figure's posture didn't seem at all stealthy or self-conscious, as it hurried up the alley.

"Do you know who that is?" Munoz asked the shopkeeper.

The man peered at the screen. "It's hard to get a good look."

Munoz prompted, "Someone said they thought the victim might be selling drugs."

"Maybe," the man agreed warily. "I think that *gringa*'s been around here, before."

"Who would know what she was doing here, one way or the other?"

He shrugged, as his gaze fell to the floor. "I don't know," he replied, and you didn't need Doyle's perceptive ability to know that this was not true.

Rather than press him, Munoz nodded. "We'll need to take a copy of this video, please. Thank you, we appreciate it."

After obtaining a download of the relevant footage, they exited the building to find Acton waiting for them, his arms crossed as he watched the SOCOs process the scene. "Anything, Sergeant?" he asked Munoz.

"Video of the victim walking past, sir; her murder is out-of-frame, though. There looks to be another woman, following her. It might be a customer—didn't look to be a killer, and she wasn't carrying a visible weapon. Hopefully, she's a witness."

"Could you get a code on the other figure?"

This referred to the police codes that were used to identify the different ethnicities to be found in London, and Munoz shook her head. "No, sir. She was wearing a hoodie, and I can't be positive it was even a woman. We'll pull the CCTV tape, and between the two films get the best image we can—hopefully, there will be a facial recognition match. And we'll show a snap around the neighborhood, too."

"Didn't look like the killer," Doyle agreed thoughtfully. "May have been a customer—she didn't seem a'tall self-conscious about wanderin' about at that hour."

"That's a good point, Doyle." Munoz was no fool, and not above complimenting the wedded wife of her superior officer. "But she still might be a witness to whatever happened."

Acton then asked, "Could you see if the victim was wearing her security lanyard, in the video?"

Both Doyle and Munoz paused in surprise, and after thinking about it, Munoz replied, "I don't think so. We'll have to have another look, but since it's white, it would have been obvious."

"The killer put her lanyard on her body?" asked Doyle in some puzzlement, since this seemed to be the only logical conclusion.

Acton nodded. "I would imagine. It would have been foolish for the victim to wear it in this neighborhood—and she would know this, since she's worked the tip-line."

This seemed a good point—albeit a very strange turn of events —and Munoz nodded. "Right, sir; I'll tell the SOCOs that her handbag should be handled with priority, and dusted for prints— the lanyard, too."

"Did the shopkeeper know anything?"

"He says no, but he didn't volunteer the tape when we first spoke to him. DS Doyle and I think he may sell drugs from the shop, and doesn't want to be caught-up."

Doyle added, "And another person who was reluctant to say somethin' was the PC who first reported the body. He didn't report that she was a Met worker, even though it was obvious from her lanyard."

"Which?" asked Acton, as he lifted his gaze to consider the field personnel.

"The blond fellow on the right, sir."

Munoz continued, "And it does seem unusual that he was dispatched to this neighborhood." She added fairly, "DS Doyle pointed it out. He did seem a little nervous, when we pulled up."

With his thoughtful gaze resting on the PC in question, Acton offered, "He wears a wedding ring. There may have been a romantic liaison, between himself and this victim. It would comport with what we know about her."

The two other detectives paused in surprised silence for a moment, and then Doyle offered, "Well, there's a wrinkle."

In an even tone, Munoz asked, "Should we consider him a suspect, sir?"

But Acton only replied, "Unlikely. I would imagine the last thing he'd want is this particular scenario—and he'd not place the lanyard around her neck, certainly. It seems more likely that hers was an admonishment-murder."

The other two nodded in agreement. An admonishment-murder was the term used by detectives when the murder appeared to be a warning to other players to back off; usually the victim had only a minor role in whatever the scheme was, so as to avoid the open turf-war that would result if a kingpin were to be killed by a rival kingpin.

"She's selling drugs on someone else's territory," Munoz reasoned.

"That would also explain why there's a code of silence; everyone's reluctant to grass," Doyle agreed. "They're worried they might wind-up as the next admonishment-murder."

Acton asked, "Who found her?"

"A vagrant, sir; looking for bottles to recycle. He'd no mobile, and so he reported it to the grocer."

Acton checked his watch. "I must return, but if you would forward a copy of the tape to me, please."

"Yes, sir," said Munoz.

He's worried about something, Doyle realized. Which is understandable, I suppose, given what we've found out so far. An already-dicey person from the Met has died under questionable circumstances, with her lanyard having been pulled as a rather nasty message—small wonder, that Acton is thinking it may be necessary to do a bit of damage-control.

Therefore, as she followed Munoz back to the scene, she was unsurprised to feel her mobile vibrate with a message from Acton. "Need to discuss," it said. "Will drive you home."

"OK," she texted back. She was working part-time, which meant that usually she'd be in the field two or three mornings every week, and then do any follow-up paperwork at home whilst her two young sons were napping. When she was first pregnant with their eldest, Acton tried to persuade her to stay home full-time but he'd finally realized that she was reluctant to step down, being as she was a valuable asset in the fighting-of-the-good-fight. Therefore, they'd worked out this part-time compromise—it was a definite boon, to be married to your commanding officer.

As was the protocol, Doyle and Munoz lingered at the perimeter for a few minutes more—oftentimes a reluctant witness had to work-up the courage to approach the police—but no one came forward. Into the silence, Doyle commented, "You know, Munoz, there's a huge problem with our workin'-theory that this was an admonishment-murder. If Flynn was indeed sellin' drugs, why on earth would she come here to do it? That you'd wind-up dead shouldn't be the least surprisin'—I imagine there's more than a few ugly customers who'd take immediate offense."

Munoz thought this over, and said, "You know, Doyle, that's a good point."

"Don't sound so surprised."

Munoz continued, "It's not as though there's no demand closer to where she lives. Maybe she was trying to stay away from anyone who might recognize her?"

"Mayhap," Doyle agreed. "But it's dangerous, for someone like her to be wanderin' about here—which she would very well know."

Thoughtfully, Munoz added, "And if it's an admonishment-murder, you'd think the fact that she was murdered would be made crystal-clear."

Doyle raised her brows. "Now, there's a very good point, right back at you. Mayhap she wasn't murdered a'tall—best not get ahead of ourselves."

And they were to get no confirmation from the Coroner's Assistant, who reported, "I've completed the field investigation, and there's nothing that leaps out. No marks, no wounds, no injection sites. Nails are clean."

"She just keeled over," Munoz offered in a dry tone. "Case closed."

Not this time, thought Doyle, as she watched the team zip-up the body bag. There's something here that's being withheld from the coppers; some of these people know very well what happened to this victim, but they're not saying.

"Call me with the preliminary autopsy report, please," Munoz directed.

"Straightaway, ma'am," Corso replied, and Doyle was startled to realize that this was, in fact, not true.

CHAPTER 5

One by one, he extinguished the candles that he'd lit on the makeshift stone altar. He'd prayed for the orichas to advise him, and their words were wise; it would be best if those who had knowledge hid themselves for a time. He must not underestimate The Husband.

*A*fter having spent the remainder of the morning at her desk going through the relevant CCTV tape, Doyle made her way upstairs to Acton's office so that he could drive her home. As she approached down the hallway, she smiled a greeting at Nazy, Acton's Assistant, who was seated at her desk outside his office.

"Good morning, Officer Doyle; the Chief Inspector is meeting with Mrs. Williams, and he has asked that they not be disturbed."

Lizzie Williams worked at the CID's forensics lab, and the young woman was one of Acton's staunchest henchmen—or henchwomen, more correctly—since she originally hailed from Trestles, his hereditary estate, and the people who hailed from Trestles tended to have a Middle Ages mindset. Lizzie was quiet and reserved—the sciencey-type—which meant that she was an entirely different creature from the impulsive Doyle. They were both devoted to Acton, of course, but aside from that, they didn't have much in common, save for their mutual fondness for Thomas Williams, Lizzie's husband who was also Doyle's closest friend.

Doyle had first met Williams when they were attending the Crime Academy, and he'd helped Doyle study for some of the harder tests, being as she was by no means as brainy as he. She hadn't realized that Williams carried something of a torch for her until she'd married Acton in a whirlwind, and then he'd demonstrated his extreme dismay at this turn of events by going a bit wobbly. As a result, they'd weathered a few rough moments together, but then had settled into a strong, enduring friendship. Williams had eventually married Lizzie, and the couple had an adopted son with another baby on the way.

Because Lizzie worked in the lab, Doyle immediately surmised she was meeting with Acton about the dry-labbing scandal—the one where lab results were being mocked-up. Doyle was already aware that Lizzie had been quietly working on that investigation with Acton, being as she was in the perfect position to do so and could be trusted to keep a tight lid on the scandal—it would be catastrophic, if the public-at-large became aware that the CID's lab was faking results.

Aloud, Doyle joked to Nazy, "I'd best not interrupt them, then—mayhap he's rakin' our Lizzie over the coals."

Nazy cast her a look. "Now, Officer Doyle; I do not think the Chief Inspector would rake anyone over the coals."

You'd be very much surprised, thought Doyle, but instead she said lightly, "Whist, Nazy; the poor man could use a cat-o'-nine-tails, betwixt me and the boys."

Nazy gently chided, "I think you are teasing me, Officer Doyle."

"I am indeed, Nazy; in truth, he only gives me the back o' his hand when I *truly* deserve it."

Whilst Nazy tried to decide how best to respond to this sally, the office door opened, and Lizzie emerged.

Faith, thought Doyle in surprise; she's brimful of misery, is our Lizzie.

Seeing her, the young woman paused to offer in her subdued manner, "Good morning, Lady Acton."

"Hallo, Lizzie." Since Lizzie originated from Acton's estate, Doyle was always "Lady Acton" to her, and there seemed to be little Doyle could do to change this particular mindset. "How are you feelin'?" Lizzie was in her last trimester of pregnancy, with only a couple of weeks left.

"A bit slow," Lizzie replied, with an attempt at a smile.

"At least you're in the home stretch," Doyle offered in an encouraging tone, and tactfully did not mention that having a newborn was going to make every little thing in the universe slow down to a massive, grinding halt. Lizzie would find this out for herself, soon enough, and besides, it seemed to Doyle that the usually stoic young woman was already knocked off her pins.

Lizzie departed, and then Acton emerged from his office, greeting his wife as he shrugged into his suit jacket. "Ready?"

"I am," she agreed easily, and thought—now that's interesting; I think he's not happy with Lizzie, and Lizzie is well-aware of this unfortunate fact. Faith, mayhap there truly was some coals-raking going on.

As she fell into step beside her husband, she decided she may as well ask, "What was that about?"

"I will tell you in the car," he replied in a mild tone. "Did you manage to get an ID for the potential witness?"

Doyle reported, "The best CCTV camera had a shot-out lens—I suppose that's only to be expected, in that area of town—and there wasn't enough on the grocer's footage to do a proper facial recognition—I'd over ten-thousand 'possible' hits. First things first, though; Munoz has expedited the autopsy, since we're not even sure we can open a homicide case as yet."

As they stepped into the lift, she debated whether to tell him that Corso did not seem inclined to speed the report along; the poor woman was already in Acton's black book, and mayhap the fair

Doyle had her wires crossed—it seemed unlikely that the Coroner's Assistant would interfere with such a priority report.

He nodded, and then as the doors slid closed, he bent his head close to hers. "How disappointed would you be if Munoz is promoted?"

Doyle smiled. "Not a'tall, husband—my hand on my heart. And besides; how I feel about it should have no bearin' on the matter, one way or the other."

"Nevertheless, it would be impossible not to consider your feelings."

"My feelings shouldn't trump the protocols, husband."

He made no reply to such heresy, and with great fondness, she tucked her hand into his elbow as they left the lift, and walked out through the parking garage. There was a time—and not so very long ago—when she would have thrown the crockery upon hearing such news, but her feelings on the subject had changed dramatically, and she'd the very sure sense that Acton was well-aware that her feelings had changed. Life was a wonder; the things that used to make you incandescently angry no longer seemed nearly as important as time went by, and other priorities emerged. Indeed, she felt a bit foolish that Acton tended to indulge her in the first place—not only did he manipulate the cases so as to suit his own notions of justice, he was also willing to manipulate cases so as to protect his wedded wife—oftentimes from her own recklessness.

"I may place Munoz in the Financial Crimes Unit; she would be well-suited."

She smiled, seeing straight though this ploy. "I truly don't mind workin' under her, Michael—we do good work, together. And shame on you, for thinkin' that I'm so petty."

"Not at all," he demurred, and she laughed, because it was not exactly true.

CHAPTER 6

fter they got into the car, Doyle mentioned, "We thought of a funny little wrinkle in this morning's case; why would Flynn go over to that area to sell drugs, if that's indeed why she was there? Seems a high-risk proposition."

"She had to be circumspect?" he suggested, as they turned into the street. "It was unlikely she would be recognized in that neighborhood."

Thoughtfully, she knit her brow. "Aye, that's what Munoz thought."

He glanced over at her. "But you don't think so?" Acton had great respect for Doyle's perceptive sense—as well he should. There'd been many a time she'd helped him solve a thorny case—not to mention many a time she'd helped him avert personal disaster.

She blew out a breath, and admitted, "I truly don't know *what* I think. The spectators this mornin' were—were *wary*, I suppose is the best way to describe it. Well, not everyone—but a lot of people were; they know somethin', but there's a code of silence in place."

He pointed out, "Wouldn't that be the case with any homicide in such an area?"

With a knit brow, she tried to put her feeling into words. "This was different; I'd the sense that—that there was more to it, than your run-of-the-mill admonishment-murder. And Munoz pointed out that it wasn't much of an admonishment-murder in the first place, if the killer didn't make it clear that the victim had been murdered as a warnin'."

As he didn't answer, she decided she may as well press him a bit; she'd the sense that he truly didn't know who'd killed Mallory Flynn, but that he did know *something* that was making him unhappy, and he was doing his best not to let her catch a glimpse of whatever-it-was. "I think you know more than you're sayin', husband. Can't you tell me?"

There was a small pause, and then he confessed, "Lizzie Williams believes Flynn was involved in the dry-labbing scandal."

After a moment's surprise, Doyle decided that it wasn't truly much of a surprise, after all. "Well, if we think she was usin' her work at the tip-line to squash any tips that might have exposed the Public Accounts scandal, I suppose it makes sense that she was also helpin' to squash any evidence that might come through on the other end, from the forensics lab." She paused, thinking this over. "Although I'm not sure why the Public Accounts embezzlers would need to fiddle with lab results—it doesn't seem connected."

"It may involve a different scheme altogether. Lizzie believes Flynn was pilfering drugs from the Evidence Locker so as to sell them on the black market."

Doyle raised her brows. "Mother a' Mercy—was she indeed? I suppose that's only in keepin', too."

This, unfortunately, was not an uncommon occurrence; personnel with access to the Evidence Locker would sometimes pilfer from the drug hauls that were locked away whilst the defendants were awaiting trial. It was a huge temptation to someone on an administrative salary, and one of the main reasons the Met kept stringent watch over anyone with access.

He added, "The false lab reports would then conceal the fact that the drugs brought into evidence at trial had been replaced with look-alike substances."

Doyle turned to stare at him, thoroughly astonished. "Holy *Mother*, Michael—there's some brass, for you. And no one would know about the switch, since the lab reports wouldn't be questioned at the trial, and after the trial was over the fake drugs would be destroyed in the usual course. Faith, it's a *crackin'* good scheme."

He nodded. "Obviously, there were more personnel involved."

Thoughtfully, Doyle followed his reasoning. "Aye—someone on the inside had to fake the lab results—that's not somethin' Flynn could do."

She thought over this revelation for a moment, and concluded, "Then that first witness was right, and Flynn *was* dealin' drugs. And her death may have been a containment-murder instead of an admonishment-murder; the net was closin'-in, and someone got nervous that she would grass them out."

But her husband tilted his head in mild disagreement. "There is the small matter of the security lanyard."

Reminded, Doyle could see his point. "Aye—a panicked cohort wouldn't have placed the lanyard 'round her neck."

"Yes. Instead, the lanyard seems to indicate an admonishment-murder."

Slowly, she nodded. "Someone's sending a warnin' to anyone else at the Met who may have been involved with this pilferin' drugs scheme. It *must* be a turf-war, then—not to mention she wasn't robbed, and if someone wanted to make it look like a random murder, they'd have taken her money."

He nodded. "I think that is the aspect I find most perplexing; she'd been dead for hours, yet no one took the opportunity to steal her money. No one interfered with her body."

Doyle added, "Not to mention it seems very strange that the killer took her lanyard out of her handbag, yet left her wallet within."

He went silent, thinking, and she respected the process and left him to it, as she watched out the window for a few minutes. As they neared home, Doyle observed, "It's a shame she's met a bad end, but she has no one to blame but herself—thinkin' she could go over to Lambeth and clomp about on someone else's drug-turf."

"Yes. I am hoping to unwind the dry-labbing scandal, now that Flynn is dead, and so I would ask that you say nothing of this connection."

Oh, Doyle realized; that must be why Corso is slow-walking the autopsy, and why my husband has taken custody of all pertinent surveillance tape—he's trying to make sure no one connects all these rather alarming and scandalous dots.

Reluctantly, she had to concede that this may indeed be the appropriate course; she was well-familiar with the dilemmas the brass often faced when competing public interests had to be weighed against each other, and in this case it was more important —to Acton, at least—that the dry-labbing scandal be quietly rolled-up with as few people knowing about it as possible. And—as much as it went against her principles—sometimes it was more important not to call-out the wrongdoers and instead to leave sleeping dogs to lie.

Nevertheless, it made her uneasy—that he felt he could decide who was going to pay for their sins, and who was not. She understood his thinking, but she'd been raised by nuns who firmly believed that wrongdoers should be called out—no matter the consequences—because otherwise, the weighing of consequences tended to be skewed in favor of one's own preferences, with Acton standing as the perfect example.

Reading her aright, he glanced over to assure her, "Steps will be taken to make certain such a thing never happens again. But I'm afraid the consequences may be worse than the crime, in this instance."

She made a face. "There's nothin' wrong with a strong dose of 'consequences' Michael—that's the whole point of the justice system."

"Nonetheless, I'd like to keep the matter private, please."

She sighed. "All right, Michael; wretched Flynn's wretched secrets are safe with me."

CHAPTER 7

The Husband was her acolyte. He was a wrathful man, and his gaze was penetrating.

$\mathcal{A}$s they pulled into their building's parking garage, Doyle suddenly realized that her husband hadn't mentioned what he'd scolded Lizzie about—hoping she'd be distracted, he was, and to be fair, he was a past-master at distracting her. But he hadn't succeeded this time around, and so she noted in a casual tone, "I think you must be losin' control of your minions, Michael; you're unhappy with Lizzie and you're unhappy with Corso—jawbonin' at the both of them, and all before lunchtime."

He tilted his head in a mild disclaimer. "Corso is not one of my minions."

She glanced over at him. "Oh? I'm that surprised—she seems just the right fit."

He admitted, "I did consider it. I asked Lizzie Williams to meet with her socially, and to put out some feelers."

There was an odd little nuance to his tone, and she prompted, "So, what happened?"

"Unfortunately, I discovered that she is attracted to me."

Thoroughly astonished, Doyle stared at him, agog, as he pulled the car into their parking slot. "*Truly*? Mother a' *Mercy*, Michael, but you're a hazard. I'm that surprised—she doesn't seem the type."

"No. I will confess it was something of a surprise."

This—unfortunately—came along with the territory, when it came to Doyle's wedded husband. Acton was titled, wealthy, famous—and handsome, to boot. It was a rare woman who could resist such a potent combination, and the fact that he was devoted to his wife didn't seem to be much of a deterrent to many.

The penny dropped, and Doyle drew her brows down. "Oh—I didn't think about it at the time, but she knew you were comin' on-site this mornin', even before you got there."

"Yes. She was not on the team originally assigned to the case."

"So, you gave her a scoldin' for actin' like a teenager."

"We should not allow inter-personnel relationships to jeopardize case-work."

At this pronouncement, she couldn't help but smile. "Speaks the man who needs my blessin' to promote Munoz."

"Touché," he acknowledged, without a shred of shame. "I did not want to make mention, but I think it would pay for you to be aware, in the event Corso approaches you."

"She harbors no ill-feelin's toward me," Doyle informed him thoughtfully. "Which is probably why such a thing never even occurred to me. Remember Cassie Masterson, who was so determined to steal you away? She was crackin' nasty to me, and very much enjoyed the thought that she was goin' triumph over the likes of me. This is different—I don't get the sense that Corso resents me a'tall; instead, I think she's someone who doesn't know how to handle real, live people, and she has no idea how to handle her feelings, either. I almost feel sorry for her."

"She should know better."

This was a fair point, in that Acton was not only a legend at the

Met, but he was also famously married—small wonder that he was annoyed with the woman. "What will you do?"

"If she steps out of line again, I am afraid she will have to be transferred."

Doyle nodded. It was a shame, since the woman was good at her job, but if she was yearning after the illustrious Chief Inspector it probably meant that she'd a wire crossed, anyway. Doyle wondered, for a moment, what had happened to make him aware of this—it was hard to imagine the Coroner's Assistant openly confessing her feelings to him.

It's that uncontrollable love-and-longing thing, she thought; and —unfortunately—the CID is often called-in to handle the resulting wreckage that occurs when it all goes awry. The head has a hard time, trying to control the heart.

Thinking on this, she asked, "Is that how you knew that Mallory Flynn was somethin' of a lightskirt? Was she another one who was chasin' after you?"

"No. I had no interaction with her."

With dawning alarm, Doyle ventured, "Williams did, though; he interviewed Flynn when he was investigatin' the Public Accounts case. Holy Mother, Michael; d'you think she cast her lures at him?" In the past, Williams had shown an unfortunate tendency to be a bit too susceptible to women with ulterior motives.

"I do not believe they had a relationship, but I cannot be certain."

This sounded ominous; Williams' marriage with Lizzie was something of a contrivance, in that Acton had basically put them together so as to keep Williams out of female-trouble. And since both of them were heavily involved in Acton's shadowy doings, it must have seemed a practical solution from his point of view, even as Doyle had warned him that such things weren't so easily orchestrated.

Struck with a troubling implication, she immediately declared, "Williams wasn't the one who killed Mallory Flynn, Michael—he would never do such a thing."

"I would tend to agree, but I would like to enlist your aid so as to be certain."

Doyle fell silent, very much dismayed by his words. Williams was her friend, but oftentimes they'd have divided loyalties, due to his aiding-and-abetting Acton in his shadowy doings whilst knowing that Doyle strongly disapproved of the aforesaid shadowy doings. If her husband was worried enough to ask for her help, it was a very serious matter; after all, Acton knew of her loyalty to Williams, and he wouldn't ask unless he felt it was necessary.

"All right, but how would you pull it off?" Other than her husband, Williams was the only person Doyle had told about her truth-detecting abilities, and therefore he'd know exactly what was afoot if the fair Doyle tried to casually raise the subject of dead-people-who'd-been-potentially-threatening-to-wreck-his-marriage.

"I thought it may be helpful to promote a social setting at our flat—perhaps a small celebration for the Savoies."

Thoroughly aghast, Doyle regarded him with undisguised horror. "Holy Mother, Michael; not another dinner-party—I barely survived the last one."

"Certainly not," he soothed. "Instead, a small gathering with a few friends."

She eyed him with deep suspicion. "That sounds very much like a dinner-party."

But her husband deftly changed the subject. "I will admit I have another motive. Do you think Melinda may be right for McGonigal?"

Dr. Timothy McGonigal was an old friend of Acton's—truly, the only one he had. The kindly doctor was a loyal supporter of the House of Acton, but unfortunately, he wasn't the sort to pluck a chord when it came to women's hearts—just the opposite of Acton, when you thought about it. And Melinda was someone who also went way back, in Acton's life—a rather annoying woman, who'd lately been underfoot more than usual.

Doyle warned, "I don't know, Michael; it's very sweet that you'd try your hand at matchmakin'—and you've a better record than me, that's for certain—but Melinda once told me she thinks Tim is plain-vanilla. And he's got completely different taste in women, lest we forget." The two times McGonigal had ventured into a serious romance, the object of his affections had been an African immigrant.

He pointed out, "I do think Melinda would benefit from a stabilizing influence."

This was true, in that Melinda tended to drift about, unaware that she was bringing mayhem in her wake. With some trepidation, Doyle agreed, "All right, then—let's do our worst."

As they made their way up the lift to their flat, however, Doyle entertained the niggling suspicion that there was more to this dinner-party plan than an attempt at matchmaking—or even her husband's expressed desire to sound-out Williams on the subject of Mallory Flynn. After all, when it came to Acton-minions, Williams was atop the list, and he could be confronted at any time—Acton was not one to avoid touchy subjects when it came to his stronghold within the Met; only see how he'd scolded both Yandra Corso and Lizzie Williams in short order. No; instead, her husband wanted to get this dinner-party together for reasons unknown, and Katy-bar-the-door because he didn't like hosting dinner-parties any more than she did.

CHAPTER 8

He'd already admonished The Foolish Child, using sharp words, but she hadn't heeded him—it was often this way, with the young ones. And so, a stronger message had been sent. She brought them all into danger, with her foolishness.

*A*cton had returned to work, and Doyle was now supervising lunchtime, seated at the kitchen table with her two young sons. Edward was home from his preschool—he was now old enough to attend, two mornings a week—and baby Tommy was sitting in his high chair and making an impressive mess of his oatmeal, which plastered every inch of his tray and much of the surrounding area. Doyle always felt that it was a shame that babies didn't come ready-made to feed themselves, because if there was ever a true test of motherhood, this was it. And it didn't help her uncertain mood that she'd come to the realization that Acton had successfully distracted her, yet again, from finding out why he'd scolded Lizzie. Ran rings around her, he did, and shame on her for not following-up.

In fact, after musing over their conversation in the car, it occurred to her that there'd been no real reason for Acton to drop everything so as to drive her home—the man had a high-priority homicide on his plate, and he wouldn't be dilly-dallying with his wife unless he felt it was important. Not to mention that—during that conversation—he hadn't volunteered any information about Mallory Flynn and her wayward ways; instead, she'd had to pull it out of him. In point of fact, there didn't seem to be anything they'd discussed that couldn't have kept till he came home from work this evening.

With a mental sigh, she acknowledged—from long experience—that the most likely reason he'd dropped everything to drive her home was because he wanted to make certain she hadn't figured something out.

I hope, she thought crossly, as she mopped-up a dollop of baby-oatmeal from her sleeve, that I'm not yet again investigating a murder that my wretched husband has committed.

This seemed unlikely, however—and the thought gave her no small measure of relief—mainly because she'd the sure sense that he was genuinely puzzled about this Flynn case. After all, he was the one who'd noted the grocer's surveillance camera, and the strange circumstance of the lanyard even as the victim's wallet remained intact. In any event, this particular homicide didn't bear the usual hallmarks of a smooth-as-silk Acton-crime—although it was truly a shame that she was able to recognize such a thing.

And aside from the crime not comporting with Acton's style, she also held the general conviction that he was truly trying to mend his ways. The wife of his bosom was very unhappy when he went about murdering people—no matter how seemingly well-deserved—and they'd had a few serious confrontations about it in recent months. She was cautiously optimistic that his devotion to her was winning over his compulsion to right all perceived wrongs, and that he was now trying to turn his talents to less bloodthirsty solutions. Fingers crossed, anyways.

So; if he hadn't killed Flynn—and she was fairly certain he

hadn't, and that he didn't know who had—then what had he been trying to sound out, in the car?

Because his mother was distracted, Tommy managed to grab the spoon—she needed to pay closer attention; the boyo could strike like a snake—and as she wrested it from his hand she remembered that the first thing her husband had asked was whether she'd managed to identify the hooded figure in the surveillance tape.

She paused, thinking about this. The woman—assuming it was a woman—was a prime witness and perhaps a suspect, and so discovering her identity should be a top priority. But Acton had let the subject drop, and he hadn't offered any suggestions to help make an ID. Did he not want the wife of his bosom to discover who it was? But wait—that didn't make sense, since it was Acton, himself, who'd led them to the grocer's camera so that they knew there was a witness in the first place. So; that seemed to be a dead end—and besides, why would Acton want to protect such a witness? It didn't make much sense.

"Mum; Miss Cherry said we could go feed the ducks, next time."

Doyle smiled at Edward, who'd been making short work of every chicken sausage that Reynolds laid before him. "That's grand, Edward; I do think the ducks have looked a bit sharp-set, lately."

Edward laughed as he returned to his meal, and Doyle decided she should take her mind from more troubling thoughts, and instead focus on household matters. To this end, she asked the butler, "Is everythin' goin' well with Miss Cherry, Reynolds?"

They'd had a bit of trouble keeping a nanny, thus far, and so—as a temporary measure—Acton had enlisted Miss Cherry from Meryton, the village near his estate. Their limo-driver was a young man named Adrian, and Cherry was Adrian's aunt; a friendly, easy-going woman who'd also lived in Meryton all her life, which meant she'd be less likely to engage in treachery. Or one would hope, anyways—hard to believe that nannies could be treacherous to begin with, but there you were.

"I have no complaints, madam. And Master Edward and Master Tommy do enjoy her company."

As she managed to insert a spoonful of oatmeal into Tommy's mouth without suffering any repercussions, Doyle hid a smile, because Reynolds was well-aware that the temporary nanny had been hand-picked by the Master of the House, and therefore she was to be given his whole-hearted support. Although to be fair, Reynolds hadn't objected even when their other nannies weren't what the very-correct butler would expect from such an exalted household. They'd first hired Mary—who'd been a witness in one of Doyle's cases—even though she'd no experience, and after Mary, they'd hired Miss Valerie—who wasn't very good with children. And in-between, they'd had some help from Acton's half-sister, Callie, who'd been a dose of high-drama, all by herself.

Callie had started out as a young servant at Trestles—again, from one of the local families—but they'd all been astonished to discover that she was actually Acton's half-sister, as a result of his awful father's having taken advantage of Melinda, who'd been Acton's youthful girlfriend.

This recent revelation had churned-up some rough waters, since the normally good-hearted girl had turned a bit rebellious when she'd discovered her true identity, and Acton did not deal well with rebellion. Plus, it didn't help matters that Melinda—Callie's newly-revealed birth mother—was now smothering poor Callie with long-suppressed maternal love.

It was all a bit tricky—mainly because everyone involved had been knocked off their pins—but nevertheless Doyle held the fond hope that they'd all sort it out soon, short of strangling one another.

Reminded, she advised Reynolds with little enthusiasm, "Acton wants to have a dinner-party. Has he said?"

Reynolds immediately perked up, being as he was one who very much enjoyed putting on such events and was severely hampered by the fact that the Master and Mistress tended to bar the door, and avoid social engagements of any kind. "Is that so, madam? How many guests?"

"I've no idea—I'm tryin' not to think about it. He says we should hold somethin' for Savoie and Mary."

"Certainly, madam. A very happy occasion."

Diplomatically, Doyle glossed over the very rugged road they had all taken to arrive at this particular happy occasion, and only replied, "Aye, that."

As she attempted another spoonful—this was a war she wasn't winning, and she was past-ready to surrender and let the boyo drink bottles for the remainder of his days—she added, "You know, Reynolds, Munoz says that she thinks Savoie has been sweet on Mary for a long time; he just kept it well-hidden."

But Reynolds was seen to be skeptical of this observation. "I must say that I would be surprised if someone like Mr. Savoie would be content to admire from afar, madam."

Doyle could see his point, as she continued with her dogged attempts to teach Tommy the joys of solid food. "Well, she was married, and so even if he did admire her, there was little to be done. Although a weddin' ring doesn't necessarily matter to a lot of people, apparently."

She blew a tendril of hair from her forehead, thinking about what Acton had told her about Yandra Corso's infatuation. "It's a shame, that this love-and-longin' business is so very messy and uncontrollable. Faith, if Acton had thrown me over so as to marry someone else, I'd not hang about; instead I'd pull-up stakes— quick-as-a-cat—and move far away, rather than live in hopeless yearnin' for the whole of my life. Although I suppose that's easy for me to say, since I've never walked that path."

"Certainly not, madam. If I may say so, Lord Acton is devoted to you."

Doyle decided it would be best to avoid the topic of Acton's unique brand of devotion, and so instead she scraped up another spoonful from the bowl and asked, "Who's that girl from the story —the one with unrequited love, who wound up dyin'?"

"Éponine, from Hugo's *Les Misérables*?"

Doyle paused to eye him sidelong. "Not a clue, Reynolds—

speak English, for heaven's sake. I'm thinkin' about the one who wound up floatin' down the river, due to a broken heart."

"Elaine, madam?"

Doyle frowned, as her spoon deftly avoided Tommy's slimy hands. "Remind me who's Elaine."

"She nursed Sir Lancelot back to health, and then he spurned her."

Impatiently, Doyle shook her head, which inspired a giggling Tommy to shake his own head so that bits of oatmeal flew about, with Edward immediately joining in so that there were a few seconds of vigorous, giggling, head-shaking. "No—not her. Faith, Reynolds, you're overestimatin' your audience, here. I mean the one from that famous Shakespeare play—the play with the mopin' fellow, where everybody dies."

Reynolds' brow cleared. "Ophelia."

"That's the one. Faith, I'd no idea there were so many famous broken-heart stories."

"Unrequited love is rather a universal theme, madam."

"Aye," she agreed thoughtfully. "It's that hard, for the head to control the heart."

The concierge buzzed, and Reynolds went over to answer the intercom. He then informed Doyle, "Miss Melinda is downstairs, madam. Apparently, she is set to meet with Lord Acton, and has arrived early."

"I suppose they're meetin' about the Father Clarence investigation—faith, what a tangle-patch. Send her up, then."

CHAPTER 9

*a*side from her secret-baby scandal, Melinda had managed to get herself embroiled in yet another scandal in that she'd engineered a secret-marriage and—as the icing on the scandal-cake—the secret-marriage was to an RC priest, of all things.

Her priest-husband had conveniently died shortly after their marriage, which had left Melinda a wealthy widow due to a few well-placed family trust-funds. Hard upon this strange and unlooked-for turn of events, the truth of Callie's parentage had been revealed—that Melinda had borne a child as a result of some long-ago brutality at the hands of Acton's awful father—and in truth, it was very like one of those unbelievably dramatic stories that people liked to write—the story about the moping fellow came to mind—where it all seemed thoroughly over-the-top, even for fiction.

Meanwhile, Melinda's erstwhile mother-in-law—the dead priest's mother—was up-in-arms about these events, with Melinda taking it all in stride in that she was the sort of person who seemed to glide effortlessly through life without worrying overmuch.

Doyle mopped-up baby Tommy so that he was semi-presentable, and then smiled as Melinda came in through the door. "You're just in time for lunch, Melinda."

"I'm too upset to eat," the other woman advised, as she gracefully settled into the open chair, and gazed benignly upon Edward. "Hello, little boy."

"Edward," Doyle reminded her. "What are you upset about?"

"What am I *not* upset about?" Melinda asked, and propped her elbows on the table. "My miserable mother-in-law is breathing fire, and Callie's got no time for me."

Doyle ventured, "Callie has a new beau, I hear."

The other woman sighed rather dramatically. "She does. He's nice enough, but I'd rather hoped she would travel to Paris with me this fall, and I can see that it's not going to happen."

Doyle lifted the sticky Tommy at arm's length, so as to carry him over to the sink for a washing-up. "Faith, Melinda—give her a bit of space. She's agreed to live in the same buildin' as you, and it's a blessin' to have her so close by instead of back in Meryton. A blessin' for us, too, to be within walkin' distance of you both." This, said a bit firmly, because Doyle was hoping that Acton would soften a bit toward his newly-discovered half-sister. Thus far, the half-sibling road had been a bit rocky.

With the air of a martyr, Melinda took a long breath. "You're right, of course. And it is a nice, quiet neighborhood—I will grant you that. Speaking of which, do tell me all about the fracas, yesterday."

Doyle raised her brows, as she dried Tommy's face and hands. "Which fracas is this?"

"I was walking by The Grenoble Hotel, and Acton was having a *passionate* argument with some Spanish-looking girl in the lobby."

Doyle paused to stare at her in surprise. "He was?"

"Oh." Melinda waved a languid, apologetic hand. "You didn't know? I shouldn't have said, perhaps." She then leaned over, to indicate Edward's grapes. "Are you going to eat those?"

With some confusion, Doyle asked, "What time was this?"

Melinda considered, as she lifted the cluster of grapes from

Edward's plate. "I think it was just after four. I was walking back from tea at Bertram's."

Doyle slowly hoisted Tommy to her shoulder, wholly bereft of words for a moment. What Melinda said was true, but it strained all credulity to imagine Acton having a public argument with anyone—let alone one with Munoz, and in the lobby of The Grenoble Hotel.

Eying her reaction, Melinda thoughtfully plucked a grape. "If Acton's going to have an affair, he should at least have the decency to give me the right of first refusal."

Crossly, Doyle retorted, "Acton's *not* havin' an affair, Melinda."

"Touchy," the other woman observed with a small shrug. "Sorry —my husbands always did." She popped a grape in her mouth. "It rather goes with the territory."

Her face aflame, Doyle snapped, "Well, Father Clarence was never given the chance to cheat on you."

Melinda laughed. "Now, there's a direct hit. Good for you."

"Come along, Master Edward," Reynolds said, as he hurriedly led the little boy away from the table. "Let's get you ready for your nap."

With a mighty effort, Doyle took hold of her temper and felt a bit ashamed of herself for the unkind remark. There was a logical explanation, of course, but she'd been nettled by Melinda's implication. The Grenoble Hotel was a posh, discreet establishment in their Kensington neighborhood, and Doyle regarded it with great fondness in that it was where she and Acton would whisk away when they needed a bit of privacy; there was nothing like having servants and children to interfere with a spontaneous bout of sex, when the mood hit.

So; it was not beyond the realm of possibility that Melinda had seen Acton there, but the circumstances seemed almost unbelievable; Acton did not engage in fracases—he would consider it beneath him. And besides that, why hadn't Acton told her that he was unhappy with Munoz, for some reason? Perhaps it was some sort of professional rebuke—and therefore none of her business—but it all seemed very out-of-keeping.

With some dismay, she suddenly remembered her sense that Acton had been carefully sounding her out during their car ride home, and couldn't help but wonder if the two events were connected. Faith—he'd also asked if she'd be upset if Munoz was promoted.

No, she thought immediately. You're jumping at shadows, lass; that husband of yours is loyal to the bone.

She excused herself to go put Tommy down for his nap—Melinda was still working her way through Edward's neglected fruit—and after the baby was settled-in, she went over to Edward's room where Reynolds was engaged in the pre-nap ritual of placing the correct stuffed animals in their correct places. After kissing Edward and tucking him in, she then apologized to Reynolds as they closed the door behind them. "I'm that sorry, Reynolds; I let my temper get the best of me."

The servant bowed his head in understanding. "Not at all, madam. Miss Melinda has always been a bit scattered, if I may say so."

In all fairness, Doyle advised, "She's a lot shrewder than she seems, my friend." In fact, Doyle was fast-coming to the conclusion that Melinda's early visit was to give Doyle the heads-up on this exact subject—not that she needed a head's up, truly, since Acton certainly wasn't doing anything shameful. But it would be interesting to hear his explanation.

Aloud, she said to Reynolds, "Best keep this whole fracas-subject under your hat, though. I shouldn't be surprised if there was an undercover operation afoot—especially if it involves Munoz."

"Certainly, madam," the butler agreed in a wooden tone.

CHAPTER 10

The memory was still fresh, of what had happened to The Old One. The Husband feared The Old One would tell the secrets of The Red-Haired Policewoman, and so The Husband had waged death.

Although she was beyond curious, Doyle didn't have an immediate chance to ask her husband about the contretemps at The Grenoble Hotel because as soon as he came home, he retreated into his downstairs office with Melinda for their meeting.

Doyle was therefore forced to possess her soul in patience, and seated herself at the kitchen table to type-up the morning's report whilst the boys napped—she shouldn't put it off any longer, what with the house blessedly quiet for a couple of hours.

Reynolds was doing the washing-up from lunch, and Doyle decided she should make it clear that she wasn't a'tall flustered by Melinda's revelation, since her initial reaction may have indicated otherwise. Therefore, with this in mind, she remarked in an airy tone, "Speakin' of Munoz's assignments, we'd a wrinkle in this morning's case; the victim was a young woman who worked at the Met."

"So, I'd heard, madam. Did you know her?"

"I didn't," Doyle replied. "And I don't want to victim-shame, but she was in a very dodgey area of town and probably up to no good." She paused, suddenly struck. "Although we'd a Queen's Counsel murdered in that same area, once, and it turned out that he was on the side of the angels, so I suppose I shouldn't judge." Remembering, Doyle lifted her gaze out the windows. "Now, there was a wrinkle to beat all wrinkles; the killers were tryin' to pin the QC's murder on a witch-doctor who lived in that area."

"I do recall that case, madam. The victim's shoes were missing."

Doyle smiled. "Faith, you've a good memory, Reynolds. And the poor witch-doctor met a bad end anyways, even though he was shown to be innocent—a nasty case, all around."

"I am not certain that a witch-doctor deserves our sympathy, madam," Reynolds remarked, in a disapproving manner.

"Whist, Reynolds," Doyle teased. "A lot of people think there's not a hair's breadth of difference betwixt Santeria and my own church. To them, it's all the same superstitions, only with feathers and beads mixed-in."

"Certainly an unenlightened view, madam."

Doyle smiled to herself, since Reynolds was one who knew upon which side his bread was buttered; as a result of Acton's unexpected marriage to an Irish mackerel-snapper, he'd been confirmed in the Catholic faith. "Well, at least the RC church doesn't try to sell magic outright, like the Santero did. I wonder if anyone's taken over his grift?"

"I would hope not, madam," said Reynolds, with a full measure of distaste.

Doyle made a wry mouth, as she returned her attention to her neglected report. "Well, it's a ripe area for it, unfortunately; lots of new immigrants there, mostly from the West Indies and Africa. They tend to be superstitious, and they don't much trust anyone other than their own—they definitely don't trust the coppers. There was a shopkeeper this mornin' who was hopin' we'd not realize he had surveillance film."

She typed in silence for a few minutes, trying to put together a decent synopsis of the facts—she tended to be more scattered than Melinda, truth to tell, when it came to setting things down in any kind of logical order. She was an intuitive creature at heart, and always wanted to leap to conclusions without setting forth the path she'd taken to get there—which was not good protocol; the reports should be written with painstaking accuracy so as to allow a fresh pair of eyes to see exactly what the detectives had seen, in the event that a new theory was needed for an unsolved case. When she'd first married Acton, he'd sat down with her to try to teach her how to make a better report, and she felt she'd improved somewhat as a result. Not that it was easy, to slog through all the tedious and minute details.

She paused to review what she'd written thus far, and frowned to contemplate the many odd details that seemed to exist, in this strange case. They'd been called-in by a PC who shouldn't have been there—he wasn't an ethnic match for the area—but Acton thought the man was one of Flynn's light-o'-loves, and that might explain his presence. Although—although it truly didn't, unless the two were supposed to rendezvous in a Lambeth alleyway—which seemed unlikely, since the PC was on duty and in uniform.

She paused to consider this. Acton had downplayed the PC's involvement, but the fact remained that he shouldn't have been at the scene, and if he was having an extra-marital affair with Flynn it was certainly possible that the man should be a considered a suspect—it would also explain the nervousness that she'd sensed, despite his best efforts to hide it.

Strange, that Acton would downplay the PC's presence, even though she was certain Acton did not know who'd killed Flynn. But her husband had pointed out that it was unlikely the man would hang about the crime scene, or place the lanyard 'round the victim's neck—which made complete sense, and did indeed seem to indicate that he wasn't a suspect.

Idly, she tapped a finger against the table, thinking about this. Mayhap she should ask Williams whether or not to follow-up with the fellow—after all, they hadn't any other suspects to speak of. She then remembered that Williams was not the SIO on the case—Gabriel had been called-in at the last minute. Which was also a bit unusual, since Acton tended to put her on Williams' cases—he trusted Williams to keep her safe when she was out in the field.

With a knit brow, she lifted her gaze out the windows. So; she'd a case where both the reporting PC and the SIO were not who they should be. Which didn't truly mean much, of course—try to concentrate, lass, and write your report.

As she doggedly bent her head to resume typing, Reynolds ventured, "Shall I set a place for Miss Melinda at dinner, madam?"

Quirking her mouth, Doyle replied, "She may want to stay for dinner, but I doubt Acton will allow it. He's one to make no bones about heavin' her out the door."

"Certainly; Lord Acton makes his preference quite clear, if I may say so."

She had to smile, because it seemed the butler had been offended by Melinda's remark about a potential affair with the aforesaid Lord Acton. To sooth him, Doyle disclosed, "She was just teasin', Reynolds. They were an item, back in the day."

She was fairly certain Reynolds already knew this—he kept himself very well-informed—but the servant feigned surprise. "Is that so? You are very tolerant, madam, if I may say so."

Doyle shrugged. "She's harmless enough—not pinin' after him in the least." She paused, thinking about it. "It's more as though they've survived a war, together."

"It appears they have another war on their hands, madam."

He was referring to the Lady Madeline situation, which was indeed in the nature of a war. Melinda's aristocratic mother-in-law was understandably outraged that the likes of Melinda had not only persuaded her naïve-and-priestly son into a clandestine marriage, but had stolen a fortune as a result of his unexpected death. Consequently, Lady Madeline was certain that Melinda was a murderess, and had put private investigators on the matter with no expense spared.

Doyle remarked, "Aye, although it's a bit surprisin', actually. I wonder that Acton spends so much of his time tryin' to sort it out—it's not as though he can't throw his weight around, and tell Lady Madeline's people to push-off."

"I would imagine," Reynolds offered a bit carefully, "that Lord Acton wishes to avoid any unfavorable press on the subject of Father Clarence's death."

This, because Father Clarence had died at Acton's estate—which would ordinarily be something a journalist might be eager to explore, but Reynolds was not aware—as Doyle was—that Acton had some well-placed allies in the press, just as he seemed to have everywhere, and that therefore this would not be much of a concern.

Indeed, someone who was not as well-versed in the ways of the House of Acton might think Acton was being careful because he was worried that law enforcement might start asking some troubling questions of his mother and his cousin. But someone who was well-versed—which Doyle was, in spades—knew that Acton could squelch any such investigation without so much as turning a hair.

It was a bit of a puzzle, actually, that her husband was being so accommodating, and it occurred to Doyle that mayhap she should look into the matter of Lady Madeline's investigation a bit more carefully. Her husband was not behaving in his usual manner—his usual manner being to protect the House of Acton at all costs, and to the last inch—and in her experience, any deviation usually meant he was cooking-up something that was sure to turn her hair grey.

"Will you require Miss Cherry tomorrow morning, madam?"

Recalled from her abstraction, Doyle nodded. "I think so; Munoz is up for promotion, and so she'll want to leave no stone unturned—what with this case involvin' one of our own."

"As is only right," the butler agreed, and then lowered his voice.

"I might mention that Lord Acton was concerned enough to ask—through back channels—that the Coroner's top team be sent out, instead of the one that was first assigned."

Doyle's hands stilled for a moment, and then she continued typing—nonsense letters, just so as to appear unsurprised by this disclosure. In an offhand tone, she observed, "Well, he'd want to be extra-careful. And you wouldn't want to hurt anyone's feelings, by outright givin' the order to change one team over to another."

"Precisely, madam. I imagine that is why he asked me to phone-in the request to Ms. Corso, rather than have his Assistant do it."

"Yandra Corso is top o' the trees," Doyle managed in a casual tone. "You can hardly blame him."

CHAPTER 11

*R*eynolds left to run some errands, which was a welcome break since it allowed Doyle to stop her pretend-typing and frowningly stare out the window in extreme puzzlement.

So; another person had been switched-out in this case, and that made three—between the PC, the SIO and the Coroner's team. And it could be presumed—based off Reynolds' remark—that it was *Acton* who'd switched them all out. Why would he do so? And why on the quiet? It made no sense; he was unhappy with Corso and he'd discreetly rebuked her—Doyle was certain of it. But it was hard to believe that he'd switch the entire Coroner's team solely because he wanted to rebuke the young woman at the scene—he could rebuke her in private any time he wished. It was all very strange.

And he'd been unhappy with Munoz, too—if Melinda's observation was correct about yesterday's fracas at The Grenoble Hotel. But—again—such a thing didn't seem to add up with the events of the morning; Doyle hadn't held the sense that Munoz and Acton were being anything other than professional with one another. It seemed much more likely that Melinda had misinterpreted whatever it was that she'd seen.

Although—although Doyle realized that she was jumping to conclusions again, instead of being a good assemble-the-facts sort of detective. She'd assumed Melinda's reference to a Spanish-looking girl meant Munoz, but Yandra Corso was just as Spanish-looking as Munoz.

Oh-oh, she thought with a jolt of dismay. When Acton had confessed that Yandra Corso carried a torch for him, it was true. But —but what if that torch was a mutual one? Melinda had described the argument as "passionate," which was not a word anyone who knew him would use to describe Acton, and Melinda knew him well.

No, Doyle chided herself yet again; you're being fanciful, lass— you are the center of that man's world.

But on the other hand, now she'd two verified reports of Acton behaving in a way that was completely out-of-character, and both times seemed to involve the Coroner's Assistant—although she should double-check about Corso's involvement in the hotel fracas. Therefore, with no further ado she phoned Munoz.

"Doyle."

"Will you be needin' me tomorrow mornin'? I'm sortin' out child care, so as to be ready."

"Yes. Let's do a more thorough canvass of that area at mid-morning when there are more people around, and show the snaps we have of the person who was following the victim. They're not the greatest, but someone may recognize who it is."

"Aye then. And we should probably check-in with the staff at The Grenoble Hotel, too."

There was a pause. "And why is that?"

"They may know somethin'."

Annoyed, Munoz replied, "I have no idea what you are talking about, Doyle. Where's The Grenoble Hotel? It's definitely not in that area."

"It's a hotel in my neighborhood, and they've some West Indies staff," Doyle offered lamely. Truly, she should have thought of a better explanation for the question ahead of time, but it didn't really matter since it was now confirmed that it wasn't Munoz who was arguing with Acton at The Grenoble Hotel. To bolster her fake-excuse, she offered, "There must be a connection betwixt Mallory Flynn and that community, else why would she be there? Since the people who live there don't want to say, we may have to look further afield."

But Munoz, who was very much an assemble-the-facts sort of detective, was understandably skeptical of this made-up theory. "We can't just go barging-around to harass a certain ethnic sector, Doyle—we need a lead." This, because—despite the fact London was an amazingly diverse city—Hispanic ethnicities tended to be vastly outnumbered by other minorities.

Since Doyle couldn't very well speak of Acton-fracases, she could only insist lamely, "It doesn't make sense that Flynn was sellin' drugs in that neighborhood, but there she was; mayhap she was a mule, actin' for a drug network."

"What do her electronics show?"

"Nothin'," Doyle confessed. "She probably knew enough to use a burner phone."

This was—unfortunately—one of the by-products of seeing the ins-and-outs of law-breaking up close; Met personnel might succumb to bribery—or might even try a hand in the wrongdoing themselves after having learned the tricks of the trade, so to speak. It was why police officers were given integrity-checks on occasion —they'd come across drugs or money, left lying about, so that the brass could test what they would do in such a situation. Unfortunately, there were no integrity-checks for administrative personnel, being as they were less likely to be directly confronted with temptation.

Reminded, Doyle ventured, "Should we canvass her department?" This would be a sticky wicket, since if any Met personnel admitted they had knowledge that a coworker was stealing illegal drugs, they'd be promptly fired.

"Acton said he'd handle it, which is fine by me."

"I suppose that makes sense—it's a sensitive subject," Doyle agreed thoughtfully, but noted that—once again—someone was being switched-out of position on this case. "Are we settin'- up a Case Management Meetin' with Gabriel?" This was a preliminary step in any homicide case, so that the SIO could approve of an investigative plan and set the parameters for a budget.

"He says we should wait for the Coroner's report, since we're not even sure we have a homicide, yet."

"I suppose that's a good point," Doyle conceded, even as she knew—in the way that she knew things—that Mallory Flynn's death was indeed a murder. "I'll see you tomorrow, then; what time d'you want me at the scene?"

"I'll pick you up," Munoz offered. "Nine o' clock."

"Got it," Doyle replied in her best support-officer voice. She then rang off and reflected, for a moment, on how much her attitude had changed. It used to rankle when Munoz had the lead on a case, but now it didn't rankle at all. No doubt this change in attitude was the direct result of being the support-officer for various small children on a daily basis; it tended to change one's perspective.

But Doyle was still left with her strange husband-puzzle, and it gave her pause. She could ask him outright why he was switching-out personnel like a house afire, but she was hesitant; she needed to know more, and besides, she didn't want to land poor Reynolds in the soup for grassing Acton out—or Melinda either, for that matter.

On the other hand, she tended to lay all Acton-cards on the table, mainly because she didn't want to behave like one of those stupid heroines in an over-dramatic story who didn't just *ask* the hero why he'd done what he did. Most times, when she confronted Acton, it turned out to be the right thing to do—mainly because it made him think twice about whatever scheme he was trying to mastermind behind her back.

But in this particular instance, she felt as though the reports she was receiving were almost too bizarre to be true—especially the one where Acton was having a public argument with an underling.

Although the discreet Grenoble Hotel wasn't exactly public, of course. Still and all, it was very, very strange.

She could always wander into the hotel, herself, and try to find out what had happened. Unfortunately, it was beyond her powers to come up with an explanation as to why she wanted to know whether her husband had been arguing with an attractive young woman in the lobby—or at least, an explanation that didn't point to an imminent divorce. And if The Grenoble Hotel staff thought that a divorce was in the offing, the last thing they'd do would be to side with Doyle against the illustrious Earl-who-was-also-a-Baron-not-to-mention-a-Chief-Inspector; she'd no illusions about who held all the power in their relationship—or at least, according to the general public.

On the other hand, she did have a staunch ally at the CID, and presumably the hotel would have CCTV tape of the comings and goings in the lobby.

Doyle paused for a moment, weighing this possibility. She could ask Williams to take a look, but Williams might not be the best ally in this situation. Indeed, that one time she'd thought that Acton was having an affair with nasty Cassie Masterson, Williams had wanted to speak to Acton on her behalf without her knowing—he was the chivalrous type, who'd try to take matters into his own hands. So; it may be better to ask her other ally at the Met to take a look at the hotel surveillance—Gabriel had been with MI 5, after all, and he could probably access the hotel's security tape without the hotel even being made aware.

She paused again, and tried to decide whether she was indeed being the over-hysterical heroine to even consider such a course of action. If the tape showed what Melinda had described, then Gabriel would be in possession of some very interesting information, and in the end, she wasn't absolutely certain she could trust him with it. Gabriel was a friend, but he'd his quirks; he'd been addicted to drugs, once, and seemed to be addicted to Munoz, too—no other reason would explain why he continued to pine after her, even as she was now firmly out of his reach. And the last needful thing would be to allow Gabriel to have useful leverage over Acton—not because Acton would be compromised, but because if Gabriel ever attempted to use it, he would likely disappear, never to be seen again. Acton may be trying to mend his ways, but Doyle had no illusions about what would be the result if he were ever directly threatened.

I'm going to wait and think it over, she decided. This turn of events is a little too personal to trust anyone with it—anyone else might think Acton was succumbing to temptation, but anyone else doesn't know what makes the Chief Inspector tick, and that his pendulum is firmly and permanently wrapped around his unlikely Irish bride.

CHAPTER 12

He'd sent word around The Remnant that everyone was to stay quiet, and out of sight—even the orishas. Especially the orishas.

$\mathcal{W}$hen Acton's meeting was finished—and as Doyle had predicted, Melinda was promptly shown the door—his wife did not raise the subject that was uppermost on her mind, but instead asked, "How goes the battle with Lady Madeline?"

Acton let out a breath, as he settled-in beside her at the table. "You can hardly blame the woman for her suspicions. I confess I sympathize with her."

This, because—in truth—Father Clarence had indeed been a victim. Acton's mother, the Dowager Lady Acton, and Acton's wretched cousin, Sir Stephen, had been conniving to kill-off the overweight priest and seize his fortune, but Melinda had sussed-out their plan and promptly married the man in secret, so that she'd inherit, instead of them.

But Melinda's sleight-of-hand made no matter to the late

priest's bereaved mother, who was sparing no expense in her quest for justice. In turn, Melinda—now possessed of a fortune—had hired a tenacious solicitor who was well-known for giving as good as she got, in a legal knife-fight.

It was all very distressing of course, but there was one element to this tumultuous tale that made little sense to Doyle; when it came to a legal knife-fight, no one could hold a candle to Doyle's wedded husband. Yet for some reason, he seemed content to watch from the sidelines.

Made thoroughly uneasy by this fact, Doyle asked bluntly, "What's afoot, that Melinda feels she needs to consult with you?"

He replied, "The investigators would like to interview Melinda, as well as the staff at the Dower House at Trestles. And so, we are negotiating the parameters of those interviews."

This, because due to the fact the investigation was being conducted by a private firm—and not the police—the interviewees were under no compulsion to cooperate. Which immediately prompted Doyle to ask, "Remind me why the coppers aren't involved in this mess."

"Because there is nothing to suggest Father Clarence died of anything other than cardiac arrest."

But Doyle pointed out, "Well, there's the dodgy marriage and the dodgy inheritance. The poor man may have been overweight, but he was young—you'd think it would raise a small doubt."

But Acton only demurred, "The police in Yorkshire do not believe there is enough to open a formal investigation."

Doyle caught a nuance to his tone, and thought, oh-ho—this must be how he's handling it; he's made certain that law enforcement would not rush to be involved—mayhap he's dropped a word in their ear about his own conclusions—and he must believe the private investigators will not uncover enough for the police to bring charges; as a Chief Inspector, he'd know exactly how much they'd need. And that would explain why he was content to let Lady Madeline rattle Melinda's cage, and content to let the investigators tread upon the sacred grounds of Trestles—he knows they won't come up with enough evidence to prompt the police to take an interest. On the other hand, he doesn't want any hint of a cover-up from his corner, which is why he's going out of his way to cooperate.

Rather relieved that she'd figured out his plan, Doyle asked, "Will you attend the interviews?"

"No. Melinda's solicitor will attend."

Although his own presence would have done more to intimidate the opposition, Doyle felt she understood his motivation, yet again; if he stepped in, it would appear that he was trying to interfere with the investigation, and he would want to avoid any such appearance if he was fairly certain that nothing would ever come of it.

He was idly reading her report on the laptop screen—keeping tabs on what she'd gleaned, he was—and this prompted her to ask in a casual tone, "D'you have any advice about handlin' this strange case? Munoz wants to go canvass a bit harder tomorrow, but we've precious little to go on."

"You are unlikely to gain much from the community," he conceded. "It would be better to go at it from the victim's end."

"Well, her 'end' is fairly sparse, unfortunately. Her electronics are far too clean, which only seems to verify that she was sellin' drugs and usin' burner phones."

"I would tend to agree."

"Which in turn tends to support the theory that hers was an admonishment-murder, if she's peddlin' her wares in a Lambeth alley, bold as brass."

He reminded her, "It is not yet clear that her death is a murder."

This seemed a perfect opening, and so Doyle took it. "Aye; and there's another puzzle—what was the cause-of-death? Did Yandra Corso stop moonin' over you long enough to have any bright ideas?"

"She could find no obvious indications. We will hope that the autopsy can shed some light."

Frustrating, it was, that the man was parrying her questions with unhelpful generalizations and hoping she'd not notice. A bit more pointedly, Doyle asked, "D'you think Corso's competent, in the first place? She's not used to field-work."

"We can only hope," was his equivocal answer.

Since it seemed clear he wasn't going to offer any more insights—and because she didn't want to appear over-curious—Doyle reluctantly changed the subject. "Speakin' of which, Munoz doesn't want to say, since she's up for promotion, but I think she'd rather not have too many assignments where Gabriel is her SIO."

He raised his brows. "Do you think the past relationship interferes with their work?"

"I don't think so—although that's a clear case of the pot and the kettle, my friend; ours does, and it never seems to bother you in the least."

He drew her to him, and kissed her temple. "On the contrary, we have an excellent track record."

Leaning into his shoulder, she agreed, "That we do. I wouldn't mention it, but I do think he still pines for her, and it makes her a wee bit uncomfortable."

"I will see what I can do."

"Don't let her know I said," Doyle cautioned. "She hasn't complained, but I know it irks her."

"I won't say anything; she is fortunate to have you as an ally."

Doyle made a face. "Fortunate only in that I'm married to you. If it was me complaining about you, I'd have no allies whatsoever —there's not a soul alive who thinks I'm more important than you."

"Williams does," he offered. "It gave me more than a few sleepless nights."

She decided this sentiment should be rewarded, and twined her arms 'round his neck to kiss him wholeheartedly. "It's rather sweet, to think that you were worried, Michael."

He pressed his forehead against hers and admitted, "I was worried enough to put it to the test."

"Then I owe Williams one—little does he know that he inspired your proposal."

"You are loyal by nature, and so I had to acquire first rights."

She laughed, because this was probably true—if Williams had acted first, she'd have probably stayed loyal to him; Acton was a shrewd judge of character. "Well, I hope he's loyal to our Lizzie—unfortunately, I get the feelin' that she's miles more invested than he is."

"Perhaps," he agreed.

She sighed. "It's a shame, that this love-and-longin' business isn't easier to control, with everyone sorted-out for happily-ever-after."

"I would agree. And oftentimes, we see the unfortunate results."

But she shook her head. "No—when people resort to murder, that's not out of genuine love, Michael; instead it's thwarted-love—which is a nasty sort of selfish-love, where nothing else matters save that you punish the person who's dared to spurn you."

"I suppose that is a fair assessment."

"'Tis," she insisted. "That one time I thought you were havin' an affair, I didn't want to murder anyone—I didn't even want to fight for you; I just wanted to curl-up and die like that girl with that famous knight."

He considered this. "Elaine?"

"Aye, that's the one."

But he tilted his head in mild disagreement. "I don't know as Elaine is a good example of selfless-love; she made certain that her death was a public rebuke of Lancelot."

"Oh. Not that I'd have any idea, of course—I'm cribbin' from Reynolds."

"Believe it or not, I'd guessed as much."

She laughed, and fondly played with the hair on the nape of his neck. "You wonder why people chafe so much, when their love isn't returned. If it's not meant to be, it's not meant to be—no need to kick up a fuss and embarrass yourself."

"I suppose that all depends on one's personality."

She quirked her mouth. "You'd fight like the dickens."

"I would fight like the dickens," he agreed, and kissed her again.

"Well, we're lucky you'll never have to, then. And speakin' of such, Savoie's weddin' is Saturday."

"Yes. I thought we'd hold our dinner-party the following evening."

She sighed. "Faith, I was half-hopin' you'd forgot that little plan."

Teasing, he bent his head to look at her. "Surely, it will not be so bad?"

"If you insist. They're not takin' a honeymoon?"

"Apparently not."

Thoughtfully, she said, "I suppose that's in keepin'. They're both all about family, and stayin' in the daily routine."

"We didn't take a honeymoon, either," he reminded her.

"We're not the honeymoonin' type," she pronounced, and then decided to add, "We're more the sneak-away-to-The-Grenoble-Hotel type."

But he didn't show the least trace of self-consciousness, and instead teased in turn, "Speaking of such, what does the remainder of your afternoon look like?"

"Too late," she replied. "There's Tommy, on the monitor."

CHAPTER 13

$\mathcal{T}$hat night, Doyle had one of her dreams. She had them, on occasion; strange and vivid dreams which seemed very real but which were clearly not, since they usually featured someone who was no longer alive. Ghost-dreams, where the ghost in question seemed determined to convey some sort of message to her—a message that often was connected to the various challenges she faced in her casework or in her personal life—and sometimes both.

The ghost-dreams used to upset her, but she'd learned to tolerate them—as uncomfortable as they were—mainly because the message that was being delivered always turned out to be important. Unfortunately, the message itself was always rather vague and unclear—you'd think whoever was going to all the trouble wouldn't tax the fair Doyle's wits to the extent that the ghost-messengers did, but she didn't seem to have much choice in the matter, and so she coped as best she could.

Sometimes the ghost was someone Doyle had known in life, and sometimes the ghost was a stranger to her. This time, to Doyle's great surprise, the dream featured both.

She frowned, as she stood in the darkness and reviewed the two women who were arrayed before her. "I'm not sure what to make of this," she admitted into the silence.

The first woman was seated in the foreground—slumped over and thoroughly miserable—and Doyle recognized Cassie Masterson, the nasty brasser who'd thought to steal Acton away from his wedded wife. With a great deal of satisfaction, Doyle observed that Masterson looked to be reaping what she'd sowed in that she wore manacles on her wrists; the old-fashioned kind, with a heavy chain hanging betwixt them.

The second woman stood behind Masterson—very straight and still—and Doyle recognized her immediately from the portrait that hung in the long gallery at Trestles—not to mention the woman wore Doyle's tiara, atop her red curls. She'd been Lady Acton way-back-when, in medieval times, and she wore an elaborate dress made of stiff brocade and velvet so as to emphasize this fact. The medieval ghost made no movement, but instead stood still-as-a-statue behind Cassie Masterson, gazing into the distance with her hands folded before her.

"I'm only here to translate," Cassie Masterson groused, thoroughly annoyed. "I'd just as soon never see you again."

"The same to you, and twice-over," Doyle retorted. "You're an out-and-out brasser, and I'm that happy you're sufferin' your just desserts."

"It's *none* of your business—" the other snapped, but then suddenly quieted whilst taking a conscious over her shoulder at her companion—as though the medieval ghost had spoken to her, even though the lady hadn't moved an inch. Settling into a sulk, Masterson explained, "I'm supposed to translate, because she doesn't speak English."

Doyle blinked in surprise. "She doesn't? But—isn't she English?"

Masterson scoffed, "Shows how much you know; the nobility spoke French, in her time."

Doyle could not hide her skepticism—mainly because she was not inclined to believe anything that came out of Masterson's mouth. "I thought her husband hated the French—there was some big battle that he always goes on-and-on about; some battle in France that he fought with King Hal." Doyle had met the lady's husband—a fearsome ghost-knight—on several occasions when she'd stayed at Acton's ancestral estate.

Impatiently, Masterson chided, "Let's move on, shall we? She wants you to listen to what she has to say."

Doyle resisted an urge to argue some more—truly, it was a fine feeling to see Masterson suffering such a well-deserved comeuppance—but with a mighty effort, she swallowed her temper. "Fine, then."

The lady continued to gaze into the distance, very still, and didn't seem inclined to say anything. To Doyle's surprise, however, Masterson acted as though she'd indeed spoken, and translated, "She says you must admonish the sinner."

"Oh—oh, does she?" asked Doyle, a bit confused. "Does she mean 'admonish the sinner,' like they tell you in the Seven Spiritual Acts?" According to the RC church, one of the Seven Spiritual Acts of Mercy was to admonish the sinner, so that he or she could put their feet on a better path and not lose all chance of heaven.

"I have no idea," Masterson returned in a terse tone. "I'm just the translator."

Doyle reasoned doubtfully, "I know that's what we're *supposed* to do, but it's easier said than done—especially in modern life. You don't want to come across as preachy, and holier-than-thou. I think everyone just leaves the admonishin' to the priests, nowadays, since they are given leave to be preachy and holier-than-thou. Otherwise, you'll be hard-pressed to find anyone who goes about admonishin' the sinners."

Masterson listened to the silent, serene woman. "You must not draw back," Masterson translated. "It is important."

"Right," Doyle reluctantly conceded. "Are we talkin' about Acton?" This seemed likely; unfortunately, Acton had a bushel of sins piled up in his name and despite his wife's best efforts, the man didn't look to be changing his ways any time soon.

"No; he is shielding the sinners."

Slowly, Doyle nodded. "Aye; he's changin' people out, and makin' sure I don't know what's happened."

Masterson paused as though listening, and then said with palpable relief, "She says that's right. Good; hopefully, we're done here."

The medieval ghost remained still, but Masterson suddenly pressed her lips together mulishly. "Never mind; I guess we're not done."

Into the silence, Doyle offered, "I think there's somethin' that he doesn't want me to find out—somethin' truly awful." She frowned, thinking about it. "I've that 'deja view' feelin'—as though the same thing has happened before—but I can't put my finger on it."

Exasperated, Masterson chided, "It's *déjà vu*, you idiot."

"*You're* the one who's the idiot," Doyle retorted. "Try to be more helpful—ask her to give me a hint, and steer me in the right direction."

Bristling, Masterson retorted, "I don't take orders from you."

"Mayhap you should have, and then you wouldn't be in this pickle—you nasty two-penny *brasser*."

"Shut *up*."

"No, *you* shut up."

Brought up short, Masterson paused to listen again, and with a sour, subdued attitude she repeated, "You must admonish the sinner."

"Who's the sinner?" Doyle asked, in all confusion. "And what's the sin?"

But she was suddenly startled awake, and found herself staring at the bedroom ceiling with her heart hammering in her ears.

CHAPTER 14

The Husband was her acolyte, and mighty in the land. The Foolish Child could not see the coming Devastation, but he could. He'd seen it before.

The next morning, Doyle found herself in an uncertain mood as she parried baby Tommy's attempts to seize his spoon. There seemed little question that last night's ghosts were connected to the Mallory Flynn murder, even though she couldn't make heads-nor-tails of how they might fit in.

Obviously, there's a sinner lurking about, Doyle reasoned. Could the ghost be referring to Flynn's murderer? That the murderer was a sinner shouldn't be a news-flash, and Doyle had the sense that the ghost was referring to someone who wasn't quite so obvious. And it was all the more confusing, because Flynn herself was something of a sinner; come to think of it, it might not be a coincidence that Masterson was featured in the dream, and Masterson was another brasser like Flynn, who thought nothing of having affairs with married men. They were peas in a pod, but since Flynn was good-and-dead, she definitely wasn't in need of admonishment; she was heaven's problem, now.

And Doyle decided that she probably shouldn't forget that yet another brasser had come to light; Yandra Corso was coveting another woman's husband—that was a sin, too, although Doyle shied away from the thought of admonishing the Coroner's Assistant. After all, Corso probably didn't know that Doyle knew, and it would be *horrendously* embarrassing. Besides, Acton had already done some admonishing, himself—didn't seem as though a second dose was needful nor necessary.

All in all, the two ghost-visitors seemed a very strange pairing, if the dream-topic was supposed to be unscrupulous brassers who went about trying to steal people's husbands. Whilst Masterson had tried to brazen her way into Doyle's role as Acton's wife, the knight's wife—by contrast—hadn't brazened her way anywhere; faith, she hadn't even wanted to be Lady Acton in the first place. Brave, she'd been; even though the Trestles knight had ruined her family and seized their holdings, she'd stepped-up to marry the man, so as to broker a peace between their peoples.

Indeed, the lady seemed a far cry from her husband; when the Trestles knight had visited Doyle's dreams, he'd been all thunder and demanding, mainly because—as it turned out—he'd been worried about his legacy, and making certain that Acton's cousin didn't get his questionable mitts on the reins of the House of Acton. By contrast, his wife seemed a very gentle sort of person—not demanding a'tall, and willing to stay back so as to let Masterson to do all the message-sending.

It was passing strange, that such a lady had been paired-up with Cassie Masterson to tell Doyle to admonish the sinner—which was in itself a very strange and rather old-fashioned message. Faith; when you thought about it, if the believers spent all their time admonishing the sinners in this fallen world, they'd have little time for anything else.

Reynolds was bent over the kitchen counter, busily making lists for the coming dinner-party—in his glory, he was, and it was a crackin' shame he hadn't landed somewhere where they held fancy parties, day and night. In his precise voice, he asked, "Have you any preference when it comes to canapés, madam?"

Blankly, Doyle stared at him. "Aren't we holdin' it indoors?"

With some confusion, the servant glanced her way. "Indeed, madam. It is my understanding we are holding the dinner-party here."

"Then why do we need canopies?"

The servant's brow cleared. "Canapés, madam. *Hors d'oeuvres.*"

Doyle considered this. "Appetizers, d'you mean?"

"Exactly," the servant agreed with some relief. "I thought perhaps we'd offer pass-plates of *gougères.*"

"Of course, you did," she said a bit crossly. "You may suit yourself, because I've no idea what's appropriate. If it were left to me, we'd have pasties straight off a street-cart on Ringsend Road."

The butler condescended to explain, "*Gougères* is French for cheese-puffs, madam."

Doyle brightened. "Oh—well, that's fine, then." Reminded, she asked, "Did you know, Reynolds, that the English aristocracy spoke French, way back when?"

Reynolds had returned to his list, and answered rather absently, "Yes, madam. Until the time of King John, I believe."

Doyle frowned. "Seems very strange thing to do, if the French were their hated enemy."

In a distracted tone, the servant explained, "It stemmed from the Norman invasion, madam."

Doyle decided not to follow-up on this seeming *non sequitur,* and instead persisted, "It doesn't make a bit of sense; why would they go and fight the French at that big battle? Aggocore, or somethin'."

Reynolds offered, "It is rather a long story, madam." This, said in a tone which indicated that the speaker was not inclined to recite chapter-and-verse, just now.

With some amusement, Doyle eyed him. "I'm not *completely*

ignorant, Reynolds; one of Acton's ancestors fought in that battle, I'll have you know."

Somewhat aghast, Reynolds immediately put down his list and hastened to say, "Forgive me, madam; I meant no such implication."

Doyle smiled. "You're readily forgiven, Reynolds—not to mention that I *am* completely ignorant, when it comes to the stupid English and their stupid history."

Reynolds was seen to struggle with how best to respond to such a remark, and settled upon, "If you say so, madam."

"D'you know anythin' about Acton's ancestor—the one who fought in that battle?"

"I know a bit, madam. I believe he was rewarded for his heroics with a grant of land taken from another Baron, whose allegiance to the current king was more questionable."

Doyle raised her brows. "Ah—that makes sense. And then he married the man's daughter, so as to keep the peace—not that theirs was a love-match by any means, but they got on well, together; she's the one who originally wore my tiara. He wasn't very faithful, though, and shame on him."

Doyle paused, suddenly struck; the knight had once mentioned that Lizzie Williams was a descendant of his, through one of his illegitimate children. Lizzie was now pregnant—could it be that the medieval lady was worried about *Lizzie,* for some reason? That would be very kind of her—to be concerned about a descendant of her husband's by-blow. So; was the sinner-warning about Lizzie and her marriage, mayhap? Williams had been showing an unfortunate inclination to stray—could he be the sinner who was in need of admonishing? After all, Acton was concerned enough to ask the fair Doyle to sound-out Williams at the dinner-party, even though such an attempt would be a trick-and-a-half, since Williams was no fool.

It might also explain why Acton had suddenly switched-out Williams as the SIO on the Flynn case, and had substituted Gabriel, instead. But try as she might, she could not convince herself that this was the solution to the puzzle; there was something going on here that went much deeper than whether Williams was inclined to stray—something rather—rather *dark*, for lack of a better term. Dark and messy.

Suddenly, she realized why she'd the sense that it felt so familiar—it reminded her of that time they'd gone to Dublin, and Acton had been called upon to handle poor Timothy McGonigal's disaster—which her husband had ably done, even though he'd had to move heaven and earth, and do it fairly quickly. Was this situation something similar? Whose disaster was Acton fixing, and why didn't he want her to find out?

Reynolds' rather surprised voice interrupted her train of thought. "I must say that you are very well-informed, madam."

Hastily remembering that she shouldn't be quite so well-informed when it came to people who were long dead, Doyle offered as explanation, "There was a reporter who came in to Trestles once, to do a bit of research in the archives—Cassie Masterson, she was. Although mainly she spent her time makin' sheep's eyes at Acton."

Reynolds nodded discreetly. "An unfortunate episode, I understand."

With no small satisfaction, Doyle thought—unfortunate for our Ms. Masterson, anyways; Acton well-and-thoroughly cooked her goose, and no one deserved it more. Aloud, she advised, "Aye; she was a nasty piece of work, Reynolds, and met a bad end, for her sins."

Doyle paused, because she was once again struck by the—the *oddness* of the ghost-pairing. Usually, the identity of the ghost was an important factor in whatever message Doyle was supposed to be receiving, but Doyle hadn't the first clue as to why the dastardly Cassie Masterson was having to play handmaiden to the knight's gentle wife. It could be a strange form of penance for the former journalist, but Doyle didn't have the impression that the awful woman was remotely sorry for her sins.

Her mobile pinged, and thus reminded, Doyle hastily took a last gulp of coffee and stood up. "That's Munoz; I'd best get downstairs, so I'm afraid you're left with our Tommy, here. Best of luck."

"Quite happy to, madam," the butler said, as he discreetly reached for an apron.

"Text me if you need more advice on canopies and cheese-puffs."

"Very good, madam," Reynolds replied, and then took-up Tommy's spoon with a stoic air.

CHAPTER 15

$\mathcal{T}$he doorman saluted Doyle as he pulled open Munoz's passenger car door, and Doyle obligingly slid within. "Mornin', Munoz."

But the other detective was not interested in social niceties, as she pulled the vehicle into traffic. "Listen Doyle, I need a favor."

Aha, thought Doyle—the penny drops; that's why she wanted to pick me up this fine morning. "That depends on the favor."

Munoz blew out a breath. "It's about the fertility issue."

"Oh—what's up?" The last Doyle had heard, Munoz's obstetrician had advised that the couple wait a year before visiting a fertility specialist, since Munoz was young and there were no apparent roadblocks.

"I really want to go see a fertility doctor—just as a preliminary, to see what my options are—but Geary's kind of against it."

"Geary and your OB," Doyle reminded her.

"I don't need to hear your opinion, Doyle."

Doyle shrugged. "Touchy, you are, for someone who's wantin' a favor."

"I made an appointment today, but I need you to cover for me."

"What do I have to do?" Doyle asked suspiciously.

"I don't think it will even come up, but if it does, I need you to say I was with you when you were interviewing a witness."

"You're not goin' to the canvass?" Doyle asked in surprise.

"Yes—of course I am. We just need to save a witness for later this afternoon, when I have my appointment."

Thoughtfully, Doyle offered, "I could go talk to the staff at The Grenoble Hotel—see if they've heard anythin' about the victim. See if anyone knows why she died where she was."

Munoz glanced at her. "You've got a bug about that hotel, don't you?"

"I do," Doyle readily admitted.

But Munoz was clearly skeptical. "I think it's a stretch."

Doyle played her trump card. "Then it's perfect; no one's goin' to look too closely at whether you were there with me or not."

"All right, go ahead. Just keep it short, and be careful we don't get a complaint about harassing minorities."

"Right." There was a small silence before Doyle added, "You're actin' a bit crazed, if I may say so."

Hotly, Munoz retorted, "You wouldn't understand, Doyle; my relatives think I made a big mistake, and they are counting the days until I come to my senses."

Munoz's relatives were high-blooded Spaniards, and the last thing they'd expected was that the pride of the family—who would have her pick of the crop—would turn around and marry an Irish working-class copper. They'd offered grudging support, but were no doubt hoping she'd reconsider her marriage before any children resulted. And—true to form—such an attitude only made Munoz more determined to put paid to it, and immediately.

But Doyle only raised her palms. "Calm down, Munoz—I'm in the same boat; Acton's relatives will be hopin' he dumps me all the way to their graves. Why d'you care what they think?"

The other girl's brows drew down, and she admitted, "I'm just —just so surprised, I guess. Elena got pregnant right away, and so did my cousins."

Doyle nodded, and decided she'd said enough—it was similar

to the unrequited love subject; any comfort that one might offer would seem patronizing, if the comforter didn't have any experience in the matter. Come to think of it, it was very much like the "admonish the sinner" instruction from the Seven Acts; it was hard not to come across as sanctimonious, and superior.

Thinking to change the subject, Doyle asked, "You never told me; how was Ireland?" Munoz had taken a holiday to Ireland a couple of months ago so as to visit her Irish in-laws.

"Good. We laugh about how it's so different from visiting my family."

Doyle had to smile—Munoz's family were by heritage very rigid and formal, whereas Geary's boisterous family were happy if he was happy, and therefore had accepted Munoz with open arms. "Leave it to the Irish."

Munoz made a face. "Well, they're hinting about babies, too."

"Leave it to the Irish," Doyle repeated. Still hoping to change the subject—a sleeveless task, apparently—she offered, "Did you take a drive anywhere?"

"No—the last time we visited we drove around quite a bit, and so this time we stayed mainly in Dublin, and did Dublin things. We visited the Guinness factory."

Doyle smiled. "Of course, you did; I think it's a requirement before you're allowed to leave the country."

Munoz glanced at her. "Believe it or not, we ran into Gabriel there."

Doyle stared at her. "*Gabriel?*"

"He was on a Code Five, and so he couldn't talk about why he was."

A Code Five indicated an undercover operation, which was of interest, since Gabriel was supposedly no longer working for MI 5, and therefore shouldn't be on assignment outside London. Mayhap he was coordinating with the Irish Garda, for some reason? "Faith, there's a surprise. Was it awkward?"

"No, not really. Geary always handles it well—he's the same way with Savoie."

Doyle smiled. "He won, they lost, everyone moves on."

But her companion grimaced. "I only wish Gabriel could move on; he's another one who's hoping I'll come to my senses."

With a small grimace, Doyle could only agree. "Aye—he fell for you hard, my friend; but that's water well-under the bridge, by now. And he's a handsome boyo; I'm amazed he hasn't met someone new."

Munoz confided, "He's kind of sensitive, beneath it all."

"Aye," Doyle agreed, as she'd figured this out for herself. "His jokin'-about is a shield, I think."

But Munoz had tired of the subject, and informed Doyle, "DC Shandera's coming to help canvass this morning—Acton suggested it."

Jerry Shandera was a Detective Constable who hailed from the West Indies, and Doyle could immediately see why he'd been suggested, in light of the Met's "matching-up" policy. "A good thing—I'm worse than useless. The locals take one look at my red head and clam up."

"I'm not much better."

"You speak Spanish, though."

"It's not the same Spanish; they consider me an outsider, too."

They drove in silence for a few minutes—the rain starting to patter on the windscreen—and as they neared the Lambeth neighborhood, Doyle remarked, "This is such a strange case; it has all the earmarks of an admonishment-murder, but we can't find a shred of evidence; you'd think that the whole point of an admonishment-murder would be to make it clear why the victim was killed."

"Exactly. Although we're not even sure we have a case yet, so we don't have a budget. I've got to be careful; budget-management is something they look for in the promotion process."

Doyle nodded, but this remark made her suddenly alert to the possibility that Acton's strange and secretive behind-the-scenes maneuvers were to ensure that no formal homicide case was ever opened. After all, if no formal case-file was ever opened, no one would be delving into Mallory Flynn's questionable doings—both personal and professional. It would explain why he was switching-out personnel and hoping that the wife of his bosom did not catch wind of whatever-it-was that he was covering-up—something that featured a public fracas in a hotel lobby, apparently. Good luck to the man; she was on high-alert, thanks to two mismatched ghosts and Melinda's timely tip-off.

But—thinking this over—she frowned yet again, because this epiphany made little sense. When Acton was in cover-up mode, his trusty stalwarts were Williams and Dr. Chiu, the head Coroner; both men had shown themselves perfectly willing to sidestep the protocols so as to help Acton cover-up whatever he'd decided needed covering-up. But this time—this time he was switching-*out* his trusty stalwarts. Why? Were they compromised? Acton had hinted that Williams might be compromised, but if that was the case, all the more reason to have Williams help with any and all coverings-up. So; mayhap in this particular instance, he felt he could better rely on Gabriel and Corso to help with a cover-up. And she mustn't forget that the one witness thought Flynn was selling drugs, and Gabriel had been in drug-trouble himself, once upon a time.

Doyle's scalp started prickling—which is what it did when her intuition was telling her to pay attention—and she ventured, "Tell me, Munoz; could Gabriel have been involved with Mallory Flynn?"

As she parked the car, Munoz threw her a scornful look. "I don't keep track of Gabriel, Doyle."

Thoughtfully, Doyle replied, "I think you do. You worry about him."

Munoz blew out a breath, and then sat with her hands resting on the wheel for a moment. "All right; I do check-in with him once in a while—just for a quick cup of coffee. I'm a little worried about his having a re-lapse, if I completely cut him off."

Doyle shook her head and said softly, "Poor man."

Munoz added, "I don't know if he was involved with Flynn, but

I did see him talking with her once, at the Deli. I was walking over to meet-up with him, and he didn't know that I'd seen them. He didn't say anything about it."

Doyle found that she wasn't much surprised by this interesting little revelation. So; there did seem to be an Acton-style cover-up underway, and Gabriel must have been involved in misdeeds that had need of covering-up, which was why Acton had abruptly recruited him onto this case. The pieces were starting to fall into place, and half-joking, she offered, "Fingers crossed that Gabriel's not a suspect."

Munoz gave her a look. "He'd just be another on a long list, Doyle—Mallory Flynn had something of a reputation. But I don't think they had any kind of relationship, or Gabriel would have recused himself from the case."

"Of course," Doyle agreed, since Munoz was unfamiliar with Acton-operations.

As she grabbed her umbrella, Munoz reminded her, "Although we're not even sure we have a homicide case yet."

Acton thinks we do, Doyle thought; but he doesn't want anyone else to know, including me.

CHAPTER 16

*The Harlot's death was a reproach to The Foolish Child, and now he would
see whether she would heed that reproach. It troubled him; the young ones
had not wisdom.*

Once again, they approached the alley were the body had
been found and saw that DC Shandera was already on-
site, waiting for them in the smattering rain.

"Jerry," Doyle greeted him. "How's the family?"

He smiled. "Another baby, on the way."

"That is excellent," Doyle said, and quickly changed the subject.
"We've somethin' of a mystery here, since we're not yet clear on
cause-of-death."

"Wow—Dr. Hsu is stumped?"

"We're workin' with Yandra Corso, this time around."

"Huh," he said thoughtfully.

Munoz eyed him. "Huh, what?"

"I'm just surprised she's on this case."

This was a fair point, since Corso was not experienced in field-work, the case was top-priority. Munoz offered, "I'm sure Dr. Hsu will step in, if he thinks he's needed. We definitely need to get some answers—although I should warn you that DCI Acton has hinted there may be information that should be suppressed, if it's not relevant."

"Got it," he replied easily, and Doyle decided that he must know about Flynn's reputation. Hopefully, he wasn't another one caught in her toils.

Munoz continued, "We're taking a canvass, and asking whether anyone saw anything on the morning of the murder, and whether they'd ever seen Flynn here before." Munoz produced two photos, and handed them to him. "We're also asking if anyone knows this woman—or at least, we're presuming it's a woman; she was on surveillance tape following Flynn that morning."

He reviewed the grainy image of the figure wearing a hoodie. "Is she a suspect?"

"Maybe. She doesn't have a visible weapon, and from the tape, she looked more like a customer—we think Flynn may have been selling drugs. No one was willing to talk when we canvassed the day-of, but since we've given it a day, maybe the photos will prompt someone to give us a lead."

Munoz indicated the south side of the street. "I'll send you along this side—no one would open their doors, day-of. Maybe you'll have better luck."

Shandera admitted, "I've been asked to stay with Officer Doyle, ma'am."

Both women stared at him for a moment, and then Munoz asked, "By DCI Acton?"

"Yes, ma'am."

"No arguing with that," said Munoz in a brisk tone. "All right; both of you take that side, and I'll take the other."

"Stay within shoutin' distance," Doyle cautioned. It appeared that that Acton was uneasy about the fair Doyle wandering in this area alone, which seemed rather ominous.

Shandera began knocking on doors, and after the first few no-responses, they were stepping down from a doorstep when an elderly woman came 'round the corner and halted on the front walk, clearly dismayed to behold a brace of detectives at her door. She shifted the bag of groceries she was carrying and uneasily backed away, in an apparent desire to retreat with all speed.

"*Mai*," Shandera offered, spreading his hands. "Come now; nuttin to fear."

The woman paused, and fixed her gaze on the cracked sidewalk before her. "I don't want no *bochinche*," she muttered to Shandera, and then added a phrase in Spanish.

"No trouble, *mai*; none," the officer assured her, as he gestured toward Doyle and Doyle promptly smiled her most friendly smile. "We tryin' to find out what happen to the *gringa*." He held up Flynn's photo. "You seen her, before?"

Doyle noted that he'd copied the sing-song cadence of the resident, as he took a cautious step toward the woman. For her part, she seemed disinclined to move forward as she condescended to give the photo a cursory glance. "No, mon."

This was not true, and Doyle was left with her usual dilemma in such a situation, being as she couldn't very well call-out the witness for lying. Instead, she urged, "Are you certain, ma'am? Her poor family needs answers."

The woman's gaze again dropped to the ground, as she shuffled back a step in her slipper-scuffs. "No—no answers."

This seemed another indication that the woman knew more than she was saying—that she was reluctant to look Doyle in the eye—and so Doyle continued in a gentle tone, "We've another woman we're lookin' for; can you look at her photo? Have you seen her?"

The woman raised her gaze for a moment to review the second photo that Shandera held up before her. Nodding slowly, she said, "*Oloricha. Sal-up condenar.*"

There was a slight pause, and then Shandera explained, "She says she is doomed."

As Doyle blinked, Shandera persisted, "Who she, *mai*?"

Slowly, the woman shook her head. "Don't know."

Interestingly enough, this was true, and Doyle asked, "Why d'you think she's doomed, ma'am?"

Again, the woman seemed to want to look anywhere but at Doyle, and finally muttered, "*Los fantasmas.*"

Those wretched ghosts, again, thought Doyle in exasperation; they've got a lot to answer for, they do.

"You know sum one who knows bout this *gringa, mai*?" Shandera asked. "I won't say you said."

"No, mon," she replied firmly, and then indicated her door with a rather defiant gesture.

"Thank you," Doyle offered as they stepped out of her way, but the woman did not respond, and could not close the door upon them fast enough.

After they'd moved down the pavement a small distance, Doyle observed, "Well, that was interestin'."

Shandera explained, "A lot of these people are superstitious, ma'am. Old habits die hard."

"Aye; it reminds me of the Santero investigation, with the code of silence—although in that case, no one dared to grass-out the local witch-doctor."

"We're in that same neighborhood," he noted.

"Well, I'm glad you were here—at least she didn't drop her groceries and run away, although I think it was a close-run thing."

"Yes, I think she was startled to see you; she warned me about 'the red-haired policewoman'."

Doyle had to smile. "That's exactly what I told Munoz; they take one look at this red head and clam up. I'd no idea I was half so alarmin'."

Chuckling, Shandera offered, "She reminded me of my granny —she was making the sign against the evil eye."

"Faith, was she? Poor thing; between me and the ghosts, she seemed scared out of her shoes. Although apparently, we have our case-breaker, and it was the ghosts who killed the victim. The reportin' witness also said there were ghosts on the scene, so that seals it."

He smiled as he knocked on the next door. "Who was the reporting witness?"

"A little homeless man, who was collecting bottles. He claimed there were ghosts about, and that they were annoyed with the victim for causin' trouble."

There was no answer to their knock, and as they turned toward the next house Shandera ventured thoughtfully, "Any chance the homeless guy was a mule? Keeping people in fear is a tactic used by the drug runners."

But Doyle shook her head. "No—he hadn't seen as much as a fiver in years, you could tell; I felt a bit sorry for him. Although Flynn herself could have been actin' as a mule—with the lanyard 'round her neck, we were wonderin' if hers might be an admonishment-murder. It doesn't seem to fit-in with what we know, though; we haven't heard a whisper about who might be sendin' a message, and it's hard to imagine that someone like Mallory Flynn would get involved in a turf-war in the first place; she'd know better than to try to muscle-in over here."

"I suppose," he agreed, as they walked to the next door. "Although she'd a brass neck, from what I hear."

This seemed a good opening, and so Doyle asked casually, "Did you know her?"

He smiled. "Not in the Biblical sense, if that's what you're getting at."

She winced. "Sorry—didn't mean any insult. She'd a reputation, it seems."

"Yes," he agreed, and said no more.

Sensing that he was holding back, Doyle urged, "If you know anythin' that might be useful, Jerry, you should say."

As they turned toward the next house, Doyle could see that he was debating what to tell her, and then he slowly replied, "There were rumors that the only reason she kept her job after the Public Accounts scandal was because she had compromising sex-tapes."

Doyle came to a halt and stared at him, agog. "Of higher-ups?"

He turned to face her, and shrugged. "I suppose that goes without saying."

Blowing out a breath, she exclaimed, "Faith—if that's true, that would be a *massive* scandal. And it would explain why she didn't get the sack—or get herself indicted."

"Yes, ma'am."

Doyle frowned. "Mayhap that's what Acton was referrin' to, when he said we might need to suppress information, dependin' on what we find out."

"I wouldn't be surprised," her companion agreed.

Hearing a nuance to his tone, she gave him a sharp glance. "Acton wasn't involved with her, Jerry."

He immediately disclaimed, "No—of course not. I hope you didn't think I was implying."

She eyed him sidelong. "D'you know who was?"

He gazed out over the street for a few seconds, as the rain started to fall in earnest, and then replied, "I don't know anything for certain, and I don't think I should speculate, if DCI Acton is trying to keep a lid on it."

But Doyle insisted, "It may be relevant, though—she'd be a mighty handy victim, if she's doin' a bit o' blackmail. Not to mention we'd have a ready list of suspects, if we knew who it was she was blackmailin'."

But he pointed out, "Maybe not, ma'am; if I know as much as I do, plenty of other people know, too."

Doyle had to concede that he had a point; the people who were compromised wouldn't dare kill her, if they were worried others already knew about the sex-tapes and therefore a finger would be immediately pointed their way—and the penalties for murder were a lot worse than for corruption. "Well—all I'm sayin' is, if that was her m.o it seems a happy coincidence that she's now dead."

"Although she was obviously taking big risks."

This seemed evident, and Doyle could only agree as they resumed their canvass. "Aye—she was definitely temptin' fate.

Which brings up yet another puzzle; it seems very odd that she was comin' out here to deal drugs—assuming that's what she was doin'. It seems a strange choice."

"I'd agree—it doesn't make much sense."

They'd come to the end of the row, and as they turned back, Doyle decided she should try to gain some insight on her closer-to-home problem. "Why did you think it strange that Corso was put on this case?"

He thought about his answer for a few steps, and then offered, "I think she's a bit too—a bit too naive to be working out in the field. She's better suited for lab-work."

Thinking of what Acton had revealed, Doyle could only agree. "Aye. She's one of those sciencey-types, who's not very good at handlin' interactions with real live people."

He nodded. "That's about right."

She could sense that he was reluctant to tell her more, and—with Acton's troubles close to mind—she coaxed, "Is there anythin' in particular I should know? If you think she's incompetent, we should tell DS Munoz."

"No—I don't think she's incompetent. But she did ask me, once, if I'd ever heard whether the old Santero had been replaced by an *ahijado*—one of his assistants."

Once again, Doyle stopped walking to stare at him. "*Corso* practices Santeria?"

He had to smile at her reaction. "I think she's RC, but she's Cuban, and there's a lot of Santeria there, mixed-in with RC beliefs."

"I don't know a lot about it," Doyle confessed, as she resumed walking. "Just what I learned from the old case—that Queen's Counsel who was killed."

"That was a crazy case."

In wonder, Doyle shook her head. "It makes no sense to me; why would someone like Corso want to speak with a witchdoctor?"

He shrugged. "She may be superstitious enough to want to keep a bit of Santeria in her back pocket. Like I said, old habits die hard."

Doyle offered, "I suppose it's similar to the RCs who only go to Mass on Christmas and Easter. You figure it can't hurt to keep your hand in."

"Exactly."

Curious, Doyle glanced up at him. *"Has* the Santero been replaced?"

"Not that I've heard; his shop hasn't reopened."

"We should ask your gran," she joked.

"I'll be happy to pull her in on a known-associates warrant."

Doyle laughed, and as they walked back toward the car, she thought over this puzzling homicide case and her equally puzzling husband, who'd assigned the Coroner's Assistant—last minute, and via Reynolds—to the aforesaid case for reasons unknown. It's all connected, somehow, she thought—although I haven't the smallest idea how it could be.

It was that frustrating; she'd this feeling often—tantalizing wisps, that dissolved like cobwebs when she tried to examine them. And it didn't help matters that there was some sort of code of silence in place, so that no one wanted to talk—not even DC Shandera, it seemed; Doyle would bet her teeth that he'd been assigned to her so that Acton could keep tabs on what she found out. A shame, that she'd found out absolutely nothing.

Thoughtfully, she suggested, "Let's go put the grocer back on the rack for another round, and see if he'll give us anythin' more."

"Yes, ma'am," Shandera readily agreed.

CHAPTER 17

$\mathcal{B}$ut as it turned out, the shopkeeper was not manning his usual post. Instead, a sullen teenage girl reluctantly set down her mobile phone long enough to inform them that he'd gone to visit relatives.

Frustrated, Doyle asked, "D'you have their contact information?"

The girl shrugged. "No."

This was true, and Doyle persevered, "Where are these relatives, d'you know? Here, in London?"

If it was possible, the girl's expression grew even more sullen. "I dunno."

"Are you one of his relatives?" asked Shandera, with his charming smile. "Do you live nearby?"

With palpable reluctance, she replied, "No; mi papi told me to come and watch the shop this morning till someone else could come."

"Would your papi know how to reach the shopkeeper?" Doyle persisted.

The girl shrugged again. "I dunno."

Doyle held up the two photos. "Have you ever seen either of these people before?"

The girl gave the photos the barest glance. "No."

They thanked her and left the shop, and as soon as they were out of earshot, Doyle said, "Well, that doesn't look good—it seems as though the grocer's done a bunk."

Shandera agreed. "And it wasn't planned; that girl wouldn't be anyone's first choice to man a cash drawer."

"No; although that may be why she was put there—she's not goin' to give us anythin' useful."

"Good point."

Doyle advised, "When Munoz and I first questioned him, he didn't mention the surveillance tape he had—we had to come back and wrest it from him. His tape was where we got the two pictures."

Shandera glanced at her. "Do you think he's a suspect, ma'am?"

Doyle thought about it. "I'm inclined to say no, mainly because he didn't seem a'tall alarmed until Munoz started askin' whether he sold drugs."

"Should I do a whereabouts check?"

"Let's ask DS Munoz," Doyle replied, as a gentle reminder that Munoz had the lead. The two detectives then walked to meet-up with Munoz, who was already waiting for them at the field cars.

Doyle asked, "Any luck, ma'am?"

"No. In fact, two of the people I managed to talk to claimed they didn't even know that a dead body had been discovered a few feet from their doorsteps. How about you?"

"Only another witness who blamed the ghosts," Doyle said. "Everyone's clammin' up. Either they're afraid, or they're protectin' their own."

Her scalp started prickling, and she paused in surprise. What? It was no surprise that immigrant communities often came together against the coppers—often to the point of protecting a murderer, unfortunately. And in this case, the murdered girl wasn't one of their own, so they'd even less incentive to be helpful.

Her scalp prickled, yet again, and she closed her eyes briefly, trying to concentrate. If the killer was being protected, could it be *Acton* who was protecting him? Acton was in cover-up mode, and worried about what his wedded wife would find out—she'd the sense that the man was busily stamping-out a prairie-fire, the same as he'd done in Dublin. And—now that she knew there were sex-tapes involved—this seemed to be a likely incentive for the aforesaid covering-up. Acton must be protecting Flynn's killer.

She opened her eyes, thoroughly frustrated, because she realized that couldn't possibly be the case; Acton honestly didn't know who'd killed Flynn—she was certain of it. So—for some reason, he was running a cover-up even though he didn't know who the guilty party was. Which meant that he was probably trying to keep a lid on the other unsavory aspects of the case—which would only make sense; the last needful thing was to have a sex-tape scandal atop the dry-labbing scandal atop the pilfering-drugs-from-police-custody scandal. Small wonder the man was trying to keep a lid on everything; there were a lot of pots ready to boil over.

Shandera's voice broke into her thoughts. "Maybe everyone thinks that Flynn deserved it," he suggested. "They know what happened, but they're not very outraged about it and think it would be best left alone."

"She didn't deserve to die," Doyle said firmly. "No matter what she'd done."

"No argument, here," Shandera replied. "But it might explain why no one's talking, and why the shopkeeper's done a bunk."

Munoz made a sound of annoyance. "Has he? He's worried about a drug investigation, I'll bet."

Doyle advised, "DC Shandera's wonderin' if he should be considered a suspect."

"I'm not inclined," Munoz replied. "But let's do a quick whereabouts check, and a known-associates to see if there's anything of interest."

"Me, or DC Shandera?" Doyle asked, as she typed these instructions into her tablet.

"You," said Munoz. To Shandera, she said, "Thanks so much; if you will coordinate with DS Doyle's report, I'll discharge you until further notice."

"Yes, ma'am."

As the two young women returned to their field unit, Doyle immediately disclosed, "Here's a wrinkle, Munoz; Shandera said he'd heard rumors that Flynn had sex-tapes, and was blackmailing some higher-ups."

There was a small pause, as Munoz closed her car door behind her. "I'd heard that, too."

With some exasperation, Doyle said, "Why didn't you mention it, then? Seems very pertinent to this investigation."

In a level voice, Munoz replied, "Because your husband's a higher-up."

Hotly, Doyle retorted, "He *wasn't* involved, Izzy."

"No—but notice that he hasn't mentioned that aspect, either."

Doyle blew out a breath, and reined-in her temper. "Aye. And I suppose that's why he's steppin' so carefully, here. But the Met's personnel problems shouldn't impact an investigation."

Munoz gave her a glance as she started-up the car. "Maybe in theory, but you and I both know that they do, Doyle. So, let's just keep processing the case until someone tells us otherwise."

Doyle realized that she wasn't practicing what she was preaching, and so—after a moment's internal debate—she disclosed, "Here's another wrinkle; Acton said Flynn may have been sellin' drugs out of the Evidence Locker."

Munoz raised her dark brows. "Wow."

The penny dropped, and Doyle exclaimed, "Oh—that might explain why she went after the sex-tapes; she needed someone on the inside, since she wouldn't have level-access to the Locker."

But Munoz was frowning, as she thought this over. "You know, Doyle, that doesn't really add-up to me. Any drugs in the Evidence Locker wouldn't be penny-cache—the Crown Prosecutors tend to target only the high-level dealers for trial. So, why is she going to the risk of stealing from police custody, and then selling high-level stuff to the sort of people who live in this neighborhood?"

"It doesn't make a lot of sense," Doyle agreed. "Unless she's tryin' to cover her tracks by sellin' bits and pieces to low-income, on the side."

Munoz raised a skeptical brow. "That's a big risk to take, just to sell bits and pieces."

"Aye; there's somethin' here that we're missin'; there's a key to all this, but we haven't got it, yet."

Making a decision, Munoz started up the car. "Let's look at her finances—although I'd be surprised if she left any kind of trail, considering the state of her electronics."

"Right," Doyle agreed.

"Just a quick look, though; remember we haven't got a budget." As she turned to back out, the other girl glanced over at her. "Are you still going over to that hotel?"

"I am," Doyle replied. "I've a hunch, I do."

Munoz quirked her mouth. "All right. Gabriel used to say that your hunches were always spot-on, and it was a shame you couldn't give a class on it over at the Crime Academy."

Since it had long seemed to Doyle that Gabriel had come to his own conclusions about her perceptive abilities, she moved quickly to make light; "It's an Irish thing, I think; we had to sharpen our wits so as to hide from the English."

Munoz smiled. "Geary has good hunches, too."

"There you go."

She cautioned, "Don't forget I went with you to the hotel."

"I won't."

"Thanks, I owe you."

CHAPTER 18

*a*fter she'd finished her follow-up tasks from the morning's canvass, Doyle's husband once again offered to drive her home, which only confirmed her suspicion that he was keeping a close eye on what she was learning about the fair Mallory's mysterious death.

Doesn't want me ferreting-out something, she thought; which is a bit disheartening, given that the decedent was a lightskirt. Not that I think for one moment that the man's been unfaithful, but it does seem a bit troubling.

Therefore, rather than wait for him to ask his innocent-sounding questions, she decided to go on the offense, once they were in the car. "Tell me, husband, why you decided I needed a watch-dog this mornin'."

In an even tone, he replied, "It is not the safest of neighborhoods, Kathleen. I'll not apologize for being cautious, when it comes to your safety."

She eyed him thoughtfully. "Usually, Williams is my watch-dog. And usually he's my SIO, too. Are we worried that he's compromised, in this case?"

"No; he would protect you, come what may."

This seemed to be one of her husband's patented non-answers, and so she persisted, "*Is* he compromised? I'm given to understand Flynn had a few sex-tapes, stashed away in her lingerie drawer."

As was his usual, Acton didn't confirm nor deny this, but only said, "I can find no indication that Williams has ever met with Flynn outside of work."

She blew out a relieved breath. "Well, that's to the good. How about that field officer—the blond fellow?"

"I am afraid I cannot say the same for him."

"Not a surprise, I guess. Now what?"

"He will be disciplined. The protocols should be respected."

She made a sympathetic sound. "His poor wife." It was always a fundamental problem amongst law enforcement; human nature was human nature, and personnel who worked together were often susceptible to love-affairs, even with married colleagues. But such a thing was mightily discouraged, due to the fact it could easily impact an officer's work—make him or her vulnerable to blackmail, or otherwise affect the quality of decision-making. Faith, Acton himself was a perfect case-in-point; there'd been many a time he'd protected the fair Doyle from the consequences of her own missteps, even when he shouldn't have.

Her scalp prickled, and she remembered that it had done the same thing earlier, when she'd wondered if Acton was protecting someone. I think that's the key, she decided; I'm fairly certain Acton doesn't know who the killer is, but he's sweeping this whole tangle-patch under the rug because he is protecting someone—or multiple someones—from the fallout. He knows who Flynn was blackmailing, and he doesn't want that aspect to see the light of day—there's nothing like a tawdry sex-scandal to undermine the Met's reputation. It would also explain why he wanted to set-up this wretched dinner-party so as to test-out Williams; he must be worried that Williams might be involved, somehow. And—say what you will about him—Acton always protected his own.

Although—although he was apparently protecting Yandra

Corso too, for reasons unknown, and Doyle had a hard time believing that he'd consider the Assistant Coroner 'one of his own'.

Struck with a possible explanation, she asked, "Was Yandra Corso buyin' drugs from Flynn? Is that why you scolded her at the crime scene?"

Ah—she could sense his flair of alarm, quickly suppressed. "I am afraid I would rather not say."

Which was understandable, if it concerned personnel matters. Nevertheless, she suddenly saw a plausible scenario for what Melinda had seen at the hotel; Acton was over there for some reason—paying the bill?—and he must have run into Corso, who was meeting someone—Flynn herself?—for a drug deal, and Acton had promptly given the young woman a thorough blistering. That made perfect sense. Faith, it was amazing that he hadn't fired Corso, right there on the spot. Which, of course, he should have. He should have; but instead he'd had Reynolds phone her up on the sly so as to send her in on the next morning's crime scene—the crime scene where Flynn lay dead.

With an acute sense of disappointment, Doyle acknowledged that this promising theory would have to be discarded. Instead, the facts on the ground made no sense whatsoever—especially since the fair Doyle was forgetting the strangest fact of all; Acton would never berate an underling in a public place—not in a million years. But for some reason, he'd berated Corso twice—although the crime-scene scolding was miles more discreet, since Melinda had deemed the hotel-lobby scolding a "fracas." Funny, that she'd used the word; it made it sound as though it was an out-and-out donnybrook, with fists flying.

But for whatever reason, Acton seemed to be moving heaven and earth to protect Corso from suffering any consequences for her fireable offenses. Corso, who was preparing Flynn's autopsy report, and was being a bit cagey about it.

Reminded of this troubling fact, Doyle asked, "What did the autopsy say?"

"Nothing definitive. The tox-screen shows some indicators for a fugitive poison."

Doyle nodded. There were indeed certain poisons which disappeared in the body without leaving much of a trace, and she frowned, thinking this over. "Any needle marks?"

"None were found."

Blowing out a breath, Doyle lifted her palms. "She just keeled over, then. Faith; mayhap it *was* the ghosts."

He gave her a glance. "What's this?"

"A witness today thought ghosts were after her, and the reportin' witness said that there were ghosts about, when he found her."

There was a small pause, and then Acton brought himself to ask, "And were there?"

"None that I could see."

He was silent, and she then added fairly, "Of course, they may have been hit-and-run ghosts—the kind who don't hang about, waitin' for the coppers."

He gave her a look, and she laughed. "Sorry. It was just too temptin'."

They drove in silence for a few moments, and then he offered, "Unless we can come up with more evidence, we may have to categorize her death as misadventure, instead of homicide."

"I suppose that only makes sense," Doyle replied. And then, to show she wasn't as dumb as she looked, she added, "The people featured in the sex-tapes will be that relieved."

He tilted his head in concession. "Indeed. But nevertheless, we don't have enough to open a homicide case."

"Oh—I understand, husband; I'm only sayin' it's a lucky thing all around. Do we happen to know who will wiggle off the hook?"

"Not me," he replied immediately.

"Fah, Michael—I wasn't worried about you." Truth to tell, it had been a bit troubling, that both Shandera and Munoz had known about the sex-tape rumor but hadn't wanted to tell her. Foolish, that she hadn't asked Acton immediately—she'd indeed been acting like the stupid heroine in the over-dramatic story. Although—although, there remained the mystery of why Acton hadn't fired Corso, and seemed to be doing his level-best to protect her.

Once again, she teetered on the edge of asking him outright, but drew back; hopefully, she'd have a better grasp of what had taken place in the lobby after she made her visit to the hotel this afternoon. He may not have been meeting the young woman to have an illicit affair, but he was definitely trying to pull the wool, for some reason, and—if past experience was an indicator—it would behoove the fair Doyle to find out why.

CHAPTER 19

More trouble to come. It was only to be expected; The Red-Haired Policewoman walked in the sight. He prayed to the orishas, but he held little hope.

*A*s soon as the boys were down for their naps, Doyle walked over to the hotel, planning her interview strategy along the way. Since Corso had been on-premises for the fracas—and Corso was apparently a customer of Flynn's—then it seemed likely there was a drug-selling angle at play. This would actually be a godsend, in that it could stand as an excuse as to why the fair Doyle was nosing-around. Good; it was a huge relief that she wasn't having to ask her questions whilst wearing a wronged-wife hat, and that she could instead wear her detective-hat.

But in this she spoke too soon, because whilst the staff at the desk gave her smiles of greeting, behind their polite expressions they were on high alert, and wary—she'd the immediate sense that they were closing ranks so as to protect their illustrious client from any wifely questions.

With a pang of dismay, Doyle mustered up an answering smile; she'd been half-hoping that Melinda was mistaken about exactly what she'd seen, but it seemed—based on this covert reaction—that she was not.

"I'm afraid I'm here on a bit o' business," Doyle explained. "We've had a report of drug sales on-premises."

Still a bit wary, the desk clerk carefully replied, "Yes; Lord Acton has inquired into personnel records."

Hiding her surprise that her cover-story appeared to be the actual truth, Doyle nodded. "Yes; may I—may I please speak with whoever supervises HR?" This was another unlooked-for blessing; she'd been worried about how she was going to bring up the subject of the Acton-Corso fracas with the Hotel Manager, but now an alternative had presented itself—hopefully she'd speak to someone who was not quite as inclined to protect the hotel's illustrious customer.

"Certainly. Please follow me, ma'am."

Doyle followed the clerk through the door that led to the hotel's administrative offices, walking down the hallway and past the kitchen area, where preparations for the evening's meals were underway. Several workers looked up in curiosity and she smiled in a friendly fashion, just so as to make it clear she wasn't about to haul anyone away in flexcuffs.

She was taken into the office of the HR Manager—a competent, middle-aged woman who greeted Doyle courteously, even as she carefully suppressed a twinge of alarm.

A bit discouraged by this reaction, Doyle began, "Good afternoon, ma'am; I hope you don't mind, but I'm followin'-up on the troubles here, day before last."

Cautiously, the woman replied, "Hermano. Yes—well, we didn't even have the chance to dismiss him; he disappeared straightaway after the incident. Lord Acton took his contact information, and I believe he is trying to trace him."

Yet again, with a mighty effort Doyle hid her surprise. A hotel employee had been involved in the fracas? This was unexpected, but on the other hand, it would explain why Melinda had called it such.

Feeling her way, Doyle took a cast. "D'you think Hermano was involved in sellin' drugs?"

A bit defensively, the woman shook her head. "I didn't know enough about him, either way. It was his first day on the kitchen staff, but everyone is drug-tested—we're very careful about our employees."

"Of course," Doyle soothed. "You run a top-drawer place, here, as we well-know."

A bit mollified, the woman added, "Of course, I told Lord Acton that I couldn't vouch for the agency that put him forward. I can't vouch for the vendors, either—I'll admit that I wouldn't be surprised if some of those people were taking drugs—between the recycling center, and Sunshine Bakery."

Doyle's ears perked up, and she tried to decide if this was of interest; Sunshine Bakery had been a link in the distribution chain for illegal smuggling in an earlier case, and—come to think of it— Igor Denisovich's awful son had worked at Sunshine Bakery. Denisovich was a Russian mafia kingpin she and Acton had interviewed a few months ago, in connection with his ex-wife's rather gruesome death.

She ventured, "Was one of the bakery people a young man named Denisovich—or Lanska, mayhap?"

The woman frowned, trying to remember. "I don't think so; I remember that Rory Flynn was one of them."

Rory Flynn—faith, I've heard that name before, thought Doyle, as she frowned in concentration. Oh—Denisovich's awful son had mentioned him during the interview. The awful son had fingered Rory Flynn as a potential suspect in that homicide case, even though Doyle had gained the sense he'd only done it to cause trouble. But now—now the HR Manager seemed to be verifying that Rory Flynn was a bit dodgy.

Thoughtfully she asked, "So; you'd the sense that Rory was trouble?"

"Well, I wouldn't say *trouble*, necessarily. He was cheeky—always chatting up the girls here." She added, "I haven't seen him since the fire, though—we had to contract with a different bakery."

This, because Sunshine Bakery had been burnt in an arson fire—mainly to cover-up all evidence of dark doings. Doyle paused for a moment, trying to decide if she was being distracted from her purpose by going down this particular rabbit hole. On the other hand, you didn't need to be a detective to think it all a bit too coincidental; not only was The Grenoble Hotel potentially involved in Flynn's drug rig, the hotel had also dealt with Sunshine-Bakery-of-the-Russian-mafia-connections.

And besides all that, this Rory Flynn fellow may well be a relative of Mallory Flynn; Mother a' Mercy, it was entirely possible that the fair Doyle had stumbled upon the distribution rig for the Evidence-Locker drugs—here were the high-end clients that Munoz thought would be more likely.

And that would certainly explain why Acton was in the hotel lobby in the first place; he must have figured this out, too, and was now trying to trace a kitchen staff worker who'd resisted arrest and fled.

Immensely relieved that this massive ball-of-snakes was *finally* starting to make sense, Doyle decided she should make some notes, even though it seemed she was re-treading ground that her husband had already trod. To this end, she pulled her tablet. "Could you describe Hermano for me?"

"Older fellow—rather slight, and a bit rough around the edges. He was a candidate from a job-project agency for the homeless, and so we didn't look too closely."

"Hispanic?"

"Yes."

"And how about Rory?"

"Thirties, I'd guess. Tall and slender—dark-haired, rather handsome."

"Caucasian?"

"I don't think so," she said doubtfully. "He may have been Hispanic, too."

Not with a name like Rory Flynn, thought Doyle, but she decided not to challenge this assessment. She'd compare notes with Acton on this—although she was certain he was miles ahead of her anyway—and she mustn't get distracted from the main reason she was here. Therefore, as she shut down her tablet, she remarked with a knowing air, "It certainly sounded as though there were drugs involved—what with that little kerfuffle in the lobby."

"Yes," the woman agreed carefully. "Not the kind of thing we usually see here."

With a light laugh, Doyle added, "My poor husband—I understand it was quite the fracas."

Unbending a bit, the woman agreed. "We can't have people accosting guests in the lobby, for goodness sake."

Doyle decided that the witness was diplomatically omitting some very pertinent information, and so she added, "I believe one of the Met's personnel was present—not that she was much help."

"Well—yes."

Doyle's heart sank, because her companion clearly had been hoping she needn't mention Yandra Corso's involvement to Acton's wife—which seemed rather ominous, if supposedly Acton was wearing his detective-hat and not his philandering-husband hat.

But rather than press the point, Doyle changed tack. "Did we ever find out what possessed Hermano to go after my poor husband?"

Palpably relieved by the change in subject, the HR Manager shook her head in bemusement. "I don't know—I wasn't there. The desk said he was gabbling in a foreign language and grabbing Lord Acton's arm, trying to scratch at his face. Security rushed over, of course, and escorted him from the premises."

Doyle nodded, all the while trying to hide her abject astonishment; the more she learned, the more utterly fantastic the tale seemed. Acton was one of those people who didn't like being touched—save by his wedded wife, of course—and he was not about to let a strange kitchen-worker run up on him, let alone get close enough to grab him and claw at his face—Acton was a seasoned police officer, after all.

Struck with a possible explanation, Doyle wondered if her husband had been drinking; he used to drink quite a bit—so as to beat back his personal demons—but the demons had receded, somewhat, and he'd tapered-off—thank God fastin'. But that theory seemed another dead-end, since Acton would never go out in public after having downed a goodly half-bottle—when he drank, he tended to drink in private.

Back and edge, the whole tale was almost too crazy to believe, save that it seemed clear that it had actually happened. And there seemed little point, anymore, in trying to get hold of the lobby camera footage—between this woman and Melinda, it seemed clear the incident had happened just as described. It was all so strange and out-of-keeping.

After thanking the woman for her time—the witness being thoroughly relieved that she hadn't been asked to expand on the Yandra Corso portion of the tale—Doyle followed her down the back hallway toward the lobby again, and noted a kitchen-staffer hauling plastic bags out the delivery door, the bags marked, "Gipsy Hill Recycling."

Yet another coincidence—that homeless fellow, Alfonso, had said that he turned-in his bottles there. Of course, since Gipsy Hill was located in Lambeth, this seemed a very ordinary coincidence—and not one of the more ominous coincidences she seemed to be tripping over, left and right. Although she'd the niggling feeling that she was forgetting a big one—something important, that someone had said. About Alfonso? About the recycling center?

Frowning in concentration, she wracked her brain as she made her way across the lobby and out the front door. Alfonso had found the body, of course, but he seemed harmless, and hadn't set off any alarms. Nonetheless, mayhap it would behoove the fair Doyle to shake her stumps and go over to take a gander at the Gipsy Hill Recycling Center.

With this in mind, she pulled her mobile phone. We'll do two birds with one stone, she decided, and rang-up Thomas Williams.

CHAPTER 20

*W*hen Williams pulled up, she gratefully slid in, and said, "Thanks for droppin' everythin', Thomas. Hopefully, this won't take more than an hour or so."

"No problem. Why are we going over to the recycling center?"

"Because I've run across far too many coincidences, and I'm wonderin' if I've stumbled across the distribution network for Mallory Flynn's drug-rig."

He raised his brows. "Mallory Flynn had a drug-rig?"

"Oh—that's right, you're not on the case. I was at the hotel because there's a question of drug-sales, with Mallory Flynn as a source."

She decided it would be best to exclude any mention of her husband's brawling in the lobby till she knew a bit more—she was being circumspect, for a change, since she tended to unburden her heart to Williams. Not that she didn't trust him, of course; there was nothing like having a good friend, to keep you level.

Her scalp started to prickle, and before she could decide why this was, Williams asked, "Is that why she was killed? She was selling drugs?"

Recalled to the conversation, she nodded. "Not only that, but—

hold on to your hat—we think she was pilferin' drugs from the Evidence Locker to do so."

He made a whistling sound. "Wow."

"Lizzie hasn't mentioned? I think she was doing a covert operation."

"No—but when she's working on assignment for Acton, she tends to be tight-lipped."

"Aye; I've learned that lesson, myself—she's loyal to the bone."

Williams frowned slightly. "Mallory Flynn wouldn't have access to the Evidence Locker; she must have had someone on the inside."

Doyle ventured, "She may have twisted someone's arm." After a slight pause, she offered in a level voice, "I understand that she was makin' sex-tapes, for blackmail purposes."

"Not of me," he replied immediately.

Unashamed that she'd been so easily caught out, she said, "Well, that's a massive relief, Thomas; I was a bit worried, truth to tell."

He shrugged a shoulder, as they headed toward the Lambeth area. "At the risk of sounding puffed-up, I've had to sort through a lot of women like her. You get so that your radar starts pinging."

She nodded thoughtfully. "Aye, Acton's the same way—he can spot 'em a mile away. More likely our Mallory targeted men who would be flattered, and weren't wise to her ways—like the bureaucrats in government, who'd never had a pretty girl give them a second glance."

Her scalp prickled, and she thought in some surprise—what? It went without saying, really, that men like Williams and Acton were not going to fall victim to a brasser like Flynn—they'd had plenty of experience side-stepping such snares. Which gave her yet another reason to goggle at the idea that Acton had been physically wrestling with someone in a hotel lobby, with Yandra Corso standing at his side. Mayhap the fair Doyle should try to take a peek at the security tape, after all—although such tapes usually didn't include sound. She'd love to find out what this Hermano-fellow had said to him—although the desk said it was not in English. Why would he think to speak to Acton in another language, though? Mayhap he was on drugs, and not in his right mind. But if that were the case, why wouldn't Acton mention the encounter to his wedded wife; surely such an occurrence would make the list of things you recited to each other at day's-end?

With a knit brow, she asked, "D'you speak Spanish, Thomas? It seems that a lot of the people involved in the Flynn case speak Spanish."

"A little—mostly secondary school level."

"Does Acton?"

"Some, I think, He's good with languages."

Thoughtfully, she nodded. "Aye; I wouldn't be surprised if he spoke a smatterin' of just about every language we come across. And speakin' of such, did you know that all the nobs in England spoke French, a long time ago? Seems very strange, if the French were their blood-enemies."

He shrugged. "It's like a club; the nobs all tend to support each other, no matter where they're from."

"Aye," she agreed. "We haven't a chance, us ordinary folk. Best to keep our heads down, and hope we don't get noticed."

"Well, it's supposed to work both ways, you know. The nobs are supposed to look out for us ordinary folk."

She made a wry mouth. "Name me one time it's worked-out that way."

He tilted his head in concession. "I think it happened more often in the olden days, and at the risk of pointing out an awkward fact, you're a nob, yourself."

But Doyle only shook her head. "No—not me; I'm miles more an 'ordinary folk' than a nob, and that whole allegiance-thing is strange and mysterious to me. Lizzie's got it; she'd protect Acton to the last yard, and think it blood well-spilt."

"You may be right."

Hastily, Doyle added, "Not that she's not loyal to you, too."

He laughed, "I know what you meant, don't worry."

Doyle glanced at him. "D'you know why Acton is cross with her?"

He raised his brows. "Is he? She's been quiet, lately; I just assumed it was the baby."

After sifting through all the various loyalties involved, Doyle decided it was safe to say, "I think Acton gave her a bear-garden jawin', yesterday in his office."

"Really? I can sympathize—I've been there," he commiserated. "But I don't know what it was about, and she hasn't said."

Doyle knit her brow, trying to decide what she was worried about; it was a bit strange, that Acton would rake Lizzie—of all people—over the coals. But she was certain that Acton had been very unhappy with Lizzie, even though he'd made a mighty effort to conceal this fact from his wedded wife. It was rather similar to the way he was concealing the fracas at the hotel from the aforementioned wedded wife. Was it possible that the two events were connected?

She mentally shook her head so as to clear it, since this stray thought didn't make much sense. The only possible connection was that Corso had been using Flynn as a drug-source, and Lizzie had been working behind-the-scenes to put a stop to the dry-labbing scandal, and the dry-labbing scandal was apparently the cover-up for Flynn's stealing drugs from the Evidence Locker. So, Acton shouldn't be *angry* at Lizzie, he should be thanking her for a job well-done, since the Met managed to avoid a horrific scandal and all's well that ends well. Well—maybe not *well*, since Flynn had been killed, for her sins. Although even that was not yet clear—cause-of-death was still unknown.

Faith, Doyle thought a bit crossly; this is all too confusing, and my poor brain can't make heads-nor-tails.

Williams interrupted her thoughts. "If this interview involves the Flynn case, shouldn't Munoz be here, instead of me?"

Leave it to Williams, to remember the protocols—he was that annoying, sometimes. Vaguely, Doyle replied, "She's unavailable, just now."

"All right. Do I get a briefing, or am I going in blind?"

She sighed. "I'll readily confess that we've haven't much to go on, Thomas. I went over to ask some questions at the hotel, because there's been a few clues that seem to show Flynn was distributin' drugs there."

Patiently, he asked, "And how does the recycling center fit in?"

"Well, the homeless fellow who found Flynn's body said that he redeems his bottles there, and the hotel sends their bags of recyclin' to this self-same center."

He lifted a brow. "That's not much of a tie-in, Kath."

She could only agree, "I know it's not much, but it's pingin' my radar."

He thought this over. "So; you have a hunch that the hotel and the recycling center might be involved in distributing the drugs? If that's the case, then it's a high-level operation; why would Flynn be out selling on a Lambeth street?"

This, of course, was a very good question, and only showed you why Williams was a Detective Inspector whilst Doyle would remain a Sergeant till the end of her days.

Raising her palms in concession, she replied, "That's a good point, Thomas. Mayhap we can find some answers at this recyclin' center—I'd like to rule it out, at least." She knit her brow. "And I've the feelin' that I'm forgettin' somethin'—some little detail that's important."

He made no further argument, as he was well-familiar with Doyle's "feelings," and besides, it wasn't his case-budget that was being spent on what appeared to be a wild-goose chase. "All right; do I have the lead, or do you?"

"I suppose I do; they already know who I am."

Again, he raised his brows. "They do?"

Suddenly, she sat up straight, and turned to him with some excitement. "Oh, *that's* what it was—the little fact that I'd forgot; the homeless fellow who found the body referred to me as 'the red-haired policewoman', and so did one of the locals—she tried to warn Shandera to be careful."

But Williams didn't seem to think this was very significant. "You do have red hair," he pointed out. "It's an easy identifier."

"I've never met either person before, though, and it makes we wonder if I'm on the right track about a distribution rig. The players are all leery of me."

Again, he shrugged a shoulder. "I don't know, Kath; you're well-known from your media coverage."

This was true—Doyle had experienced more than her fair share of coverage in the London press. "I suppose," she reluctantly conceded, as she thoughtfully sank back into the seat. "Although I don't know why they wouldn't just say 'Officer Doyle,' since that's what the media always says. When these people say the 'the red-haired policewoman' it makes it sound as though I'm a tarot-card, or somethin'."

"It may be a cultural thing. Red hair is a rarity, in their population."

"Aye," she conceded. "And a lot of new immigrants are overly-superstitious. That might be it."

As they turned into the recycling company's asphalt parking lot, though, she wondered if there was more to it than just that, and she also wondered why her scalp had started prickling again.

CHAPTER 21

He'd sent word to The Remnant; there would be no sales this week.
Everyone stay quiet. Stay quiet and pray.

*O*nce at the recycling center, Doyle and Williams approached the man who was slouched on a stool behind the battered counter—a lanky, tattooed fellow who looked as though he'd worn the same denim jacket every day for several years without a wash—and introduced themselves.

"What's this?" the man asked with some alarm. "Never say there's another complaint about the dogs? If you don't want to get your arse bit, then don't climb the fence."

"No," Doyle reassured him, and made a mental note to avoid the yard. "We're homicide detectives, and we'd like to know if you recognize this woman." She pulled-out Mallory Flynn's photo, and turned it toward him.

"Nah—never seen that bird before," he replied, after squinting at the photo. "Above my touch."

In a firm tone, Williams said, "We think she may have been

involved in a drug-running rig. Take another look—are you certain?"

"Hey, now," the fellow said, much affronted by the insinuation. "I run a clean shop."

"You don't sell drugs?" asked Williams, for Doyle's benefit.

"No," the fellow repeated adamantly. "You lot shouldn't be harassing me—I'm saving the environment, here."

"And much appreciated," Doyle assured him. She then showed him the photo of the other figure. "Can you help us identify this person?"

Again, the man squinted. "It looks a bit like Yandra, maybe?"

Doyle stared at him in astonished silence for a moment, and then managed to find her voice. "Yandra Corso?"

He shook his head, still scrutinizing the photo. "Dunno her last name. She's started coming around, once in a while—wears that hoodie, when she comes in, like she's ashamed to be seen. It does look a bit like her—hard to tell." He flipped the photo back onto the counter. "I'd be surprised to hear she's doing drugs, though—she's a prim-and-proper type o' bird." He shot a glance at Williams. "Gave it a go, but she wasn't having it."

Doyle, however, was struggling mightily with this surprising revelation, and the rather ominous prospect that Corso may have been the last person to see Flynn alive—*could* she have killed her? Was that the reason Acton had called her in on the case—to cover-up her own crime? It would fit-in with the scolding, certainly; could it possibly be that Acton *did* have feelings for Corso, and was helping her off the hook?

Stop it, she commanded herself abruptly; for the love o' Mike, lass, pull yourself together and act like a detective—Acton doesn't know who killed Flynn, and so that theory is flawed six ways to Sunday.

In an attempt to put herself back on track, Doyle asked the fellow, ""Why does Yandra come 'round here?"

The man raised his brows at Doyle, and explained as though speaking to a simpleton, "She brings-in bottles, lady."

There was a small silence, and then Williams stepped in, since he could see that Doyle was at a loss for words. "Does she live around here?"

The man shrugged. "Dunno. We don't take personal information unless the person brings in hazardous materials."

Doyle seized on a possible connection. "Does she bring-in the recycling from The Grenoble Hotel?"

He shook his head, a bit bemused by the question. "Nah—just a few bottles, now and again. She asks me to credit them to a little homeless bloke who comes 'round every week. Nice of her—helps him to keep body and soul together."

Doyle blinked. "Alfonso?"

"Oi—that's him." The man paused, and then asked warily, "Is he in trouble with the coppers?"

"No," Doyle replied slowly; "He was the one who found the dead girl."

The fellow looked at them in surprise. "Who's dead?"

Doyle indicated Flynn's photo. "She's dead."

"Oh; sorry to hear it—didn't know."

Doyle knit her brow. "Tell me what you know about Alfonso."

The fellow shrugged. "Nothing much to tell—we see a lot of homeless, turning in bottles and tins for pocket change. Always polite, a little odd—talks to himself a lot. He stashes some of the stuff he's found against the wall, over there—lights candles, sometimes, and waits around to swap bottles with the other blokes. I just leave him be—a lot of the 'em are a bit nicked."

He paused, and then screwed up his face as though thinking deeply. "Come to think of it, he had words with Yandra, last time she was here. I thought I might have to go out and send him off."

Doyle frowned. "They argued?"

The fellow nodded. "Oi. Although it looked as though he was the one tellin' her off—she didn't say much."

But this didn't seem to make much sense. "He was tellin' her off, even though she credits him for bottles?"

The man explained, "I think he's one who doesn't want looking-after; most of the homeless blokes don't want no one paying no mind to them."

But Doyle was still frowning, processing this latest wrinkle and trying to decide what it was she was thinking about. "Can you remember exactly when this was—when Alfonso had words with Yandra?"

He squinted out the window for a moment. "A week ago, maybe? It's hard to remember."

Doyle pulled out her tablet to make a note, mainly to give herself a moment to think of the next question. So; here was evidence of another scolding—that would be three, for Corso—two from Acton and one from this Alfonso-fellow. Doyle knew—in the way that she knew things—that this was important, somehow; Corso was the last person that you'd think *anyone* would scold.

Again, since Doyle had gone silent, Williams stepped in. "Did you hear what he said to her?"

The fellow shrugged. "I couldn't hear it, as much as I could see it; they were out front, and whenever Alfonso is out front the dogs always bark like crazy—they don't like him, much."

Doyle asked, "D'you know how to contact Alfonso?"

Again, the man gave her a look that questioned her faculties. "No, lady; he's homeless."

"Aye; and he doesn't have a mobile," Doyle remembered. "Does he come by on a regular basis?"

The fellow considered this. "He's pretty predictable, if that's what you're asking. Although he didn't come by this morning, even though he usually does."

Doyle handed the man her card. "If you see him, will you phone me? But do it quietly—don't scare him off."

"Will do."

The two detectives thanked him, and then turned to exit the building.

CHAPTER 22

*A*s soon as they were outside, Williams asked, "So; the manager's not dealing drugs?"

Doyle shook her head. "No. He was tellin' the truth."

"Who's Yandra?"

Doyle glanced at him in surprise, and then remembered that Williams wouldn't know much about this case, since he wasn't the SIO. "Yandra Corso is an Assistant Coroner at the Central Morgue." She teetered on the edge of saying more but then drew back, and instead asked, "Lizzie hasn't mentioned her?"

"No."

Doyle went silent for a few steps, a bit puzzled. Acton said he'd asked Lizzie to sound-out Corso about being on team-Acton, and since Williams could be considered a major-general on team-Acton, it seemed strange that Lizzie hadn't mentioned such a development to him. Of course, Lizzie was loyal to Acton and was something of a prim-and-proper bird, herself, so mayhap she'd keep such a thing from her husband, and instead allow Acton to handle what Williams would be told or not told.

To Doyle's surprise, her scalp started prickling. What? she thought in confusion; Lizzie was loyal to Acton—that was not exactly a news-flash. Not everyone was like Doyle, who couldn't seem to be able to keep a secret from her husband for love or money—

Williams broke into her thoughts. "Interesting, that this fellow hadn't heard about the murder."

Recalled to the case, Doyle advised, "Nobody claims to know about the murder, my friend. I think there's some sort of code of silence, in that neighborhood."

"Everyone's nervous about possible retaliation, maybe?"

"Mayhap," she agreed. "Although I didn't have the sense that people were afraid—it was more like they were closin' ranks against the coppers. And here's an odd little wrinkle; no one robbed the victim. Acton found it very strange, because someone— mayhap the killer—went into her handbag, and draped her Met lanyard 'round her neck."

Williams whistled softly. "Wow. That's a clear message."

"Aye; the workin'-theory is that hers was an admonishment-murder."

Williams frowned. "Who's being admonished?"

"That's the rub; you'd think whoever did it would make that obvious."

"No prints?"

"None a'tall. We haven't the ghost of a hint of a clue."

He glanced at her, as they came to the car. "What about Yandra the Assistant Coroner? Is she a possible suspect?"

Doyle weighed what to say in light of the fact that Williams would think this the logical conclusion. Of course, Williams was not aware that Doyle's wedded husband had pulled stupid Corso into this stupid case for reasons unknown, and was driving his poor wife to distraction in the process. Which was perplexing in and of itself, because—in the usual course of things—Williams was an Acton-insider.

Again, her scalp prickled, and she paused beside the car door. It was indeed strange—Williams didn't seem to know anything about anything, even though his wife was being roundly admonished and

Acton was running around behind the scenes, pulling the levers with a vengeance. Usually Williams worked cheek-by-jowl with Acton when the man was stamping-out a prairie fire—faith, you need look no further than the Dublin episode, when Acton had moved heaven and earth to protect Timothy McGonigal. In that mess, Acton hadn't hesitated to summon Williams forthwith; could it be, that *Williams* was somehow involved in this tangle?

"Kath?" he prompted, as he watched her over the top of the car.

"Oh—oh, yes; I'll report to Munoz about the Yandra Corso ID." She paused. "Best keep it under your hat, though; if she's another Met employee who's mixed-up in this, Acton may want to keep a tight lid on it."

"Understood."

They got into the car, and as he started it up, he asked, "Does Acton have any working-theories about the Flynn case?"

In light of the fact that Williams had been kept in the dark, Doyle decided it was safe to say, "He agrees that it appears to be an admonishment-murder, but cause-of-death is unclear, which is why we're so stymied."

He glanced over, as he waited for a break in traffic to pull out onto the street. "There's no apparent cause-of-death? Really?"

"It's a mighty strange case, Thomas, and you should thank God fastin' your card wasn't pulled on it." She added, "I will say that it seems a bit ominous that the homeless fellow didn't show up, today. The grocer who had the surveillance tape has also disappeared, and we can't raise him."

Understandably, Williams was a bit confused. "Do you think they've all gone doggo because they know something? Or are you worried that they're containment-murders?"

She blew out a frustrated breath. "I honestly don't know what I think, and I'm that sorry I keep throwin' out bits and pieces that don't seem to amount to much. Oh—speakin' of such, there's also a connection to Sunshine Bakery; the hotel used to order their baked goods from them."

Doubtfully, Williams glanced over at her as he drove down the road. "I'm not sure that's much of a lead, Kath. Neither was this recycling center, to be honest."

"It's pingin' my radar," Doyle insisted stubbornly. "I wish I knew why."

Williams—who was an excellent detective, separate and apart from his being an excellent friend—decided to recount what he knew in a valiant effort to understand why the fair Doyle felt the way she did. "Flynn may have been selling drugs to personnel at The Grenoble Hotel, and you are checking into their outgoing recycling deliveries as well as their incoming bakery deliveries, to see if it was all part of a distribution rig."

Rather ashamed that she didn't want to tell him the real reason she was so keen, Doyle nodded. "Somethin' like that."

"Well, this recycling center seems a dead end—unlikely they'd be distributing drugs from there with the manager unaware." He shot her a speculative glance. "On the other hand, Savoie's involved with Sunshine Bakery, and I wouldn't put it past him."

This was said semi-hopefully, since Williams didn't like Savoie much, based on a long-standing mutual animosity. And he did make a good point; Savoie had partnered with Denisovich in Sunshine Bakery's questionable doings, being as Savoie was something of a world-class smuggler, himself. But then the bakery had burned down, and Savoie had bought-out his partner's interest.

"No—Savoie's not a suspect, Thomas; faith, but you've got an unholy grudge against the man. But there was a fellow named Rory Flynn at the bakery who may be of interest—I don't know as yet if he's related to the victim. The hotel's HR Manager told me that Rory Flynn was a very smooth operator, and this was the second time his name's cropped up; Acton and I interviewed Denisovich's son on the Sasha Lanska case, and at that time the son was doing his level-best to throw Rory Flynn under the bus. I thought it was just a smarmy fellow tryin' to cause trouble, but mayhap there's somethin' to it."

Williams noted, "Denisovich would be another likely suspect—right up there with Savoie. He's a tough customer."

"Not when it comes to his son, though; he was that worried, when Acton wanted to conduct an interview."

There was a small pause, whilst Williams knit his brow. "I didn't know Denisovich had a son."

"Oh—the son poses as his nephew. Acton said it may be that his mum didn't want anyone to know she'd a grown-up son, bein' as she was a famous actress and all." She grimaced at the memory. "Mother a' Mercy, but he was a puffed-up sort of jackanapes; didn't have the first clue that he shouldn't be cheeky with Acton."

Williams laughed aloud. "I wish I'd been there; Denisovich must have been *dying*."

"That he was, my friend."

The rode for a minute or two in silence, and then he glanced over at her. "I have to say, Kath, that if I was the SIO on this case I'd need a bit more before I'd allow any more time to be spent."

With a sigh, she confessed, "It's worse than that; we don't even have a case-file opened as yet."

Surprised, he stared at her for a moment before turning back to the road ahead. "*Now* you tell me."

"I'm that sorry, Thomas; I thought this would pan-out better than it did. But there's too many coincidences for my taste—not to mention that some of the players are duckin' out of sight."

Silently, she added, And Acton's up to something—something he's truly hopes I won't unearth, and thus far, I've played along like the stupid heroine in the over-dramatic story, which is a role that does not suit me *a'tall*.

Coming to a decision—after all, she did have the sense that Williams was involved, somehow—she ventured, "I wouldn't be surprised if Acton knows more about Mallory Flynn's death than he's lettin' on."

He glanced over at her. "I don't know anything about it, if that's what you're wondering."

This was the truth, and she frowned slightly. "Then I think he's tryin' to keep both you and me out of it, for some reason."

It was on the tip of her tongue to mention that she also had the sense Lizzie knew something about whatever-this-was, but she drew back. I should be careful, she decided; Lizzie hadn't told Williams about Acton's attempt to recruit Corso, and there may be something here that Acton doesn't want him to know. Her scalp started prickling, yet again, and she knew she was on the right track.

"Speaking of Savoie, are you going to his wedding?"

Happy to change the subject, she smiled. "Wouldn't miss it, truth to tell."

"We've been invited to the reception."

Confused, Doyle turned to him. "Oh? Is the church havin' a reception?

"No, Kath; it's at your flat, and you're the hostess."

"Oh—that's right. I think I'm blockin' out all thought."

He tilted his head. "I'm not too keen on it, either, but Lizzie thinks we should go to support Mary."

"You need to support me, too, Thomas; you know I hate that sort o' thing."

He chuckled, and Doyle turned to gaze out the window again, thinking—you know, it *is* a bit strange; why wouldn't Acton just host a reception at the church hall, which would be miles easier on his poor beleaguered wife? It's almost as though he wants to gather people at the flat, like in an Agatha Christie story—

"I'll try to behave myself, this time," Williams joked.

She made a wry mouth. "Yes—try not to have a go at Savoie, this time 'round. Faith, you're lucky Lizzie was there to pack you up and take you home."

At their last attempt at a dinner-party, Williams had become drunk and disorderly and Lizzie had been tasked with taking him home, since he was in no shape to drive. Somehow, Williams had wound up married to her that night, and—despite this extremely unorthodox beginning—the relationship had stuck.

And Williams may not be aware of it, but Doyle was almost certain that Acton had enlisted Lizzie and planned-out the whole thing. It was that medieval mindset, again; Acton had arranged a marriage to suit his aims—just as his ancestors would have done— and he felt no shame in it. Faith; that was exactly how he'd got the fair Doyle to marry him in a whirlwind, as a matter of fact; he knew how to best pull it off because he'd studied her, and had then proceeded accordingly.

Williams smiled. "Lizzie's a life-saver. Me having a go at Savoie was a lot like Denisovich's son having a go at Acton—it was never going to end well."

Doyle teased, "Pulled you from the coals and patched you up, she did. She's like that heroine from the knight-story—Elaine, or somethin'."

"Not really—Elaine wound up dying of a broken heart."

"Never mind then; Lizzie would eat Elaine for breakfast."

He chuckled, but insisted, "She's sensitive, though, underneath it all—you can't judge by appearances."

Well, that's interesting, thought Doyle; Munoz just said the exact same thing about Gabriel. With a smile, she agreed, "Aye, Lizzie's got hidden depths, and no one knows this better than me, what with the Wexton Prison disaster comin' immediately to mind."

"She's a brick."

"She is, indeed."

He glanced at her. "I can't say the same for Mary, though. Good luck to her, for taking-on Savoie."

"Believe it or not, I think that particular pairin' may work out well."

He grimaced in disagreement. "You're ever the optimist, Kath."

"That's me," she readily admitted. And here we are—thanks for lettin' me impose."

"Always a treat. Will there be a report?"

"I don't think so," she said, as she slid out. "But I'll see what Munoz has to say."

"Who are you, and what have you done with DS Doyle?" he teased.

She leaned in the window. "Shame on you, for thinkin' that I'm so petty, Thomas Williams. Besides, somethin' tells me I'd best get used to Munoz bossin' me about."

He grinned. "Good on you."

"Aye; my pride has gone by the wayside, and a good riddance."

As she thanked the doorman, though, she wondered why she'd the uneasy sense that this was not exactly true.

CHAPTER 23

*W*hen Doyle arrived at the flat, Reynolds informed her that her husband was working from home for the remainder of the afternoon.

With a smile, she relinquished her coat. "Thanks, Reynolds, I'll go give him my regards. Let me know when the boys are up."

"I will, madam."

As she made her way down the stairway to the first floor, she thought; I'm in for another debriefing, it seems—although my husband will hide the fact that this is his aim. I should pay attention to what he probes me about, to see if I can garner any clues; a shame, that the man is as subtle as a serpent, and twice as guileful. On the other hand, I'm something of a loose cannon, and —for once—I have a bit of ammo to fire off.

She tapped on the office door and then entered with a smile. "Michael; here's a happy surprise."

He rose to kiss her. "I thought I'd accompany you and the boys to the park, this afternoon."

She settled into the chair across from him. "The boys will love it —best wear your wellies, it's a bit wet."

"You visited the recycling center on Gipsy Hill?"

It was not a surprise that he was keeping track—he tended to monitor her movements—and so she readily affirmed, "Aye. I hadn't the first whisper of a lead on the Flynn case, and so I went over to The Grenoble Hotel to test-out a drug distribution theory. Then I found out that you'd been there before me, with the very same idea."

"Yes," he said smoothly. "Unfortunately, my lead came up empty."

She made a face. "I should have checked-in with you, first, and saved myself the trouble. Well, this Hermano-fellow has done a bunk, along with the grocer and the reportin' witness, and it can't be a coincidence that they've all decided to disappear. So that's why I decided to go over to the recyclin' center; the reportin' witness is supposed to be a regular, over there."

In a mild tone, he asked, "Williams went with you?"

She winced. "Against protocol, husband. I'm due for a scoldin'."

But Acton only tilted his head. "Williams has a full plate, just now; in the future, if Munoz is unavailable perhaps you could enlist me, instead."

Smiling, she teased, "Because you are idle, and all your plates completely empty."

"There is always time for you."

"Thanks, Michael, but if I enlist you on all of my wild-goose chases, we'll both wind-up out of a job."

He made a sound of sympathy. "So; you discovered nothing of interest?"

With a casual air, Doyle fired-off her cannon. "As a matter of fact, I did find out somethin' of interest. The manager at the recyclin' center thought our mystery-figure on the surveillance tape is Yandra Corso, and I've the strong feelin' you already knew this, which was why you gave her a scoldin' at the crime scene."

He met her eyes, and there was a small silence.

Doyle leaned forward and offered, almost gently, "If Corso was somehow involved in Flynn's death, you mustn't cover for her, Michael. I'll admit that I'm a bit confused as to why you would."

But he immediately replied, "No—I do not believe she is a suspect. Instead, I believe she was there to meet-up with Flynn, and was in the wrong place at the wrong time."

This was true, and Doyle raised her brows, thoroughly surprised. "Wow. That's unexpected; you think someone who worked in the morgue would have access to all the drugs she'd ever want."

"Perhaps. Although we cannot be certain that illegal drugs were her aim."

Doyle lowered her head and shot him a skeptical look from beneath her brows. "That's doin' it too brown, husband—why else would she be there, meetin' up with Flynn in an alley? It makes me wonder why you're bendin' over backwards not to give her the sack."

He drew a long breath. "I'd rather she be given another chance. She is very talented."

This was true, and grudgingly, she admitted, "That's fair, I suppose—you did the same for Gabriel, when he was the one with the drug problem. Faith, husband, but you are crackin' unpredictable; there are times you come down like the wrath of God, and then there are times that you show amazin' restraint."

He pointed out, "If the Met fired everyone who dabbled in recreational drugs, we'd be hard-pressed to muster a unit."

"I suppose that should be filed under sad-but-true, but don't think I can't see that you're trying to avoid the main topic, here; you're buryin' Flynn's case in the cold files and I'd like to know why."

Meeting her eyes, he replied, "Unfortunately, there is a plentitude of possible suspects."

She quirked her mouth. "Now, there's a ten-pound word. And I suppose you can't start lookin' into that 'plentitude' without bringin' down a firestorm on our poor heads."

"Precisely."

Stubbornly, Doyle insisted, "Flynn may have been a nasty

blackmailer, Michael—and I know you have to step carefully, given the circumstances—but murder is murder."

Gently, he reminded her, "We have no evidence that this was a murder."

This, of course, was a valid point, and she could only shake her head in wonder. "Aye—it's so *very* strange. You've no workin'-theories?"

"None that can withstand scrutiny."

Hearing a nuance to his tone, she eyed him. "I've the feelin' you know a lot more than you're sayin', husband."

He lowered his gaze, and ran a hand along the edge of his desk. "I will admit that if this matter goes cold, I will not be unhappy."

She made a derisive sound. "Now, there's some backwards-speak for you. And I imagine your 'plentitudes' wouldn't be unhappy, either."

"There is that. It is a nuanced situation, Kathleen."

"It always is," she retorted a bit crossly.

He spread his hands. "What would you have me do? The Crown cannot prosecute a homicide if there is no clear cause-of-death."

Grudgingly, she had to admit he'd a point. "Aye, and so you're off the hook, it seems. Everyone should thank God fastin' that I'm not standin' in your shoes, husband, and makin' these decisions; I'm not one for nuances, no matter what the plentitudes may think."

"Indeed. And if I may change the subject, I'd like to ask a favor."

"Nothin' with a nuance," she warned.

"No—instead I am trying to make certain that Callie attends our dinner-party; perhaps you could encourage her? You may wish to make mention that Melinda will not be attending."

Doyle lifted her brows. "Oh—is that the rub?"

"I think it may be a factor."

Doyle added, "Along with the unfortunate fact that she was

hopin'—once upon a time—that she'd be the one who nailed-down Savoie."

But he only demurred, "It does appear that she has moved on."

"Aye—here's hopin'."

This was indeed a relief, that young Callie had turned the page from Savoie; Acton's half-sister had harbored a massive crush on the Frenchman, which had caused no small turmoil in their lives; indeed, they were lucky that Savoie hadn't used her infatuation to his advantage, in the recent troubles between the two men. It just went to show that—despite all appearances—Savoie was decent sort of criminal kingpin.

Reminded, Doyle asked, "I thought you were goin' to try to set-up Melinda with Tim."

"I will have to come up with a different strategy," he admitted. "I think it is more important that Callie attend."

"That's very sweet, Michael. All right, then—I'll tell her, and I'll also tell her that we're dyin' to meet her new beau; we should be welcomin', and such."

"Thank you; I appreciate it."

"Whist; I'm only happy that you're tryin' to mend fences with the lass."

He bowed his head. "I will be the first to admit I have not handled the situation adroitly."

"In plentitudes," she agreed.

CHAPTER 24

When the boys were up and organized, they made their way across the street to the park, and headed over toward the playground area where Doyle tended to meet-up with a regular crew. Mary was usually there with her two girls, and Savoie would often come over with his son, Emile, on their way home from school.

Because it was something of a novelty to have his father along, Edward was chattering nonstop whilst Acton tried to keep up, and this gave Doyle a few minutes for quiet thought, as she pushed Tommy along in his push-chair.

This latest discussion with her husband seemed to verify her suspicion that Williams—of all people—was somehow involved; Acton was unhappy that she'd enlisted Williams to take her over to the Recycling Center, and he didn't want her to rope him in on anything else—small chance of that of course, with the case destined to die a quick death.

But it was puzzling, because she'd the strong feeling that Williams knew nothing about this case—he hadn't been caught-up in Mallory Flynn's toils, he didn't know about the Evidence Locker drugs or wretched Yandra Corso, or—or about anything a'tall. He'd been well-and-truly kept out of the loop, which was itself unusual.

So; was Acton worried that she'd say something she oughtn't to Williams, all unknowing? Or that a witness would? But what could it be? It all made little sense, but then again, every blessed thing in this case made little sense, especially Acton's hands-off attitude with Yandra Corso. When he'd said he wanted to give the young woman another chance it rang true, but on the other hand, her husband was not behaving in his usual fashion—not a'tall. He wasn't the benevolent type—especially when it came to silly women who could spark a massive firestorm and bring dishonor down on the Met.

It was true that he'd been generous with Gabriel in a similar situation, but Gabriel was Doyle's friend, and that made all the difference in the world—Acton would protect her friends simply because they were dear to her. Corso, on the other hand, was not Doyle's friend; did Acton want to protect the woman for some other reason? And what would that reason be?

He's not in love with her, she assured herself, as she watched Acton take Edward's hand along the pathway. But mayhap he's negotiating a deal with the woman—mayhap she knows about Flynn's operations, and who's been featured in Flynn's sex-tapes. He's told Corso that she'll not suffer any consequences for her misdeeds as long as she keeps her lip buttoned about what she knows—that would certainly explain his forgiving attitude.

This theory seemed plausible, but—try as she might—Doyle couldn't imagine a hardened brasser like Flynn trusting the likes of Corso with anything remotely important; Corso was clearly a weak link, and coming from Doyle, that was truly saying something.

With a mental sigh, she faced the very real possibility that she may never find out, one way or the other, because in the end Acton was right—the prosecutors wouldn't bring a case without a clear cause-of-death. Mayhap she shouldn't be so certain that her husband was up to something, and that instead he was just allowing this minefield of a case to die a natural death. Faith, it was the same as the Father Clarence investigation; Acton had stepped back, because he knew that there would never be enough evidence to pursue a case.

Her scalp prickled, and it gave her pause, because she knew exactly why it would. In her Acton-experience—which was vast, and somewhat hair-raising—when the man was stepping back instead of taking action, it was usually because he'd a counter-plan in the works that was equal parts hair-raising and advantageous to the House of Acton. And—as a result of this vast experience—it would behoove the fair Doyle to be mighty suspicious of this step-back-and-let-the-justice-system-take-its-course version of her wedded husband.

But—try as she might—she couldn't see what his goal would be, if he had an ulterior motive. No question that it would be to the Met's benefit if Flynn's death sank from sight with as little scrutiny as possible, considering that the case was brimful of sex-tapes, false evidence, and dealing drugs straight out of headquarters—faith; it would be the trifecta of horrifying scandals. It was the same with the Father Clarence investigation; Acton was only acting prudently in allowing the investigators full access, since he knew it would go nowhere and therefore all potential scandals would quietly sink from sight.

But she couldn't help but knit her brow at this conclusion, because "prudent" wasn't a word that leap to mind when it came to her better half. Not to mention there was a pair of mismatched ghosts havin' at her, and she'd bet her teeth that it had something to do with this confusing Flynn case.

The playground came into sight, which inspired Edward to ditch his da and run pell-mell toward it, a bit hindered by his rain boots. Acton fell back into step beside Doyle and asked, "Shouldn't Edward wear his mittens?"

Doyle sighed. "We've gone through two pair this week, already. He'll only fling them off and lose them."

"Nevertheless, I will make the attempt—it is quite cold."

He strode over to wiggle mittens onto Edward's hands, and the boy willingly stopped his mad racing-about to allow this procedure —something he would be loath to do for his mother, but his father was another matter altogether.

Everyone responds to Acton's air of authority, Doyle thought with a touch of amusement—even my mad lad. It was always a sight to behold—that instinctive reaction to a thousand years of wielding power. Small wonder that women were always after him, and the villains gave him wide berth. I—on the other hand—wield no power whatsoever, and would rather duck out of sight like a turtle withdrawing into its shell.

Savoie and his son Emile arrived—Emile joining-in immediately with the assorted other boys who were already there, all of them happy to get some exercise after days of rain.

Doyle lifted Tommy from his push-chair—the boyo was dying to get down on the wet sand, and so he had to be distracted—and as she hoisted him to her hip, she watched Acton step over to converse in cordial tones with Savoie, who had gone to stand at the playground's edge. The two men stood casually as they kept an eye on the children, but Doyle felt a sudden and profound desire to hear whatever-it-was that they were discussing. She knew—in the way that she knew things—that the conversation was not half so casual as it appeared.

Which rapidly led to an alarming thought; Mother a' Mercy, could Acton be covering for *Savoie* in the Flynn matter, just as Williams had suggested? Mayhap the about-to-be-married Frenchman was featured front-and-center in Flynn's sex tapes— and—after all—Acton owed the man a favor.

No, she decided almost immediately; Savoie was not the sort to be ensnared by such a woman—not to mention that if anyone actually tried a touch of blackmail, he'd no doubt deal with the problem in a fashion similar to how Acton would deal with such a problem—which was unfortunate, but was nevertheless the sad-but-true reality. Still, Doyle found that she couldn't shake a feeling of uneasiness, as she watched the two men stand beside each other, seemingly at ease.

Her distraction was interrupted by the arrival of Mary, along with Gemma and little Hannah, and the two young women duly admired the other's baby in the time-honored ritual of new mothers everywhere, whilst Gemma ran off to join the other children on the playground.

With some relief, Doyle turned her thoughts away from the various criminal kingpins she tended to consort with, and instead brought her attention to the upcoming happy event. "Are you girded-up, Mary? Is there anythin' I should do to help?"

The other smiled, as she lifted Hannah from her own push-chair —the benches were too wet to sit. "Thank you, Lady Acton, but there really isn't much to worry about—it will be a small ceremony. And please—bring both of the children; we'll have ours there, too."

Firmly, Doyle shook her head. "Not a chance, Mary—I want to be able to concentrate fully on the miracle you've wrought."

Blushing, Mary laughed. "It *is* a surprise, I suppose. And a good part of the reason that the ceremony will be small—everyone will think that I'm rushing things."

Doyle made a wry mouth. "I'd be the last person to make such a judgment, Mary, seein' as I married Acton at the drop of a hat."

"Did you? Well, I've decided it doesn't really matter what anyone thinks."

"Good on you, Mary—that's the spirit."

The other woman disclosed, "My brother's family is in town; we had them over to meet Philippe, and it went very well." She paused, and then added. "I think my brother was relieved—he's been worried about what was to happen to me and the girls."

Doyle smiled. "And now you've sorted yourself out; he's off the hook, and he's got himself a rich brother-in-law, to boot. He couldn't have arranged it better, himself—just like the nobs, in the olden-days."

Mary laughed. "Maybe—but I don't think women had much choice, in the olden-days."

"Aye that," Doyle agreed, thinking of the Trestles knight and his wife. "Much better, when you can marry who you like."

They stood together, watching the others for a few moments, and then Doyle asked, "How goes the bakery plan?" Mary was slated to manage Sunshine Bakery when it re-opened, being as Mary was a prodigious baker and her indulgent husband-to-be happened to own the place.

With a happy smile, the other woman replied, "I have wonderful news, Lady Acton. I asked Philippe if we could donate a portion of the profits to Nigel's charity, and he decided that we should donate all of our profits to it, instead."

Doyle blinked. "Did he indeed?" Nigel Howard had been Mary's second husband—a reformer at heart, who'd been frustrated by the political horse-trading he'd had to do as an MP. Before his tragic death, he'd been setting-up a charitable foundation for at-risk youth, with the aim of working on it full-time once he'd stepped down.

Mary nodded. "Philippe says he has plenty of money, and it is a good cause." She lowered her voice. "I don't know if you know, but he had a hard childhood, and so I think it strikes a chord with him."

Doyle teased, "I think it's you, that strikes a chord with him, Mary."

Again, Mary smiled. "Maybe." She lowered her voice in a confiding manner as she glanced Savoie's way. "He told me that he'd been interested in me ever since Lord Acton's Confirmation, but he felt he had to wait until he was out of prison."

"That would be a stumblin' block," Doyle agreed.

"But that's when I met Nigel, and so he never had the chance."

"Faith; there was a lot goin' on, at Acton's Confirmation," Doyle noted, in a massive understatement.

"Oh, look; here's Callie," Mary said, as she waved at the approaching girl.

And there's a lot going on, right now, Doyle realized, as she waved in turn. It's that deja-view thing, all over again.

CHAPTER 25

*W*ith a small smile, Callie came over to talk to Doyle and Mary—baby Tommy reaching out and insisting that she hold him, which she willingly did.

Mary greeted the younger girl with warmth, "How are you, Callie? I miss the days when we saw you on a regular basis."

"I'm fine, Miss Mary; I miss you and the girls, too."

Doyle asked, "Has school started yet?" The last she'd heard, Callie was going to attend some classes at university, to help her decide what occupation she wished to pursue.

"I put it off," the girl admitted. "Maybe I'll take another look, next semester."

"Plenty o' time," Doyle offered in a hearty tone. "And I suppose it's understandable—you're otherwise occupied." Doyle explained to Mary, "Callie has a new beau."

Mary exclaimed, "That's wonderful—how did you meet?"

Callie smiled. "He was the real estate representative for our building."

"Which means he's handsome and charmin', because they always are," Doyle teased. "What's his name?"

"Rolph," Callie replied, and couldn't suppress a smile.

Doyle saw her opening, and took it. "You must bring him to the dinner-party, Callie—we're all dyin' to meet him."

Callie's expression changed subtly, and there was a small pause. "Oh; I don't know—"

"Nothin' like a weddin', to give a man a nudge," Doyle insisted, seeing the girl's reluctance.

"If you're not ready to bring him, I completely understand," Mary soothed. "It should be on your timetable, Callie."

Thwarted in this attempt—honestly, *such* an annoyance that Mary was always so nice—Doyle asked brightly, "Should we go to the kiosk to get coffee, Callie? Want anythin', Mary?"

"No thank you." Mary replied, as she shot Doyle an amused glance which indicated she was well-aware that Doyle was looking to buttonhole the younger girl.

With Callie still carrying Tommy, they set off down the pathway toward the kiosk, and after a few moments of trying to decide how best to broach the subject, Doyle decided—in direct contrast to her husband—that she wasn't one for nuances. "Please come to the dinner-party; Melinda's not invited."

Callie grimaced. "I don't know as I really want to, Lady Acton—whether Melinda comes or not."

"Whist; you can't yearn after Savoie anymore—the man's gettin' married," Doyle replied bluntly. "It was never meant to be, lass. And besides, you don't want to be like that Elaine-person from that knight-story, who wore her heart on her sleeve and wound-up only embarrassin' herself."

Stricken, Callie ducked her head, and made no reply.

Softening her tone, Doyle continued, "I know it's hard—this unrequited love business; but I'm your sister—even though neither one of us has the least clue how to go about it—and so it falls on me to scold you a bit."

A bit mulishly, Callie pressed her lips together. "You can't relate, though; Lord Acton is mad for you."

Doyle thought—truer words, never spoken—but aloud she said,

"You're only provin' my point, lass; you deserve someone who'll be just as mad for you."

She walked a few steps, weighing what to disclose—never her strong suit—and then offered rather cautiously, "Savoie's a different kind o' bird, Callie, and it's probably for the best that he's wound-up with someone who doesn't delve too deep, and can only see the best in everyone."

"I suppose," the girl agreed in a subdued tone, and Doyle duly noted that this wasn't necessarily true. Still, she persevered, "Tell me that this new beau has promise, at least—is he kind to you?"

Callie's face brightened a little, and she nodded. "Oh, yes—we're very similar, really; he's connected to a wealthy family too, but he doesn't really fit in, either."

A bit alarmed by this implication, Doyle decided not to argue the point, and instead changed her tactics. "Come to the party; dress up, and bring your handsome beau—you can demonstrate to our Mr. Savoie that he's missed the boat and should repent fastin'."

With a little laugh, Callie agreed, "All right. What do I say to Melinda?"

"Tell her I said she's not invited because she hasn't the first idea how to behave herself. She'll only laugh, and heartily agree—she's always been one for plain-speakin'."

Callie smiled. "That's true; she's never takes offense, either."

Doyle gave her a glance. "Beneath it all, Melinda's a good egg, lass."

The younger girl grimaced. "Lady Madeline doesn't seem to think so."

"Whist; Acton's monitorin' that little situation, and so it's slated to be a tempest in a teacup—not to worry."

After a moment's hesitation, Callie ventured, "You don't think Melinda really murdered Father Clarence, do you?"

"No—my hand on my heart," Doyle offered sincerely, since she knew very well who had actually done so. "Besides, Melinda hasn't the energy."

With a laugh, Callie could only agree.

CHAPTER 26

*a*s soon as she and Acton began their walk back to the flat, Doyle announced, "Mission accomplished, husband; Callie's goin' to come and bring her beau."

"Good," said Acton, who was a bit distracted because he was holding Edward's hand whilst the boy kept pausing to jump in puddles.

"She wasn't inclined, since she still carries a bit of a torch for Savoie."

"Yes. That pairing never held much promise."

There was a trace of disappointment in his tone, and she teased, "It didn't have any promise *a'tall*, for heaven's sake, and just as well —it's not as though Savoie would indulge our Callie the same way he's goin' to indulge our Mary. Have you heard? They're givin' all the bakery profits to Nigel Howard's charity."

Surprised, Acton glanced at her. "Are they indeed?"

"Aye; and if that's not a turn of events that makes you see God's hand behind it all, I don't know what is."

"Not something anyone could have foreseen, certainly," he agreed.

"Well, let this be a lesson to the likes of you; there's no controllin' love."

"I can assure you that I have learned that lesson very well."

He paused to kiss her whilst Edward continued to pull at him, and laughingly, she steered the push-chair closer so that he could. "With a vengeance; your well-ordered life was turned upside-down by the likes of a lowly DC—and a shant, at that."

Smiling, he pulled her fondly against him with his free arm. "My life may have been well-ordered, but I will admit it was a bit bleak."

"And now the circus has come to town, and you're far too busy to even consider fallin' back on your bleak-and-broodin' ways."

"A lucky fate," he said, and bent to kiss her again whilst Edward tugged impatiently at him.

"Fah, husband," she teased. "It was meant to be—luck had nothin' to do with it. Stop bein' so superstitious."

"And yet you call yourself an Irishwoman."

She laughed again. "A fair point. I suppose it's more accurate to say that—whilst we understand that it's God's hand that's behind everythin'—we're always tryin' to sway Him to do what we'd like."

Smiling, he glanced up at the trees overhead. "Very well put."

"And apt," she teased. "In plentitudes."

They paused to allow Edward to attack another puddle, and then, when they resumed their walk, Doyle offered, "I'm superstitious enough to wish Callie some good luck, for a change. She's had a rough go, this past year."

But this was the wrong thing to say to her husband, who'd been a bit impatient with his new-found sister's reaction to her new-found status. "I disagree; in my view, she's had the best of good luck."

Quickly backtracking, Doyle soothed, "Aye, I suppose that's true; she has a million more options than she used to—not that she didn't have options before, but you know what I mean."

"I do," he agreed. "Not that she seems appreciative."

Doyle decided that now may not be the best time to mention the girl was putting-off university, and so instead she offered, "She's young, Michael, and her world's been turned upside-down, what with findin' out about her birth parents and—as an added burden —havin' Melinda always underfoot, drivin' her mad. A bit of rebellion shouldn't be much of a surprise."

"I suppose you have a point," he replied, and it wasn't exactly true.

Thinking to steer the conversation away from ungrateful-Callie waters, Doyle offered, "Mary and I were just talkin' about the olden days, and how women had to marry whoever they were told to. Faith, but it must have been miserable; to have no choices, and to have to make the best of it."

But he tilted his head in mild disagreement. "I believe we were just discussing how little judgment the young have, oftentimes."

Trust him to see it from the side of the deciders of such things— he probably wished it was the same way, nowadays. "Well, that may be true, Michael, but love tends to find its own way without anyone's tryin' to steer it, and you need look no further than the weddin' this week-end. Munoz thinks Savoie's been carrying a torch for Mary for a long time, and against all odds." She gave him a gleam. "And—speakin' of long odds—I bet you never thought you'd be hostin' a fancy dinner-party for the likes of Philippe Savoie."

"Very unexpected," he agreed with a small smile.

Suddenly reminded, she exclaimed, "Oh—I forgot to tell you. When I was chasin' my wild goose with Williams, I managed to raise the subject of Mallory Flynn, so as to sound him out short of accusin' him of murder."

He squeezed her to him. "Did you? That was well-done."

"Aye—and I can say very confidently that he wasn't caught-up in her toils, so he's off the suspect-hook."

"That is excellent news," he replied.

With a smile, she teased, "Now that our whole reason for

holdin' the wretched dinner-party is no longer a concern, is it too late to cancel?"

"As tempting as that sounds, it may be too late," he conceded.

She made a face. "Ah, well, it was just a fond thought; we should meet Callie's new beau, after all, and even if we tried to cancel, Reynolds would probably override us."

They were interrupted by Tommy's heaving his favorite stuffed toy—a rather bedraggled giraffe—into a nearby puddle, and then watching it soak up the muddy water with great interest, as though he was conducting a scientific experiment.

"Man overboard," Acton noted, as he went over to pick it up.

"Told you, that you should have worn your wellies," she said, and then watched him thoughtfully as he wiped the poor giraffe with his handkerchief before handing it back to Tommy. She'd gained the very strong sense—during their conversation—that her husband was already aware that Williams was not involved with Mallory Flynn. Which only confirmed what she'd already guessed —he'd an ulterior motive for this wretched dinner-party that he was withholding from his wife.

But try as she might, she'd couldn't guess what it could be— whatever it was, apparently it could only be accomplished over formal place-settings that always seemed to involve far too much silverware.

With a mental sigh, she acknowledged that she'd little choice but to possess her soul in patience, and hope that no matter what went forward, nobody would start throwing the fancy porcelain plates that Reynolds always wore gloves to handle.

Her musings were interrupted when—after a measuring glance at his father—baby Tommy carefully tossed the giraffe over the side, yet again.

"I'm to be put through my paces," Doyle's husband noted, as he walked over to fetch the soggy beast.

Good, Doyle thought; the shoe's on the other foot, for a change.

CHAPTER 27

hat night, Doyle was once again confronted by the same two ghosts, the medieval ghost standing still and silent, whilst Cassie Masterson sat before her, her hands weighed down by the heavy chains.

"Still have your chains, I see," Doyle observed, and couldn't quite keep the snark from her voice. "Quite the comeuppance, for the likes of you—however do you manage to smoke?"

"Stuff it," Masterson retorted. "Acton smokes, too."

Oh, thought Doyle in surprise; I think she's right.

But any further recriminations were interrupted because Masterson reluctantly turned her head as though listening, and then translated, "She says you mustn't forget your obligations."

Doyle frowned. "Which obligations are those? Admonishin'?"

"Yes," Masterson replied, listening. "She's saying something about false idols."

"It's the Second Commandment," Doyle explained with a superior air. "No surprise that the likes of you doesn't have a passin' acquaintance with The Commandments."

But Masterson was ignoring her, listening. "You must not hang back."

In some confusion, Doyle ventured, "I'm to admonish someone for worshippin' false idols? Can't say as I know anyone who does, actually."

"You must not hang back," she repeated.

"I'm somethin' of a hanger-back, though," Doyle admitted. "I'm not a nob, I'm one of the ordinary folk. We tend to keep our heads down, and hope no one notices us."

This remark was met with a disapproving silence, and—a bit bewildered by it—Doyle insisted, "It's true, ma'am. I don't know whether you're aware, but I'm just an Irish shant, and I haven't a shred of authority to throw around." She paused, and added, "Not like Acton—he doesn't hesitate to throw himself into the breach, if there's a need for it. It's truly somethin' to behold—just like that time in Dublin, when he went on scramble-drill to save poor Tim, and was havin' to beat out one prairie-fire after another. He doesn't necessarily enjoy it, but he's hard-wired to leap to the rescue—it's that 'nobles oblige' thing."

"*Noblesse oblige*," Masterson corrected, rolling her eyes. "You are *so stupid*."

Nettled, Doyle retorted, "Not as stupid as you are—only look at what you've done to yourself."

"*He's* the one who did it to me," Masterson shot back, since she was obviously nursing this grievance well into her after-life.

"You're a homewrecker," Doyle returned hotly. "And you got exactly what you deserved."

"I was much better suited to him than you are."

"He was *married* to me, and so whether he was better suited or not is *completely* beside the point—speakin' of The Commandments. You're only gettin' your just desserts for targetin' other women's husbands, and you're no better than that awful Mallory Flynn— faith, but I'm surprised the two of you haven't met-up to compare notes."

Masterson suddenly paused, listening. Then—with a mulish mouth—she sullenly translated, "She's saying again that it's important you remember your obligations."

With a mighty effort—truly it was rather satisfying, to finally have the chance to go after Masterson hammer-and-tongs—Doyle reined-in her temper, and frowned in concentration. "Right; she keeps sayin' it, so it must be important, but who's the sinner, here? She needs to be a bit clearer."

Masterson listened, and then translated. "If love is an excuse for sin, then it is not love, it is only sin."

Doyle blinked. "Oh—oh, I didn't realize that 'love' was the topic, here. Right; 'love does seek its own interests'. She paused, thinking about this. "You know, that's an odd little coincidence; I was just havin' this very discussion—about that Elaine-person, and how selfish-love isn't truly love a'tall."

Masterson listened, and relayed, "Yes."

Holding the unhappy sense that the medieval ghost was hanging on to her patience with both hands, Doyle ventured, "I'm not sure what she wants of me—somethin' havin' to do with false idols, and selfish-love? Most of the time, my 'obligations' involve cleanin' up the consequences of selfish-love; faith, she's lucky she's not a detective, nowadays—she'd see an eyeful of love-gone-wrong, *believe* me."

Masterson translated, "Then it is not love."

Slowly, Doyle nodded in concession. "Aye. I keep forgettin', and she's right—it's not love, it's only sin—selfish-love is a far cry from the real thing. The real thing 'bears all things', even if it doesn't suit our own notions. It's a bit like what Acton and I were talkin' about, today; you might try to steer God, but you haven't got the first clue how it all fits together, and so you don't realize that sometimes it's for the best that your prayers go unanswered."

There was a small silence, and then Doyle offered, "Right, then. I've got to find the sinner and do some admonishin', because real love is unselfish. I've got to quit hangin' back."

Grudgingly, Masterson agreed, "I think that's the sum of it."

Doyle scrutinized the lady's still, pale face, and remarked, "I suppose it's a touchy subject for her; she was forced to marry someone who didn't love her, and had to try to make the best of it."

There was a subtle shift in the atmosphere, and Masterson chided, "She's trying to help you, don't criticize her."

Surprised, Doyle defended, "I'm not criticizin' her—she truly had no choice."

Masterson listened, and then translated. "She says there are always choices. That is the entire point of admonishing the sinner."

Thoroughly confused, Doyle stared at the unmoving medieval woman, and then slowly shook her head. "Mother a' Mercy, but I can't make heads-nor-tails of this; I need somethin' more to go on."

Masterson listened again, and then translated, "He admonished them. You must find out why."

Tentatively, Doyle asked, "Acton, you mean?"

But she wasn't to receive an answer as she was startled awake, her heart pounding and her eyes wide.

CHAPTER 28

The following morning, Doyle lingered at the breakfast table after Miss Cherry took the boys to get dressed for the day, mulling over her latest dream.

It did seem as though there was a theme, here, and that theme had to do with love, of all things—selfish-love versus unselfish-love. And it would certainly explain why Masterson was the designated ghost, in this instance—she was a prime example of the hazards of selfish-love.

It would also explain the presence of the medieval ghost. The lady had been married-off to the Trestles knight, and they'd managed to avoid a war in the process—unselfish-love, so to protect her people. And apparently, she'd made the sacrifice willingly since she'd said there were always choices—which was true; presumably they weren't going to drag her to the altar if she refused. Or she could have leapt from the nearest tower, or something.

It was a bit of a revelation, in fact; due to her historical circumstances—having to do whatever the men-folk told her to—Doyle had assumed the knight's wife would be meek, and mild-asmilk, but—surprisingly—she seemed rather steely; miles more steely than the fair Doyle, as a matter of fact.

So; it was one of those juxtaposions—juxstaporitons?—with the lady being a pattern-card of unselfish love, and Masterson being just the sort of nasty brasser who would have tried to steal the ghost's husband, back in the day. And atop all this, Doyle seemed to be getting a persistent message that she wasn't behaving as she ought; the ghost seemed annoyed that the fair Doyle wasn't handling her obligations.

So; it was past-time that she put some effort into figuring out who was in need of admonishment—apparently, an admonishment that was connected to selfish-love. The obvious candidate would be Yandra Corso, who was mooning after the fair Doyle's husband, but—try as she might—Doyle couldn't understand what she was supposed to do; Acton wasn't falling victim, and he'd already admonished the young woman on the subject. Surely, Doyle wasn't supposed to give Corso another bear-garden jawing? It would be overkill—not to mention it would be thoroughly embarrassing for the both of them, since Acton seemed intent upon keeping the matter private.

Although—although Doyle would go at it from a different angle than Acton; Doyle was supposed to try to redeem the woman's immortal soul—there was that reference to The Commandments, after all—whilst Acton would be trying to redeem her career—he always tended to take a much more practical view of such things.

Thinking on this, she said to Reynolds, "You remember the tale about that Elaine-person, Reynolds?"

"Certainly, madam."

"Well, Acton says we shouldn't feel sorry for her, because of how she publicly rebuked Lancelot. She wanted to make him feel guilty, and shame him in front of everyone—which was not very nice, and more than a bit spiteful."

Reynolds paused to consider this. "A fair point, madam; although with hindsight, Lancelot would have done well to marry Elaine, just as she'd wanted." He gave Doyle a significant glance.

She knit her brow. "Remind me why it is that you're givin' me the side-eye."

The butler explained, "Sir Lancelot was having an adulterous affair with Queen Guinevere, madam. Indeed, the author's major theme was that their lack of loyalty to the King led to Camelot's downfall."

"Oh." Thinking this over, Doyle replied, "I suppose that's all in keepin' with what I've been hearin' about for the past few days; on the one side it's about unrequited love—and how hard that is to deal with, and on the other side it's about the importance of being unselfish."

"That is one way to look at it, madam," the butler offered diplomatically, as he cleared away her plate.

Distracted, Doyle gazed out the windows, trying to make sense of the ghost's message. It was true that a likely candidate might be Yandra Corso, but—on the other hand—there was no need to find out *why* Acton had admonished her—faith, that was just about the only thing Doyle knew for certain, in this tangle-patch. It seemed more likely that the ghost was referring to Lizzie Williams, since Doyle's wedded husband had—rather surprisingly—also given Lizzie a scolding, just after Corso's scolding.

I should put together a timeline, she decided; just like I would at work, and approach this problem with my detective-hat on. Acton scolded Corso at the crime scene, and then he'd scolded Lizzie shortly thereafter. But before this pair of scoldings, Acton had asked Lizzie to recruit Corso for team-Acton—which is the only connection between the two women that I'm aware of.

Could Lizzie have blundered, somehow? Given Corso some information she shouldn't have, so that Corso had a means to apply pressure on Acton? If Corso was a part of Mallory Flynn's blackmailing rig, that working-theory rather made sense—although it was hard to believe that Lizzie would give away any state secrets, even accidentally.

And she mustn't forget to include the fracas in the hotel lobby on her timeline—that particular Corso-scolding happened the day before the other two scoldings. Faith; if she was a good detective, she'd find out what Acton was doing in the hotel lobby in the first place—she'd didn't know for certain, she'd just assumed he was nosing-out the drug-distribution situation, and had run into Corso. But that would be a mighty tall coincidence.

Just as it was another mighty tall coincidence that Corso had stumbled onto Flynn's dead body minutes after the victim's death; it was hard to believe this was all just happenstance—that the Assistant Coroner had been present for these two dramatic events, one hard upon the last. What was her role, in all this? Could the lanyard have been an admonishment to *Corso*, mayhap? But from whom?

Doyle frowned, thinking this over. It was a shame, that Acton seemed bent on making sure his fair wife did not catch a glimpse of whatever was at play, here, and you need look no further than the fact he'd managed never to answer her question about why he'd been scolding Lizzie Williams.

But the ghost was pressing her to find out, and so—despite Acton's clear opposition—she should do so. It was obviously important, or she wouldn't have a medieval ghost jawboning at her about the Seven Acts of Mercy.

As though on cue, her phone pinged, and—with a guilty start—Doyle saw that it was Munoz. Faith, she should have made a report before now, especially since she'd discovered that the indistinct figure on the surveillance tape was Yandra Corso.

"Munoz," Doyle answered, in the hearty tone of someone who was definitely not a dosser. "I was just preparin' a report."

"Well, put it on pause. Since we can't open a case, Gabriel's inclined to hold off on any more expenditures."

Not a surprise, Doyle thought. This unholy mess is being well-and-thoroughly swept under the rug.

"Are you going in? I'll pick you up, so we can discuss wrap-up."

Alarmed, Doyle lowered her voice. "What's wrong?"

"Nothing," the other said, and it was a lie.

"All right. I'm ready when you are."

"I'll see you in twenty minutes."

Doyle grimaced, as she rang off. Since the case was to be closed, she could only surmise that Munoz had heard some unwelcome news at the fertility clinic, and wanted to talk about it.

CHAPTER 29

The Foolish Child had stayed quiet, and he was hopeful no further action need be taken. The orishas, however, were not as hopeful.

$\mathcal{A}$fter she bade goodbye to the boys, Doyle hurried down to the front of the building to find that Munoz was already waiting at the kerb.

As they pulled away, the other girl said in a brisk tone, "I spoke with Gabriel this morning, and he's inclined to keep the preliminary file open for a couple of weeks just in case a witness comes forward. Otherwise, he wants to put everything on hold."

Doyle offered, "I doubt we'll get any witnesses, comin' in. The people in that neighborhood may know somethin', but they're not goin' to tell us—we're outsiders, and we make them nervous. It's like what you said about speakin' a different Spanish; if they think you're an outsider, the drawbridge is firmly pulled-up."

Practically, Munoz pointed out, "I don't know if it would be much help, even if someone did come forward. Acton doesn't want us talking about the decedent's selling drugs unless we think it's connected to her death, and since we've no cause-of-death we wouldn't be able to say, one way or the other."

"Now, there's a good point."

In light of the case being all but closed, Doyle debated whether to tell Munoz that the Gipsy Hill witness had identified Yandra Corso as the figure on the grocer's tape. She'd the strong feeling he'd rather she not disclose this unfortunate fact, and when he'd told her that he didn't think Corso was involved in the murder it was true—he definitely didn't think the rather hapless Assistant Coroner had murdered Flynn.

On the other hand, Munoz was the lead detective on the case, and according to protocol, the fair Doyle should make a full report; a single detective shouldn't decide what was important and what was not, which was exactly why they worked together in teams.

Therefore, Doyle revealed, "I did find out somethin' of interest, yesterday. I went over to Gipsy Hill Recyclin', and the fellow there thought the other figure on the tape was Yandra Corso."

Munoz glanced over at her. "Really? What does Acton want to do?"

Doyle blinked. "You don't seem very surprised."

"No—Acton already briefed me that Corso was a customer of Flynn's. He said we should tread lightly about making it public, unless we think there's a connection to Flynn's death."

Slowly, Doyle nodded. "Aye; he doesn't think Corso killed her, and he's tryin' to keep a lid on the Evidence Locker drugs-scandal."

Munoz glanced at her. "He told me he'd handle the Corso angle."

And that he is, thought Doyle; if by "handling it" you mean he's letting the woman off, scot-free—save for the occasional scolding, of course. Which rather supports the fair Doyle's theory that her husband had negotiated a deal with Corso, to protect her in exchange for whatever information she could give him about this unholy trifecta of scandals.

Munoz shrugged a shoulder. "I suppose you can't blame him

for trying to contain the scandal, and we don't even know for certain that Flynn was murdered."

Doyle blew out a breath. "Faith, it all comes back to that—it's so very strange. And Williams wanted to know why Flynn was sellin' where she was, if we think she's part of an well-organized distribution rig."

Her interest sharp, Munoz glanced over at her. "What does Williams think about the case?" Since Munoz was up for promotion, she wouldn't hesitate to crib a theory from Williams.

Doyle lifted her palms. "He doesn't think anythin'—he's completely in the dark, and thoroughly unhelpful." Frowning, Doyle asked, "Did Flynn speak Spanish?"

"I don't know. Why?"

"You think you'd need to, to be wanderin' around over there," Doyle offered lamely, unable to explain to Munoz that she wished she knew what had prompted the fracas in the lobby, which seemed to feature Spanish-speaking combatants. "Does Acton speak Spanish?"

Munoz shot her a look. "I don't know, Doyle—don't you know? He hasn't spoken Spanish to me."

"He spoke Spanish to your grandmother, I think."

"Don't remind me. She's the main reason we eloped."

Sensing her companion's sudden jolt of misery, Doyle was reminded of the likely reason Munoz had offered to drive to work, and so she asked gently, "What did the doctor say, Izzy?"

There was a small pause, and then Munoz cautioned, "You mustn't tell anyone, Doyle. Promise."

"Aye, then."

"She ran a bunch of tests, and she said they found a trace of a plant-based hormone in my urine."

Doyle raised her brows in surprise. "I didn't know plants *had* hormones. That's a bit disturbin'—just goes to show that leafy greens are the work o' the devil."

Impatiently, Munoz glanced her way. "Pay attention, Doyle. It's significant, because the substance is sometimes used as a natural birth control."

Doyle's brow lightened. "Oh. There's the reason you're havin' troubles, then. Well, that's a relief."

But her companion replied in a somber tone, "No, it's not a relief. The doctor said it's possible that it's just a by-product of my diet, but she was surprised it was there at all." There was a pause, and then in an even tone, she continued, "I'm wondering if Geary is giving me something to keep me from getting pregnant."

Agog, Doyle stared at her. "Holy *Mother*."

Munoz nodded. "He keeps saying we shouldn't be worried about babies, yet, and we should enjoy our time alone together. I thought he was just trying to cheer me up, but maybe he means it."

"And he'd *do* such a thing, without your knowin'?" Into the silence, Doyle considered what she knew of the bluff Irishman, and then slowly shook her head. "I don't see it, Izzy. Truly."

"Then what's going on? I didn't want to believe it, either."

"Well, gird-up your loins, and go ask the man."

But Munoz asked a bit bleakly, "How can I? If he's innocent, he's going to think I've lost my mind—and he's going to think I don't trust him."

But Doyle wasn't having it. "Faith, Munoz; you're being the stupid heroine in those over-dramatic stories—doubting him, but afraid to just *ask* him, so as to sort it all out. That approach never works out well—either in the stories or in real life. Go ask the man, and think how relieved you'll be when you rule it out."

"But what if it's true?"

Doyle made a sound of annoyance. "He's your husband, lass— the bone of your bone, and the flesh of your flesh. Quit bein' such a timid-Nell—it's as though I don't even *know* you."

Munoz was silent for a moment. "You know, Doyle, you're right."

"Every once in a while," Doyle joked, even as she realized that here was a clear case of the pot and the kettle—she was being a timid-Nell, herself, just as the ghost had accused. She needed to

heed her own advice, and quit being the stupid heroine in the story
—it was past-time to confront her husband, and ask the man about
the fracas in the hotel lobby. If there was any admonishing to be
administered, no better candidate to do it than the man's wedded
wife.

CHAPTER 30

herefore, with steely resolve, Doyle rang up Acton as soon as she was in the lobby. "Are you free?"

"Certainly," he replied.

"You're not in trouble," she assured him. "But I think it's important that I find out what's-what."

"I am entirely at your disposal. Perhaps we could take a short walk."

"Nothing I like better than a hearty walkabout," Doyle agreed with a touch of irony. She was not one for exercise of any stripe, as he well-knew.

"Excellent; I will meet you out front."

Doyle rang off, thinking it interesting that her husband seemed to have been expecting just such a call from his better half, and also thinking it interesting that he wished to take no chances that their conversation might be overheard.

Therefore—in the fond hope of keeping the walkabout to a minimum—as soon as they were underway down the pavement, she asked, "I would appreciate it, husband, if you would tell me what happened twixt you and Yandra Corso in the lobby at The Grenoble Hotel."

Immediately, he assured her, "It is not what you think."

She quirked her mouth. "That's *not* what I think, Michael—give me a thimbleful of credit. But it seems passin' strange that you've never mentioned it to me. Unsnabble, if you please."

In a mildly curious tone, he asked, "How did you become aware?"

She gave him a look. "That's neither here nor there, my friend."

There was a small pause, and then he began, "I needed to meet with Corso privately, because she'd informed me of a rather disturbing development. Discretion was advised, and so she suggested that we meet for tea at the hotel. We spoke for perhaps half-hour, and then I received a note from the staff, informing me that you were upstairs in our usual suite."

Doyle came to an abrupt halt, and stared at him in astonishment. "*What?*"

"Indeed," he agreed, as he halted to face her.

Coming to the only conclusion that seemed plausible, Doyle ventured, "Holy *Mother*, Michael; she was tryin' to lure you upstairs, so as to have her way with you?"

"I would imagine that was the plan," he agreed. "I believe the intent was to create a sex-tape, for blackmailing purposes."

Utterly taken aback, Doyle had a hard time finding her voice for a moment. "Then she *was* workin' hand-in-glove with Mallory Flynn—faith; I'd never have believed it. They must have known you were honin' in on the dry-labbin' scandal, and they needed to get some leverage over you."

"I imagine that was the case," he agreed.

Outraged, Doyle continued, "And how *on earth* did she hope to accomplish this? Did she truly think that you'd just settle-in to jump her bones, once you found out I there?"

There was a small pause, and then he said in a level tone, "I'm afraid it is much worse than that. I was fast losing my ability to make lucid decisions."

Again, Doyle stared at him for a long moment of horrified

silence. "Mother a' *Mercy*, Michael," she breathed; "you were *roofied*?"

"It would seem so."

Doyle was suddenly reminded that she'd already entertained the possibility that he'd been drunk, since the entire episode was so completely out-of-character for her polite and reserved husband. So; here was the explanation for these bizarre events, as alarming as it was sordid.

Remembering what the HR Manager had said, Doyle prompted, "But you balked in the lobby, and argued with her, and then someone from the staff tried to wrestle you into the lift."

But he shook his head. "On the contrary; a man from the kitchen-staff approached to intervene. He gave me warning that it was a trap, and broke a capsule under my nose—presumably ammonium carbonate. It cleared my mind just enough to allow me to resist."

"Hermano," said Doyle in all wonder. "So; it turns out that he was the hero, here, and not the villain."

Acton continued, "The desk personnel called-in security to clear everyone away, and then the Hotel Manager asked if I would like to lie down for a bit—I believe he thought I was drunk. I declined his invitation, and managed to leave under my own power."

Doyle stared at him. "Holy *Mother*, Michael."

"Indeed."

But Doyle had seized upon the one fact that seemed most pertinent, in this strange and alarming tale. "And yet, everyone involved is not a smolderin' corpse, lyin' dead in the street. Why is that?"

He glanced up at the horizon, as he considered her question. "I thought it best not to draw-down more attention."

The penny dropped, and Doyle added, "Not to mention that Flynn was murdered the very next mornin'."

He bowed his head. "There is that."

In all wonder, Doyle asked him again, "But you'd nothin' to do with Flynn's murder?"

"No. I do not know who murdered her, nor do I know why she was murdered." He then added fairly, "If she was."

Impatiently, Doyle chided, "Whist, Michael—a'course she was murdered, else it would be a coincidence to beat all coincidences."

"I cannot disagree."

Doyle forgave him this lapse into backwards-speak—small blame to the man, after this horrifying tale—and slowly shook her head in disbelief. "So, Corso was workin' with Flynn. Didn't see that one comin' a'tall—she doesn't seem the type."

He made no remark, and rather alarmed by his silence, she lifted her face to meet his eyes. "She's got to be punished for this, Michael."

"She will be. But not immediately."

Staring at him, Doyle voiced her theory aloud. "You're usin' her to find out what she knows—promisin' she won't lose her career, in return."

"Something along those lines."

But Doyle found his matter-of-fact manner almost unbearable, as she retorted angrily, "That's not enough, Michael; you could have been—you could have been *killed*."

Her voice broke, and as she bowed her head to control her emotions, he immediately drew her into an embrace. "No," he soothed, his arms around her and his head resting against hers. "I was much more useful alive."

"*Shame* on her," she retorted, trying to control her tears. "It's *despicable*, and she can't just get away with it."

"She won't," he assured her, and this was true.

Doyle fought an impulse to find immense satisfaction in this remark, and instead—with a mighty effort—she pulled herself together, and wiped her cheeks with her palms. "I suppose this is my cue to preach about forgiveness and mercy, and how you mustn't go about killin' people. I'm not very inclined, just now, but you've already heard it a million times. Keep it to mind, please."

"I will," he assured her, and gently moved his hands along her back.

Now I've done it, she thought unhappily as she rested her forehead against his shirtfront; I've gone and cried, and he hates it when I cry—which does not bode well for the villains in this sordid tale.

And so—despite a strong impulse to cheer him on, in this particular case—she lifted her face to caution, "Just be careful, Michael. And I was wonderin'—it's only a theory, so bear with me —but I was wonderin' if mayhap the lanyard 'round Flynn's neck was a warning to Corso."

"I think it unlikely," he replied, as though he'd already considered this. "I don't believe Corso had much involvement in Flynn's operations. That theory would hold more water if it was Corso who'd been murdered, and the warning given to Flynn."

Doyle nodded, seeing his point. "Aye—that's why it was just a stray theory—unlikely that Flynn would trust Corso with anythin' important; she's somethin' of a weak link." She remembered what Shandera had said, and added, "She's too naïve to be any good as a cohort."

"I would tend to agree. But nevertheless, she was involved in the plot, and I'd like to find out how it came about."

He was being careful not to give her chapter-and-verse about what he intended to do, but Doyle had seen this same holy-show once before. He'd manipulate the young woman into staying quiet about this mess—mayhap by letting her believe she still had a chance at him—and in the meantime, he'd be carefully defusing all potential scandals. He'd done the exact same thing to nasty Cassie Masterson, when she was going to publish an exposé about him; he'd convinced her to hold off, all the while spinning a web 'round her like a devious spider.

Taking a long breath, she leaned back to meet his eyes. "Aye, then. Just don't get too cozy with her, Michael—you might start to realize that she's miles more your type than I ever was."

He squeezed her, gently. "You are being foolish, Kathleen, if I may say so."

"I'm just jokin'," she assured him. "I knew it couldn't be what it sounded like, the moment I heard about it."

"How did you hear?" he asked in a casual tone.

"Nice try, my friend."

She stood content, within his embrace—such a relief, to finally know what had happened—and then informed him, "Gabriel's inclined to hold Flynn's file in abeyance for a couple of weeks, pending a witness."

"Yes. Although I doubt we will have one. Our CIs have heard no rumors, which is rather surprising."

She raised her brows, because the Met's Confidential Informants —who mingled with the various blacklegs in the London underworld—tended to keep a close ear to the ground, and would be eager to grass-out any suspects since they'd be rewarded for it.

She withdrew from his embrace so that they could continue their walk, and to show him that she'd recovered from her little melt-down, she teased, "I'm that worried, Michael, that you've finally met your match. Someone's got away with murder, and there's not a pig's whisker of evidence to show for it. I'm amazed that this wasn't your doin'."

He tilted his head in concession. "It is a puzzling case."

She didn't push the matter, because it seemed clear that there was more to this tale than he'd been willing to disclose—a truly alarming aspect, that Acton had been careful to avoid touching on. Flynn—or Corso—knew that Acton and his wife tended to tryst at The Grenoble Hotel—faith, they even knew the suite number, which could only be seen as an ominous development. Ominous, because it seemed evident there was someone on the hotel staff who'd been willing to plot with the evildoers—it was the only thing that made sense, and it would also explain why Hermano had been ready to intervene; he'd overheard the plan, somehow, and had swooped-in to save the day.

And of course, if Doyle had reasoned this out, then so had her wedded husband; he was always miles ahead of her when it came to reasoning things out, and so—presumably—he was well-aware of this rather sinister aspect, and was bent on finding out who the traitor was. Well—"traitor" wasn't exactly the right word, technically, since it wasn't someone in their service; instead it was probably someone on the hotel staff who took drugs or was bribed —someone at the front desk? Faith, the matter would be miles more serious if there was indeed a traitor in their own ranks.

Her scalp prickled and she stilled in surprise, thoroughly dismayed.

Noting her reaction, her husband soothed, "Please try not to worry, Kathleen. I am in the process of taking appropriate steps. In the meantime, I ask that you say nothing of this matter."

"Right, then—but no more floozies," she teased half-heartedly, alarmed by the direction of her thoughts.

"Shall I take you home?"

"I'm fine," she assured him, pronouncing it "foine" to tease him. "I had a momentary lapse, is all. And I wish I'd been the one who was there, coverin' your back. I think our poor Hermano was fired, for his pains."

"Unfortunately, he has dropped from sight, and I have been unable to trace him. He was at the hotel as part of a project to employ the homeless, and so he has no known-address."

Doyle made a wry mouth. "I suppose you can hardly blame him; he's probably worried about repercussions for thwartin' this nasty plot." With all sincerity, she lifted her face to his. "Thank you for tellin' me, Michael."

"Not at all," he replied, and she hid a smile, because there wasn't the smallest chance he'd have told her a blessed thing, if she hadn't forced him to.

CHAPTER 31

*O*nce back at headquarters, Doyle parted from her husband in the lobby and then began the walk back to her desk—happy to be alone for a few moments, so as to try to sort out whatever-it-was that her instinct was trying to tell her. Was there indeed a *traitor*, in this tale? It seemed clear that Acton knew more than he was saying—if nothing else, he'd mentioned there'd been a "disturbing development" that required him to meet-up with Corso. And not a knockin'-heads sort of meeting; instead he'd met the woman for tea, and on her terms.

So; Corso had a means to bring Doyle's formidable husband to heel—some sort of upper hand, over him. *Could* they have blackmail material on him, in some other way? It seemed so unlikely—Acton wasn't the sort of person to allow anyone to have the upper hand over him; the blackmailers were much more likely to learn a terrible lesson, and in short order.

And why had her instinct leapt to the possibility that there was a traitor, within their ranks? It seemed too unbelievable to contemplate—that someone in their household would pass on information about their visits to the hotel. Of course, it was possible that someone hadn't been able to resist a bit of juicy gossip, without realizing that the villains would seize upon it so as to set-up a trap. But even that idea seemed nonsensical; only a couple of people would even know about the trysts at the hotel—Trenton, possibly, since he was their security, but Doyle couldn't even be certain that he would know. Not Reynolds, certainly—Nazy, perhaps? But it seemed very unlikely that Acton would inform his Assistant that he was sneaking-off to the hotel to meet-up with his wife; instead he'd just tell her that he'd be out-of-pocket for an hour or two, and leave. And besides, Doyle hadn't gained the impression that Nazy was in the dog-house with Acton—the girl tended to be transparent, when it came to her emotions.

Abruptly, Doyle halted midstride and stood stock-still whilst her scalp prickled like a live thing. No—she hadn't gained the impression that Acton was cross with Nazy. On the other hand, Acton had been mighty cross with Lizzie Williams.

Impossible, she countered immediately; Lizzie would never betray Acton—not in a *million* years. But there was no denying that Acton had given the young woman the rough end of a jack-saw for some reason, which was very unlike him—Lizzie was one to never put a foot wrong.

As she stood in dismayed confusion, Doyle was suddenly reminded of the medieval ghost's parting instruction—find out why he'd admonished them, she'd said. Doyle already had a good guess as to why Acton had admonished Corso at the Flynn murder scene, but she'd no idea why Acton had admonished Lizzie on that same morning. Or at least, no idea until now. As hard as it was to believe, mayhap Lizzie had said something to Corso about The Grenoble Hotel.

There's only one way to get to the bottom of this, Doyle decided, and when the lift's doors opened for her own floor, instead she stayed within and pressed the button for the floor that would take her to the forensics lab.

With a grim sense of determination, Doyle made her way down to the basement lab, hoping Lizzie would be on-premises—the young woman was heavily pregnant, and might not be working as much as her usual. But when Doyle held her lanyard pass to the security scanner, she looked through the door's reinforced window and could see that Lizzie sat at her usual post—her white coat unbuttoned over her belly—as she peered into the scope of some sort of fancy machine, and made notes.

Watching her, Doyle was again struck by how similar the two young women were—Lizzie Williams and Yandra Corso. Both were clever, but both were very reserved—not the type to wear their hearts on their sleeves. And—come to think of it—both were the type who'd crush on Acton, who was clever and reserved, himself —aside from all the other attributes he offered the average woman. Corso carried a torch for him, and Lizzie had also harbored a mighty crush on the head of the House of Acton—until she'd met Williams, of course. She'd then had a hopeless crush on Williams for some time, until—wonder of wonders—she'd wound-up married to the man, as a direct result of Acton arranging things in true Acton-fashion.

Recalled from her abstraction, Doyle took a deep breath and pushed open the door. "Lizzie," she offered in a cheerful tone. "How are you?"

Lizzie looked up from her scope, understandably surprised. "Oh—Lady Acton; I am doing well."

Doyle paused, because—due to the nature of the conversation— she'd intended to ask the other woman to take a little walk to the Deli, so as to avoid prying eyes. But this plan had to be abandoned, in that she'd forgot Lizzie was so very pregnant. And Doyle's window of opportunity was no doubt closing fast, since her wedded husband—who tended to keep careful track of her—would soon realize that his wayward wife had gone to buttonhole Lizzie, and would quickly move to stymie any such attempt. If Acton told Lizzie not to spill, then she'd not spill—her loyalty to him was baked into her very bones. Which, of course, only made Doyle's current suspicions all the more puzzling.

"Come into the closet, for a minute," Doyle suggested. "Leave your phone."

As could be expected, upon hearing such a request Lizzie could only stare at her in abject surprise.

Rather lamely—truly, she should have thought this out ahead of time—Doyle explained, "I need to ask you somethin' privately, and this is likely to be my only chance."

"Oh—oh; I don't know, Lady Acton—"

It was on the tip of Doyle's tongue to remind Lizzie—for the hundredth time—that she was "Kathleen" and not "Lady Acton," but then she paused. To Lizzie, Doyle would always be the Lady of the House; it was time to use it to advantage, for once.

Doyle deposited her mobile phone on the stainless-steel counter, and then turned toward the closet. In an imperious tone she instructed, "Come along, Lizzie."

Unhappily, the other woman rose and followed her into the storage closet, where Doyle firmly locked the door behind them.

CHAPTER 32

The light was a bit dim in the closet, which was stacked with rows and rows of sciencey-looking things, and Doyle rather belatedly realized there was no place for Lizzie to sit. And so, with no further ado, she began, "I will hear from you, here and now, about your role in Flynn and Corso's little scheme."

Even in the dimness, Doyle could see that Lizzie went pale. "I didn't know, Lady Acton," she protested, her voice a bit strangled. "I didn't know what she'd intended—about Lord Acton. Oh, please believe me."

Firmly, Doyle commanded, "Spill, Lizzie."

To Doyle's great surprise, the other woman's face crumpled and she began to cry—bending to sob into her hands. Doyle stood for an uncertain moment—wincing a bit against the waves of remorse and misery that emanated from her companion—and then rallied herself. In a gentler tone, she asked, "Why would you be cooperatin' with the likes of Mallory Flynn, Lizzie?"

Gasping, the other women disclosed, "She said—she said she had—that she had tapes, and—and that he'd go to prison."

Doyle frowned. "Tapes of Acton?"

In an attempt to control herself, the other took a shuddering breath and raised her head. "No—of—of Thomas."

Her brows raised in surprise, Doyle stared at her. "I truly don't think Thomas was involved with her, Lizzie—and neither does Acton. She was bluffin'."

The young woman regarded Doyle with watery eyes. "She *was*?"

"Faith, didn't you ask the man?"

But this question only unleashed a fresh onslaught of tears, as Lizzie once again buried her face in her hands. "You—you don't understand," she sobbed. "It—it was *all* my fault."

"What was?" Doyle prompted, thoroughly confused.

"I did—I did an analysis, and it seemed harmless. Oh—I was *so* stupid."

Impatiently, Doyle chided, "*What* seemed harmless? Faith, Lizzie; pull yourself together—you're soundin' like me when I make a report, and I can't make heads-nor-tails."

This seemed to have the desired effect, and her companion made a visible effort to control herself and straighten up. In a subdued tone, she disclosed, "Mallory Flynn was selling potions."

Doyle stared at her. "*Potions*?"

Lizzie nodded, and wiped her eyes on the back of a sleeve. "The Santero case—remember? His potions were seized from his shop, and the bottles were still in the Evidence Locker. Flynn was selling them to the Santeria community."

Doyle stared at the other woman in astonishment. "She was sellin' *potions*?" Faith, I've got to stop repeating things, she chided herself—I sound like a deranged parrot.

Unhappily, Lizzie nodded. "They were worth a lot of money, apparently."

The penny dropped. "And Flynn was blackmailin' you about Thomas, so that you would give her access to the Evidence Locker."

With a half-sob, the other woman nodded again. "Yes. Although —although it was Yandra Corso, who first told me about them."

In all confusion, Doyle seized on the most puzzling aspect of this strange and disjointed tale. "Why on earth would the likes of Yandra Corso be helpin' Flynn sell *potions*? She's a scientist—and so are you, for heaven's sake."

Lizzie explained, "I was meeting with Yandra, to see if—to see if she'd like to become better acquainted, and she asked if I could recreate a formula, if I was given a sample."

Frowning, Doyle ventured, "What sort of formula? A roofie?"

"Oh no, no—of course not, Lady Acton; I'd never do such a thing. Instead, it was—it was supposed to be a love potion."

"A *love potion*?" For the love o' Mike, stop being a parrot, Doyle reminded herself.

Yet again, Lizzie's face crumpled, and she bent over to weep into her hands.

There was a discreet knock at the door, and a man's voice inquired, "Is everything all right? Chief Inspector Acton is inquiring."

"Right as rain," Doyle called out, and then returned her attention to her companion. "I'm lost, Lizzie; please explain, in plain terms, what on earth it is that you're talkin' about."

"She—she told me it works," Lizzie sobbed. "And—and I did do an analysis—the formula was made from harmless ingredients." She paused, sniffling. "It seemed worth the attempt. So—so I gave some to Thomas."

"You gave *Thomas* a *love potion*?" Doyle repeated, like a squawking parrot. "Have you run *mad*?"

"He doesn't love me," the other wailed in misery.

Doyle felt compelled to grasp the other girl by her forearms and give her a good shake. "Of course, he does; it's only that he's very buttoned-up, is our Thomas, and he always will be. He'll never be the sort to write poems about your eyes, or tell you he loves you every five minutes—Mother a' Mercy, only think how *annoyin'* that kind o' man would be."

But Lizzie only bent her head in abject misery. "I think he loves you—he always has."

Doyle stared at the top of the other woman's head for a moment, and then offered in a quieter tone, "Now, there's an example of exactly what I'm talkin' about, Lizzie. Even if he *was* in love with me—once upon a time—I'd absolutely no clue that such was the case. He's not one to wear his heart on his sleeve."

There was another discreet knock at the door, and this time Doyle's husband's voice could be heard. "Perhaps you would like to come out, Kathleen; I've cleared the room."

"Give us a mo," Doyle called out.

"Certainly," he replied, as though nothing untoward was going forward.

Turning back to her companion, Doyle scolded in a low tone, "Shame on you, Lizzie. You're chasin' a fantasy that will never exist, and on the fast-track to ruinin' your family in the process. You've gained your heart's desire, but you can't just be content; instead, you're takin' a wreckin' ball to it—*shame* on you."

"I'm *sorry*—I was so stupid," Lizzie sobbed.

"Aye; you were stupid to give these evil people somethin' to hold over your head, so as to make everythin' miles worse."

Lizzie took a shuddering breath. "Flynn said unless I cooperated, she'd ruin Thomas. And—and she said she had tapes."

"Well, you should have confronted your husband, but mainly you should have told Acton immediately—for heaven's sake, Lizzie, but you put him in a cleft-stick."

Because this, of course, must have been what the villains were holding over Acton's head—the reason Corso had been able to bring him to meet on her terms. Lizzie had given them access to the Evidence Locker and its drugs, and then had been forced to falsify lab results, so as to cover for it. It would have ruined her career, her marriage, and potentially sent her to prison.

It's exactly like Dublin, Doyle suddenly realized; in Dublin, Acton had scrambled to move heaven and earth so as to protect Tim from his own foolishness, and now he was doing the same for Lizzie. Faith, Williams was right; Acton's loyal retainers were bound to him but it went both ways, and he'd protect Lizzie with every ounce of power at his command.

Lizzie's emotions were finally coming under control, and she offered in a subdued voice, "I'm so ashamed, Lady Acton."

"As well you should be," Doyle replied, giving no quarter. She then weighed whether or not to press her on the particulars of the hotel trap, but decided against it; it seemed very unlikely that Lizzie herself knew the particulars—even though it appeared clear that the villains had learned about the hotel trysts from her. It wasn't hard to connect the dots; Trenton must have mentioned this fun bit of gossip to his cousin, certain that it would go no further, but Corso had somehow finessed this information from Lizzie.

It hardly mattered; however it was done, Doyle truly didn't think Lizzie knew what they'd planned for Acton, and one need look no further than how stricken the young woman had been when she'd emerged from Acton's office after her scolding. No matter how much she loved Thomas, Lizzie would never betray Acton.

And—hard on this realization—yet another dismaying thought occurred to Doyle. "Tell me, here and now, that you didn't murder Mallory Flynn."

"No," the other said, and it was the truth. "I would have liked to, though."

Doyle decided she'd done enough admonishing—the closet was getting a bit stuffy—and she eyed the other girl. "Should we hug, now? Is that what should happen?"

"Please don't," Lizzie replied with a small, watery smile. "That's not who we are."

"Which is a very good point," Doyle agreed. "I think you forgot who you are, Lizzie—you're not one to betray your principles for any paltry man."

Again, Lizzie smiled slightly. "He's not so paltry," she protested.

"I cannot disagree," Doyle replied, and then congratulated herself on this deft use of aristo-backwards-speak. "We'll say no more about it, then. Let me know when you want me to open the door."

As Lizzie carefully wiped her face on both sleeves, Doyle could only wonder—for all her fine words—what she would have done in Lizzie's situation. Although it was a bit different, of course; Doyle didn't have the any doubts about Acton's affections, and so wouldn't have had the slightest interest in a love potion. Instead, Corso must have learned about Lizzie's insecurities during their potion-talk, and Flynn had been all too happy to play on them by claiming that Williams had been unfaithful, and that it was all on tape. But Lizzie had tried to protect him anyway—even to the point of hiding his misdeeds from Acton, and allowing all the Met's lab-cases to be compromised.

I'd probably have done the same, Doyle admitted to herself. In fact, I *did* do something similar, when Melinda first told me about the fracas—I tried to fix it for Acton, even as the circumstances looked a bit dicey and I knew that he hadn't been honest with me. And so—between Lizzie and me—I suppose that's a testament to the power of unselfish-love in all its glory; unselfish-love is miles stronger than any prideful hurt feelings—miles stronger. Miles and miles and miles.

At Lizzie's nod, she opened the door to see her that her husband was leaning against one of the stainless-steel counters, as though he'd nothing better to do than wait upon his mad wife's latest mischief.

"I love you," she said sincerely, walking into his embrace. "I don't tell you near enough."

"You don't have to say," he replied, as he enfolded her in his arms. "Not to me."

CHAPTER 33

The Husband was weaving a web, and The Foolish Child was weak. It grieved him, but The Remnant must be protected.

*D*oyle sat beside Acton at St. Michael's Church, where they were waiting for the Savoie-Howard wedding to commence. There were only a few attendees seated in the front pews, and she was a bit dismayed to see that Gerry Lestrade—Savoie's dodgy brother—was present. But it only stood to reason, after all; Lestrade was Savoie's sole remaining brother, in that Doyle had killed his other one.

Reynolds was also in attendance, being as he and Savoie had conducted their own bit of business together, once upon a time, and as a result the two men were friends-of-sorts. Reminded, Doyle whispered to her husband, "I'm that surprised Lizzie's not here, too; she's another comrade-in-arms. Although Thomas would be hard-pressed not to make snarky remarks."

"They will attend the dinner-party," her husband whispered back.

Reminded, Doyle blew out an impatient breath. "I'm still gob-smacked; Lizzie was a crackin' knocker to step into that snare." She'd debriefed Acton about the potions-angle, but was almost certain that he already knew the tale—after all, he'd roundly admonished Lizzie, and so he must have known what was afoot.

"Very surprising," her husband agreed, in a massive understatement.

"There's no controllin' love—and it's foolish even to try," she continued with a bit of heat. "What *ails* everybody?"

Her husband took her hand in his—which was probably his way of reminding her that she should be a bit quieter—and she duly subsided. It was true that she was in an uncertain mood; she'd been a bit nettled, ever since she'd held her closet-conversation with Lizzie—and she'd had some trouble sleeping, which didn't help matters. She needed to stop dwelling on it—the poor girl had made herself vulnerable to evildoers, and had succumbed to their pressure. After all, it was the same old song—they saw this exact scenario a dozen times a day at work; it was a hardy soul who could withstand the pressure to do wrong in an attempt to gain one's heart's desire.

And—when you thought about it—it was the very reason why it was so important to admonish the sinner; temptation was so very *tempting*, and the wrongdoer needed to be reminded what-was-what by someone who had their best interests at heart. It wasn't wise to trade your chance at eternal happiness for a bit of temporary pleasure—such a thing never ended well, and you need only look to the Old Testament to see some excellent examples. Even the most heroic of heroes were made to pay a terrible price, when they tried to arrange things to suit themselves.

And—speaking of such—she leaned to whisper to Acton, "If you could have given me a love potion when we first met—and with no one the wiser—would you have done it?"

There was a small pause. "Possibly," he equivocated.

Blowing out another annoyed breath, she sat upright again, and then tried to rein-in her indignation; theirs was a fallen world, and

—news flash—human beings were only human. Instead, she should be grateful that all was well that ended well, and—for the love o' Mike—she should stop dwelling on it, and try to calm her tangled feelings.

Although—although she'd been rather surprised that the two ghosts hadn't made an appearance, these past few nights. After all, she'd successfully admonished the sinner, and so she'd half-expected a pat-on-the-back now that she'd figured it all out. It was just as she'd suspected; the medieval ghost had wanted to help straighten-out Lizzie Williams, who was semi-related to her even if it was from the wrong side of the blanket.

So; job well-done, and everyone moved on. If only she could shake this persistent feeling that it wasn't a job well-done—not yet, leastways—and this was the reason the ghosts hadn't come to tell her so.

Father John took-up his place behind the altar, and nodded at Savoie and Mary, who came forward flanked by their children— Emile looking as though he'd been warned within an inch of his life to behave himself, and Gemma holding a small bouquet of flowers very similar to her mother's.

I wonder, Doyle thought, as the ceremony began, I wonder if the reason that I'm feeling so unsettled is because there's yet another sinner to be admonished.

Her scalp prickled, and—a bit annoyed by this confirmation— she heaved a mental sigh and reconciled herself to sorting it out, even though she wasn't at all comfortable with her role as the scolding archwife.

Her gaze rested upon the attentive groom. Was it Savoie, who was in need of admonishment? He'd be a likely candidate—his sin-sheet was probably as long as his occurrence-sheet, and then some. But Savoie was radiating sheer happiness, beneath his grave manner, and Doyle had a hard time believing that she was slated to give the man yet another scolding—been there, done that. Mary was happy, too—not as happy as Savoie; hers was more of a measured happiness. She'd had a rough go of it, and could be forgiven for tempering her expectations.

Doyle's scalp prickled yet again, and she frowned slightly. There was someone else who'd had a rough go of it, lately. Callie? Things seemed to be settling-in for Callie, though, with the worst of it behind her. Corso, mayhap? The Coroner's Assistant would be a likely candidate for a Doyle-scolding, save that it would interfere with Acton's spider-like plans if Corso found out the man's wife knew all.

Not to mention Corso should have known better—shame on her, for pursuing another woman's husband. Faith, she was no better than nasty Cassie Masterson, who was roundly suffering her just desserts; it gave Doyle no small pleasure to witness that awful woman's humiliation—talk about a well-deserved comeuppance.

She was recalled to the present circumstances when the audience rose to their feet—it had come time for the vows, and so Doyle stood beside her husband to hear Savoie and Mary make their promises to each other. Acton squeezed Doyle's hand slightly, and she squeezed back—he was remembering their own vows, on that fateful day, and she should concentrate and not allow her thoughts to wander. If only she didn't feel as though she was forgetting something—something important.

After the ceremony had concluded, they all retreated into the church hall for punch and cake, served by Nellie, the church's Administrator. When everyone had their refreshments in hand, Doyle sidled up to the Filipino woman and observed, "I'm that surprised I don't get PSTD—or whatever it's called—every time I come into this room, Nellie. A lot of strange and unsettlin' things have gone on in here."

"Not this time," said Nellie, who gave Doyle an arch glance that contained a triumphant message.

Doyle smiled. "You have every right to say 'I told you so'; I should never doubt you." The other woman had predicted this marriage, because Nellie had a lot of experience observing the mighty power of love on a day-to-day basis.

"It was Father John who knew they'd make a match of it," Nellie confessed modestly.

"A miraculous turn of events," Doyle pronounced. "Faith, we should build a shrine on this very spot."

"Not as miraculous as yours," Nellie teased. "Yours deserves an entire chapel."

Doyle could only agree. "Aye, my weddin' was even more amazin'. A shame, that I was so nervous I can scarce remember it."

"I wouldn't know," Nellie said, a bit pointedly. When Acton had bundled Doyle off to the altar, he'd set it up with another church—mainly because it was necessarily a surprise-attack, and he'd presumed Doyle's own priest would be unwilling to cooperate. Little did he know that Father John was a huge Acton-fan, and so Doyle couldn't be completely certain that he wouldn't have been a willing co-conspirator.

As Nellie set about replenishing the punch-bowl, Savoie's brother Gerry Lestrade came over to smile his thin smile at Doyle. "We meet again."

"We do," she agreed. Doyle didn't like Lestrade much, in that he'd been up to his eyeballs in some very dicey goings-on when she and Acton were first married.

"It is a shame," the man said with a show of sadness. "A shame, that our other brother, Emile, could not be here."

"I'm sure he's here in spirit," Doyle offered brightly, having shot the man dead.

"Yes. Do you remember Monsieur Solonik?"

"I do, indeed," Doyle said—speaking of other dead people that she didn't like very much. Hopefully, Solonik was wearing his own set of chains.

Lestrade took a casual glance around the room, and continued, "Monsieur Solonik, he always thought there was more to my brother's death than we were told."

With a massive effort, Doyle hid her abject dismay at the introduction of this particular topic, and raised her brows. "Did he? Fancy that." Acton had given Savoie a whitewashed version of his brother's death by telling the Frenchman that Emile had been killed by another detective at Doyle's flat—a plausible scapegoat, who was now dead by Lestrade's own hand.

Doyle was to be rescued from this alarming conversation by her husband, who came over to politely offer his hand to the other man. "A happy occasion."

"*C'est vrai*," the other agreed, and then—reading Acton's expression aright—immediately excused himself.

"What was he saying to you?"

A bit chagrined that she was such an open book—she was never very good at hiding her emotions, especially from her sharp-eyed husband—Doyle confessed, "Somethin' about how he thought there was more to his brother's death than they'd been led to believe."

But Acton seemed undismayed by this. "Please don't worry; it is only Denisovich, stirring-up trouble. He is unhappy with Savoie."

This was only to be expected; Denisovich was the Russian kingpin who'd been lately put in his place—in rather brutal fashion—by the current happy bridegroom. But this reference was a bit puzzling, and Doyle asked, "It seems an odd thing to say; why would Denisovich claim to know anythin' about Emile's death?"

"Remember that Denisovich was affiliated with Solonik, all the way back to their days in St. Petersburg."

"Oh; that's right. I have trouble keepin' all my criminal masterminds straight, save for the one I'm married to."

Amused, he protested, "You malign me unfairly."

"Aye; you're always on the side of the angels—I keep forgettin'."

Father John came over to greet them, looking very much like the cat at the cream pot, and Doyle duly congratulated him on his match-predicting abilities.

"It was as plain as plain could be," the priest pronounced, rocking back on his heels with his hands clasped behind him. "And a good thing, I think—for the both of them."

Doyle nodded, a bit struck by this insight, since up to this time she'd only been thinking about how Savoie had swooped-in to rescue Mary—and Gemma, too. But if Savoie was slated to do a turnaround—with charitable doings, and such—mayhap Father John was right, and Mary was doing a fair bit of rescuing, herself. This was to the good, in that it meant that Doyle could finally hang up her Savoie-scolding hat, and leave such things to his new wife.

Reminded—rather unhappily—that she was supposed to be looking for another sinner to scold, Doyle allowed her gaze to rest on Lestrade, the trouble-causer. Could he be a candidate for a scolding? Nellie had gone over to speak with him, since Nellie was always watching for someone who might feel left out in a gathering.

If nothing else, I should go help Nellie, Doyle decided; and besides, I should make it clear that the comment about his brother's death didn't touch me in the slightest—no point in letting him see that he'd scored a hit. Therefore, since Acton was occupied with Father John, she walked over to join the other two.

"Kathleen," Nellie turned to include her with a smile. "Mr. Lestrade tells me he used to work at Sunshine Bakery."

"This is so," the Frenchman readily admitted.

"Fancy that," said Doyle, who wasn't at all surprised. After all, before the bakery had been set on fire, it was ground-central for criminal goings-on.

Nellie continued, "I'm so happy it will open again; Father was very fond of their soda bread. Will your friend return to work there, do you think?"

Doyle blinked. "Which friend is that?"

Nellie knit her brow. "I forget his name. A tall young man—Persian, I think; he was here for Lord Acton's Confirmation. He was always so cheerful, when I would see him at the bakery."

"Oh—yes," Doyle said carefully. If Officer Gabriel had been working at Sunshine Bakery, he must have been undercover, and it would probably behoove the fair Doyle not to say too much in front of dodgy Lestrade, who was no doubt one of Gabriel's targets in the aforementioned operation.

But before she could quickly turn the subject, Lestrade pronounced with a palpable undercurrent of dislike, "Yes; Rory Flynn. That was his name."

Whilst Doyle stared at him in abject surprise, Nellie said doubtfully, "Was that it? I'm not sure—"

"Oh—here comes our bride," Doyle interrupted hurriedly, and flashed Mary a bright smile, as she approached with Savoie. Immediately all discussion of Sunshine Bakery was dropped, as they congratulated the new couple.

CHAPTER 34

They'd come home to the flat after the wedding—Miss Cherry greeting them quietly, since the boys had already gone down for their naps. After bidding farewell to the nanny, Doyle did not hesitate to kick off her heels and head for the kitchen table, whilst Reynolds—ever quick on the uptake—promptly made his way into the kitchen to prepare her a pot of coffee.

"A very happy occasion," the butler pronounced with great satisfaction. "And with the dinner-party tomorrow, another one to come."

"How many will we have?" asked Doyle, who was vaguely aware that she should be a bit more involved.

"Fourteen, at dinner."

Doyle stared at him. "Faith; that many?"

The butler recited, "The honorees, Miss Callie and her beau, Dr. McGonigal and a guest; Miss Mary's brother and his wife, Mr. Lestrade and Ms. Davies—"

"Melinda's solicitor?" Doyle interrupted in surprise. "Never say they're a couple?"

"I do not believe so, madam. I understand Mr. Savoie made the request that she attend, and so I have paired her with Mr. Savoie's brother."

"Oh—I suppose I can see why he'd want her to come; she was a great help at the Howard murder trial," Doyle remembered. "I imagine they all know each other."

"And Mr. and Mrs. Williams will also attend."

Doyle asked, "If Lizzie's a guest, this time, who's goin' to help you out?"

"Lord Acton will bring-in two servants from Trestles," Reynold disclosed, and had a hard time keeping the note of triumph from his voice. Reynolds very much enjoyed the idea of rubbing elbows with aristocratic servants, since he'd be amongst his own species.

Making a wry mouth, she offered, "Well, tell them to keep a sharp eye on the silver; Savoie's brother is as dodgy as they come."

"I believe Lord Acton has arranged for security, madam."

Surprised, Doyle glanced up at him. "Won't our Trenton handle security?"

"It is my understanding that Mr. Trenton is unavailable."

Reynolds placed her cup before her, and with some impatience she lifted it to blow on the hot liquid. "That's just as well, I suppose—Trenton's not a Savoie-fan, and the last needful thing would be to have him armed and underfoot. Will Adrian fill in?" Adrian was their limo-driver, originally from the Trestles area, and the young man occasionally helped with their security.

"He is also unavailable, madam. I understand that Officer Shandera and Officer Gabriel will be present."

This was of interest, and Doyle lifted her gaze to him. "Will they? Faith, that's an odd pairin'—although mayhap it's because neither one of them would dare give Savoie the side-eye. And I suppose it wouldn't have been kind, to put poor Adrian in the company of Callie and her new beau." Their driver Adrian entertained a fondness for Callie, who was a childhood friend.

A bit fretfully, Reynolds disclosed, "It is not yet certain whether Dr. McGonigal will indeed bring a guest. It may be a concern, in that we cannot sit down with thirteen."

Doyle teased, "Faith, you sound like you're Irish, Reynolds. I refuse to be superstitious about it; there's good reason Acton wanted this wretched dinner-party, and he's not about to allow any paltry bad luck to interfere with whatever-it-is he's got planned."

The servant was understandably surprised by this characterization. "I am given to understand, madam, that Lord Acton wishes to honor the newlyweds. It would only be appropriate, after all."

But Doyle pronounced, "He doesn't care two pins about such things, Reynolds; he's got somethin' up his sleeve—mark me."

"As you say, madam."

The coffee had cooled sufficiently, and Doyle savored a sip as she stared out the window at the blustery day. Interesting, that Gabriel was coming—and Shandera, too. If she was the sort of person who didn't believe in coincidences, she'd duly note that these selfsame detectives had been rather unexpectedly assigned to the Flynn case, and that neither was someone you'd expect Acton to enlist for dinner-party duty—he'd just rope-in more Trestles servants, who were already at his beck-and-call.

So; what was afoot? The two were police officers, of course, but it seemed unlikely that Acton was going to arrest anyone—fingers crossed of course; you never knew. And it didn't help her suspicions that she'd just learned Gabriel had been working undercover at Sunshine Bakery—he was the elusive Rory Flynn; the fact that the hotel's HR Manager had described him as a charming rogue only cemented this revelation. Faith, they were lucky Nellie hadn't given the game away to Lestrade, all unknowing—although the operation was obviously over, since the place had burnt down. And if Lestrade was truly a target, it seemed that they hadn't come up with anything useful so as to arrest the man.

Her fingers stilled on the cup, because this didn't make much sense. It was very unlikely that Acton would be conducting a covert operation on Savoie's brother; Acton may have been unhappy with Savoie during that time, but Acton had been hip-deep in the Public Accounts scandal, himself, and therefore he would have to step carefully around Savoie and the notorious bakery. On the other hand, it was very hard to believe that Acton was unaware Gabriel had taken a covert role at the bakery. Could it be, that Gabriel had been assigned without Acton's knowledge—assigned to take a long look into Acton and Savoie's connection to the Public Accounts scandal?

These rather disquieting thoughts were interrupted when her husband leaned down to kiss her—she'd been so distracted that she hadn't noticed he'd changed into casual clothes, and was making ready to leave. "I have a meeting, unfortunately."

She mustered up a smile. "No rest for the weary."

"It should not take more than an hour."

She watched him leave, idly trying to decide whether he was handsomer in his formal suit or in his casual clothes—although nothing could hold a candle to Acton when he was wearing his tall boots to go horseback riding. And—speaking of such—mayhap they could take a quick trip over to the hotel, soon. Although—in light of recent events—she was half-embarrassed to show her face over there. It was a crackin' shame that as a result of pulling Lizzie's coals out of the fire, the people at the forensics lab thought Officer Doyle had run mad, and the people at The Grenoble Hotel thought that Acton was an unfaithful drunk. Ah, well; in all things, give thanks.

She stilled, suddenly. Wait a minute—wait a blessed minute; Gabriel had been chatting-up the staff at the hotel—could it have been *Gabriel* who told Flynn about Acton and Doyle's secret trysts?

Slowly, she sat up straighter. Mother a' Mercy—it was *surely* unbelievable, wasn't it? Gabriel wouldn't plot with a nasty piece-of-work like Flynn. But the unwelcome thought remained, mainly because in the past, Doyle had been a bit worried that Gabriel was part of an MI 5 team that was monitoring Acton's questionable doings. Indeed, the young man often hinted that he was aware there was more to Acton than it appeared—not to mention he'd been on a team that had attempted to test-out

Doyle's preceptive abilities—he'd made a few hints about that, too.

Thoroughly dismayed, Doyle set down her cup, the coffee forgotten. Could it be that Gabriel's friendship with Doyle was merely a means to lull her, and gather information to use against them? And should she mention these newly-hatched fears to her husband? The problem, of course, was that if there were any merit to her fears, Acton would first downplay her concerns and then Gabriel would sink from sight, never to be seen again. Her husband may be trying to walk a better path, but Doyle had no illusions about what would happen if either one of them were truly threatened.

Her scalp prickled, and she was suddenly filled with the certain conviction that Acton was already well-aware of all of this, and—indeed—it explained why her husband was bringing-in Gabriel as dinner-party security. Acton would have been keeping a very close eye on what going forward at Sunshine Bakery, if for no other reason than Denisovich was involved, and Denisovich—as Acton had pointed out—was yet another trouble-causer in the London underworld. Did her husband somehow discover that "Rory Flynn" was gathering information on him? And if he'd discovered this, what did he have planned for this dinner party? Because he was surely planning something—she knew it, down to the soles of her shoes.

Doyle had a sudden, unwelcome memory of how Acton had dealt with Caroline—another so-called friend who was actually a back-stabber of the first order, and with a feeling of acute dread, she suddenly knew—in the way that she knew things—that Acton's meeting—rather unexpected, on this wedding weekend—was with Gabriel, himself.

I've got to get over there, she thought in dismay, as she tamped down her panic. I've got to make sure it's not the Caroline situation, all over again.

This thought gave her pause, though, because it seemed unlikely that Acton would be moving to eliminate an enemy if that selfsame enemy was slated to handle security at their dinner-party tomorrow. But with a small shake of her head, she decided she shouldn't take the chance, and resolved to go to over Gabriel's flat with all speed—her trusty instinct was prodding her to take action, and if indeed she had her wires crossed there would be no harm done, save for another round of embarrassment atop of all the others.

Since she wasn't of high-enough rank to have access to personnel files, she pulled her phone and rang-up Munoz. "Ho, Munoz; I need Gabriel's home address."

The Spanish girl was understandably surprised. "Why?"

"Never you mind. Quickly, please, and don't you dare tell him that I asked for it."

The other girl made an impatient sound. "It's not like I see him all the time, Doyle; I just check-in once a month, or so. Or I manage to run into him on holiday."

Munoz continued to speak, but Doyle couldn't hear her, over the sudden roaring sound in her ears. *Holy Mother*, she thought, as she gripped the edge of the table to keep herself from swaying. Holy *Mother*.

"Did you hear me? Are you still there?"

With a massive effort, Doyle pulled herself together. "Sorry— you cut out. Say it again, please."

Munoz repeated the information. "Don't tell him I gave it to you," she warned.

"Don't worry," Doyle replied a bit grimly. "That's the last thing I'm goin' to say."

CHAPTER 35

*D*oyle debated whether to take the tube over to Gabriel's flat instead of the driving service, but then decided that speed was of the essence, and that it wouldn't hurt if her husband became aware that she was on her way; if he truly did have something terrible planned, it might serve to temper his actions. Because he must know what Doyle herself had figured out; Gabriel had fallen into the same sin that Lizzie had, he'd fallen into the temptation—the original temptation, that could be traced all the way back to the Garden—of trying to game the system so as to suit himself.

When she arrived at the flat, she tapped softly, and was not surprised to find that Acton was the one who opened the door for her, and that her husband—in turn—wasn't overly-surprised to find his wife on the doorstep.

"Hallo," she said. "I hope I'm not interruptin'."

"Not at all," Acton replied in a polite tone. "We were just finishing up."

Doyle looked beyond him to where Gabriel was seated at his table, gazing out the flat's windows and seemingly uninterested in Doyle's arrival on the scene. With a massive sense of relief, Doyle realized that matters didn't seem nearly as ominous as she'd feared —and she'd been a bit foolish to be fearful, truth to tell. She'd been worried it was the Caroline situation, all over again, but she'd forgot that Acton was not serving-up a cold-dished revenge, as he'd done with Caroline. Instead, it was the Dublin situation, all over again; the man was on scramble-drill trying to save the day, but he didn't want his wedded wife to catch wind of what was afoot because the sinners, here—Lizzie and Gabriel—were her friends, and her husband was trying to shield her from the knowledge of the terrible things they'd done.

But—although it was kind of him to make the attempt—her husband didn't understand that a sinner's friends were the ones who could best admonish the sinner; indeed, it was friendship's greatest challenge—to care enough to confront them, and not play the stupid heroine by saying nothing.

To this end, she told her husband, "I need to speak with Gabriel privately, please."

Acton tilted his head in mild disagreement. "I don't know as it is necessary, Kathleen."

"It's necessary," she told him, a bit unhappily. "I've no choice."

Her husband took this enigmatic remark in stride, and only nodded. "I will leave you to it, then. Shall I wait below?"

"Yes, please."

Acton quietly shut the door behind him, and Doyle approached to pull out a chair and take a seat beside Gabriel, who still hadn't looked her way. It was a bit alarming, all in all—Gabriel was one who hid himself behind a brassy, joking exterior, but it seemed—in this instance—that he couldn't pull himself together enough to even make the attempt.

Doyle blew out a breath. "I'm not good at roundaboutation, Gabriel, and so I'll speak plainly, and hope I don't hurt your feelings."

With the ghost of a smile, he offered, "My feelings are worn down to a nub, thanks all the same."

She made a wry mouth. "Aye—Acton well-knows how to blister

you to pieces, even though he's all polite and such. In fact, I think its miles worse because he's all polite and such."

Gabriel took a long breath. "I doubt he blisters you. In fact, I think I have been spared a worse fate, owing to the fact that you and I are friends." For the first time, he glanced at her. "Although I've been warned that I'm not to speak of your hunches, ever again."

"You're doin' it, now," she pointed out practically.

"Then don't tell him, I beg of you."

"I don't like to hide things from my husband, so it's far better that you mind yourself."

He nodded. "Fair enough."

Mentally girding her loins, she asked in an even tone, "Tell me what you were doin', workin' in disguise at Sunshine Bakery."

But his answer was unexpected, as he raised his brows at her, clearly surprised that she didn't already know. "Your illustrious husband wanted me to do a bit of snooping around, mainly to keep an eye on the equally illustrious Monsieur Savoie."

Doyle blinked. "Oh." So; apparently Acton had decided to enlist Gabriel for a bit of side-work, which meant that either Acton trusted the man, or he didn't trust him an inch and wanted to monitor what he'd do in the situation—the latter being miles more likely. Genuinely curious, she asked, "What did you find out?"

"Unfortunately, I am not at liberty to say."

Doyle decided not to dwell on the fact there was an arson fire at the self-same bakery, right around that time-frame, and instead re-focused on the task at hand, as difficult as it was. "Now tell me what Mallory Flynn was holdin' over your head." She paused, and then added, "I imagine it involved potions."

His gaze dropped to the table, and she prompted, "Some sort of birth-control potion, that you were slippin' to Munoz on the sly."

There was a small silence whilst her companion examined the tabletop. "I wanted to give her a bit more time, in the event she might want to change her mind."

Doyle let out an impatient breath. "*Shame* on you. Gabriel. A despicable thing to do, for the *love* o' Mike."

A bit bleakly, he replied, "I felt as though I belonged to her, and she to me. I still do."

"But you *don't*," she retorted. "It was only a fantasy, and it wasn't meant to be. You tried to insert yourself where you didn't belong, and the more you were thwarted, the more determined you became. You're not used to not havin' your own way, and in the end, it consumed you—the same as if you'd thrown yourself into a fire. The mortal sin of pride, taking the guise of unrequited love."

Thoroughly annoyed, he made a dismissive gesture. "Good God, Sergeant; can we skip the part where you preach at me?"

"No," she replied firmly. "It's one of the Acts of Mercy—I'm supposed to try to save you from yourself. St. Augustine said there's no saint without a past, and no sinner without a future."

Making a derisive sound, he scoffed, "I think I prefer your husband's blistering, if it's all the same to you."

Softening her tone, Doyle continued, "You're tryin' to force God's hand, and that never works out well, my friend."

"God has done me no favors."

She nodded, sympathetic. "Aye; we think, 'If God loves me, why isn't He helpin' me win my heart's desire?' And you don't realize that He's savin' you from yourself—He's the only one who has a clear view of everything-all-at-once. Sister Luke would tell the girls at school that they should thank God fastin' for unanswered prayers, just as much as for answered ones. And it was usually in the context that someone was longin' after some boy that Sister Luke did not approve of."

He took a long breath, and ran a hand over his face. "I wasn't trying to do any permanent harm; it was just a temporary gambit, I swear—she married him so quickly. And Corso told me it doesn't always work, in the first place."

But Doyle wasn't having it. "Shame on you, Gabriel. You caused our Munoz a full measure of misery."

"She caused *me* a full measure of misery," he returned a bit sharply.

There was a small silence, and then Doyle said softly, "Now, that's a bucketful of spite that I'm hearin', and yet you say you love her, Gabriel. Here's a news-flash; love—real love—isn't spiteful."

He contemplated the table-top as Doyle added, "And I'm not even goin' to ask what made a long-headed boyo like yourself start thinkin' that magic potions might have some merit—I'm that gobsmacked."

He was quick to respond, "The components weren't harmful—I made sure of it. And I figured it was worth the attempt." He added, rather bleakly, "I will be the first to admit that I was a bit desperate, and willing to take a flyer."

"So you say, Gabriel—but can you see how this kind o' thing is a slippery slope, once you start thinkin' mayhap there's some merit to it? Soon you'll convince yourself that you can see cause-and-effect where there is none, and the next thing you know you're as superstitious as my mum's neighbor, who practically fainted every time she saw a black cat, or a ring 'round the moon." Doyle frowned slightly. "It's akin to havin' false idols—which is the original sin of pride yet again, but in a different guise; you're tryin' to control things so as to suit yourself."

He glanced at her, sidelong. "You know, you might say it's somewhat prideful to lecture other people about their pride."

Doyle couldn't help but smile. "That's fair, I suppose. Where do I get off?"

"Exactly. It smacks of self-righteousness."

She raised her palms in concession. "It does indeed. Yet we're called to do it, so how's it possible to thread that needle? To scold the sinner, without comin' across as smug-and-superior?"

"You're asking the wrong person. I specialize in smug-and-superior."

Tentatively, she ventured, "Father John's pretty good at it—steerin' you aright, without raisin' your hackles."

He rolled his eyes at her. "You're not going to tell me to go speak to your priest again."

"It doesn't matter whether you're a believer or not," Doyle insisted. "It's just nice to have someone to help talk things out—someone who'll never tell a soul about your burdens, so that you can be completely honest."

He took another long breath, as he lifted his gaze out the window again. "My AA group was like that. Maybe I should go back."

She ventured, "D'you think you're fallin' off the wagon?"

Slowly, he replied, "I will admit the wagon's been a bit wobbly, in light of recent events."

"Aye—I think you're teeterin' on the edge. Be a role model for your little sister; she loves you so, and she deserves nothin' less."

He twisted his mouth. "Not to worry—redemption is at hand, believe me."

This was said in a self-mocking tone, and she wondered what he meant—no doubt Acton had arranged for something; mayhap a transfer to a different department?

It filled her with a sense of relief; trust Acton, to sort the worldly things out—that was miles easier than sorting-out the spiritual things—and so she decided she'd done enough admonishing and could retreat back into her turtle-shell with a clear conscience. "I'll leave you, then. I'm that sorry if I've sounded like a Dutch aunt."

"No—I appreciate it. Maybe someday it will make a dent." He examined his hands, spread out on the table. "Are you going to tell Munoz?"

Doyle rose. "I think that's up to you, my friend. At the risk of sendin' you off again, I'll mention that the Church requires repair, as part of a true repentance."

He lifted a corner of his mouth. "I'm the one who'd need repair; she'd tear me limb from limb."

"Mayhap, then, the appropriate repair would be to support her in her marriage, goin' forward. Either way, I'll not say a word."

He glanced up at her, and said with all sincerity, "I really do appreciate you, Sergeant. As I mentioned, I think you've spared me a worse fate."

She rested a fond hand on his shoulder. "It's God, my friend. I'm just the safety-ring He keeps tossin' your way."

She turned to walk out the door, and noted that he still hadn't moved.

CHAPTER 36

*D*oyle made her way down to the building's entry, where her husband was waiting for her by the door. As he held it open for her, he gave her a quick, assessing glance. "Everything all right?"

"I hope so. Thanks for clearin' out, Michael."

He glanced up and down the street. "Would you like to walk to get an ice cream?"

She mustered up a smile. "You make it sound like I'm Edward, and in need of a treat."

He put an arm around her shoulders, and gently steered her along the pavement. "You do seem a bit pulled-about."

Making a wry mouth, she fell into step beside him. "I don't fancy myself as an authority on anythin', that's why. I'm one who likes to hang back, but lately I've been scoldin' the sinners, left and right." She blew out a breath. "It's miles easier to mind my own business."

"How did you find out?"

She shrugged, slightly. "You're whistlin' in the wind, my friend, if you think I can explain it. I just realize things, sometimes."

With all sympathy, he squeezed her to him. "Right. Although sometimes I worry that you carry a heavy burden, Kathleen."

"Sometimes," she agreed. "But I've no choice, and so I make the best of things." She glanced up at him with a smile. "Which is not somethin' you could even fathom, I think. You're a lot like the Trestles ghost-knight; you're determined to arrange things to suit yourself, and cursed be anyone who dares try to thwart you." She paused, thinking about this. "You know, I think the knight's wife is a bit steely too, in her own way."

He made no comment—being as he was never very comfortable talking about her ghosts—and they walked for a small distance in companionable silence until he offered, "I would ask that you say nothing of these matters."

She readily agreed. "No fears on that front, my friend—it's all rather horrifyin', to find out that the people you think are level are so easily led atilt."

"Very surprising," he agreed.

She decided not to mention that he'd have given her his own potion, quick-as-a-cat, and instead said, "I was a bit worried when I came over, because I was reminded of the time I went over to Caroline's flat."

He squeezed her again. "I have learned my lesson, certainly."

"Aye, I gave you the mother of all scoldings, husband. I'm glad to see that it took root—although sometimes I think it only means that you try to hide your doings under more layers of guile."

"You malign me," he protested. "As you saw, the situation wasn't at all what you'd feared."

"Aye—I do appreciate your tolerance with Gabriel. He's still tryin' to sort himself out."

"A very interesting man."

She decided not to mention that Gabriel had confessed that the "Rory Flynn" caper was Acton's plan, and instead rejoice in what victories she could. Whatever her husband had been up to, it did seem that he was showing some mercy for a change—an unlooked-for turn of events which was much appreciated.

Thus reminded, she asked, "And speakin' of layers of guile, have you managed to glean any useful information from Corso? Does she know how Flynn was killed?"

"She claims she was meeting Flynn to take delivery of the latest batch of potions, and was genuinely surprised to find her dead. She claims to have no other knowledge or information." He paused, and then added, "I am not certain that she is being truthful."

Doyle eyed him and prompted, "Because?"

"Because there were no potions found at the scene."

Much struck, Doyle could only agree. "Aye—there's a good point. The Santero's potions were in bottles, so where did the bottles go? And it's hard to believe that someone would steal the potions after she was dead, but not steal her wallet."

"I would agree."

Shaking her head in wonder, Doyle said, "Faith, nothin' makes a thimbleful of sense. But if you think Corso's lyin', shouldn't we interview her, with me listenin' in?"

It seemed clear he'd already considered this option, and he replied, "Perhaps. Although I'd have to consider how to set up such a situation."

Doyle could see his dilemma. "If she thinks she's in the clear, she might relax her guard and we don't want to spook her with an interrogation."

"Exactly. I think the better plan would be to monitor her communications for the time being. She may make contact with someone, or otherwise give us a lead."

Glancing up at him, she asked, "Should we also keep an eye on the PC who was on-scene? He had motive and opportunity."

"No opportunity, actually. He was on-duty from midnight, and his field-car never hit those coordinates until after the grocer's call."

She nodded—trust Acton to do his homework. "How about the man's wife? She's someone who might want to do a bit of reproachin'. She may have not done the deed herself, but she could have arranged for the murder, and made sure the lanyard was on display so that her wayward husband got the message, loud and clear."

"A good thought, but I can find no evidence that his wife was involved, nor that she even knew of the affair."

She nodded, unsurprised. "Aye—it was just a stray thought. If that were the case, you'd think we'd have a cause-of-death. No point in an admonishment-murder unless it's clear who's bein' admonished, and who's doin' the murderin."

"I will admit I looked hard for a lead, but could not find one."

They were nearing the ice cream store, and it seemed he was tired of discussing this case-that-wasn't-a-case, because he remarked, "That is a very pretty dress; I don't think I've made mention."

She smiled, because on those rare occasions when she wore a dress, her husband's mind tended to lusty thoughts. "Instead of ice cream, shall we brave our favorite hotel? Or are we too embarrassed to show our faces there, ever again?

With a smile, he turned her 'round by the shoulders so that they headed back in the direction that they'd come. "You must never allow anyone to see that you are discomfited, Kathleen."

Taking a guess at what this meant, she teased, "Well, you're miles better at that than I am; I've got a blush you can't hide under a bushel."

"It travels all the way to your toes," he noted in a suggestive tone, and she giggled.

CHAPTER 37

he following day was the day of the Savoie dinner-party, and Doyle was coming back up the stairs after helping Miss Cherry secure the boys in the master bedroom, where they looked forward to an afternoon of watching cartoons whilst the preparations were underway.

Doyle was in an uncertain mood, and was trying to decide why this was—apart from the obvious annoyance that she was hosting a fancy dinner-party, for the love o' Mike. And although Acton said she shouldn't let anyone see that she was miscomforted—or whatever the word was—nevertheless she felt unsettled, and a bit on-end.

Her state of uneasiness was no doubt directly connected to the fact that her wily husband was up to something—she'd bet her teeth—because the last thing he'd want to do is host a dinner-party that featured the motley assortment of people who were coming over. Not to mention that Officer Shandera and Officer Gabriel were going to handle security instead of Trenton—although this might be because Trenton couldn't be trusted not to engage in a bout of fisticuffs with the bridegroom, and so it was probably a good thing.

She sank down at the kitchen table, watching with all admiration as the Trestles servants carefully set-up the formal dining table, the crystal sparkling and the silver gleaming. "D'you need me to do anythin'?" she asked Reynolds, who was busy as a bee in the kitchen. "Should I wipe your brow, or somethin'?"

"All is in hand, madam," Reynolds assured her, which was understandable since he was born for such things.

And I'm born for blundering about, Doyle thought, a bit crossly. The poor ghosts who are thrown my way must be sick to the back teeth of having to prod me along, like a tinker's donkey.

She paused, because this cranky and wayward thought seemed out-of-place. Faith, she always managed to figure out what the ghosts were seeking—despite her blundering ways—and in this instance, she'd done it yet again by admonishing the sinners, just as the lady had asked. Although it was interesting that the ghost had included Gabriel in the admonishing, since he didn't have any sort of family connection to her—not like Lizzie did.

Strange, that the medieval ghost hadn't shown up to pat her on the back, which was the usual course of things when Doyle managed to complete whatever ghostly task she'd been given. No doubt stupid Cassie Masterson was bad-mouthing Doyle to the lady—she wouldn't put it past the nasty brasser, and there was yet another person who'd been willing to destroy the happiness of others in an attempt to gain her own. But now—now she was suffering her comeuppance, and wearing her misery as heavily as her chains.

Thinking on this, Doyle remarked to Reynolds, "Remember that ghost, in that famous Christmas story? He was draggin' about chains."

"Jacob Marley," Reynolds supplied, because Reynolds was an expert at sorting-out whatever jumbled reference Doyle was trying to make.

"Aye," she said thoughtfully. "Why was he wearin' the chains, again?"

"They represented his past sins, madam."

"Exactly," she pronounced with a great deal of satisfaction. "Those chains are her just desserts."

"Marley was a man, madam."

"Of course," she agreed. "My mistake."

But Reynold had paused in his duties to add, "I believe the author wanted us to feel sorry for Marley, madam, as his was a cautionary tale. Indeed, it was why he was sent to admonish Scrooge."

Doyle eyed him in surprise. "Marley admonished Scrooge? But you couldn't choose between them, Reynolds—they were both miserable sinners."

"Yes, madam. I believe that was the point."

The servant returned to his chores, leaving Doyle to sit in uneasy silence—made all the more uneasy by the realization that she'd been behaving badly. Faith, when you thought about it, she'd been just as prideful as all the other players in this strange and sordid morality tale. Small wonder, that the medieval ghost was cross with her.

Abruptly, Doyle rose to her feet. "I'm goin' to have a little lie-down in the guest bedroom, Reynolds—best get rested-up before the big ordeal."

"Certainly, madam," the butler replied, hiding his relief that the Lady of the House would no longer be underfoot.

And so with no further ado, Doyle retreated into the quiet bedroom downstairs, drew the curtains, and fell asleep mere moments after sinking into the bed.

And—just as she'd anticipated—almost immediately she was confronted by the two ghosts; the medieval ghost gazing into the distance, still and silent, whilst Cassie Masterson looked harassed and impatient.

Gird your loins, lass, Doyle told herself, as she gazed upon her hated rival; it's a fine lesson in humility you're to be having.

"I think we're finished with all this," Masterson snapped, very much annoyed. "You've finally done what you were supposed to, and you're not needed anymore."

"I think I am," Doyle replied. "I have to beg your pardon, and tell you that I'm sorry that I've felt—I've felt triumphant, I guess you'd say, to see that you've landed yourself into a well o' trouble. I shouldn't feel that way—instead, I should be truly sorry that you've wound-up as you have."

Scowling incredulously, Masterson retorted, "Spare me your pity."

"No—I can't spare you, because I'm in the same boat. I'm called to forgive you, but my pride is keepin' me back—the same as yours is keepin' you back. There was an English saint—St. Thomas Moore—and when he was sent off to be executed he forgave everyone, and said they'd all meet-up and laugh about it in heaven. That's how we should be, you and me. We should forgive each other, and try not to hold on to our resentment."

"Just where do you get off, lecturing me?" the ghost returned in an incredulous tone. "You're nobody from nowhere, and you never deserved being Lady Acton in the first place."

Gently, Doyle offered, "It's a mighty long journey through eternity, Cassie. Just think on it, please."

With an angry flounce, Masterson turned her shoulder on Doyle and promptly disappeared.

Into the silence that followed, the medieval ghost lowered her gaze so that—for the first time—she looked directly at Doyle. She then gravely dipped a respectful curtsey, the stiff brocade rustling as she did so. "*Madame d'Acton.*"

"Same to you," Doyle replied with a smile. "Thank you, for remindin' me what's-what."

The ghost then gracefully rose and turned to leave, her manner dignified and contained. The lady's husband had come into the fair Doyle's dreams—all menace and sharp elbows—to goad her into preserving his legacy, but his wife was fighting to preserve her own legacy, too—a legacy of forgiveness, and of peace. No easy thing, in a world that had featured an unfaithful husband, the constant threat of enemy attack, and the frustration of never having a say in the important decisions that would bear upon one's life.

I wish I'd half her steel, Doyle thought humbly, as she watched the ghost fade away.

CHAPTER 38

$\mathcal{T}$he dinner party was underway, and Doyle could feel herself relaxing somewhat because—after all—everything seemed to be going smoothly, and they were amongst friends. Or the next thing to friends, anyway—Lestrade was certainly a sketchy character, but he seemed to be behaving himself as he talked with Melinda's solicitor and Savoie.

Mary's brother and sister-in-law were admiring the view out the windows—they were a bit intimidated of course, and small blame to them; Doyle had been so intimidated that Acton had to coax his wedded wife into moving in with him.

And Doyle's tranquil mood was much-enhanced by the fact that the *hors d'oeuvres* featured a tray of miniature pasties, very similar to those that were sold from the carts on the Dublin docks. She caught Reynolds' eye across the room and flashed a smile of gratitude as she took a healthy bite. They weren't quite as lardy as the originals, of course, but it was a sweet gesture, nonetheless.

As one tends to do after such an event, Doyle and Mary were fondly going over every detail of the wedding and agreeing that everything went perfectly.

"We're all moved in together," Mary reported. "Philippe wants to look at finding a larger house on the outskirts, but we're in no hurry."

"One life-changer at a time," Doyle agreed, even though she wasn't exactly the poster-child for this advice.

Mary assured her, "The children will still attend St. Margaret's of course, so we will get together just as often."

"No worries, Mary. You're to do what's best for your family."

Mary brightened as she looked over toward the entry door. "Oh—here's Callie, with her new beau."

Doyle glanced over, and then was unable to smother a gasp of abject dismay. Standing in the doorway was Callie—dressed very smartly—and standing beside her was none other than Igor Denisovich's nephew—who was actually the man's son—and as smarmy a boyo who'd ever put an arm through a coat.

"Let's go over and meet him," Mary suggested. "She looks a bit nervous."

With a feeling of acute dread, Doyle trailed Mary over to the entry area, all the while wondering if Acton was aware of this disastrous turn of events. When they'd interviewed the young man some months ago, he'd been very off-putting—sly, and full of himself. Not to mention he'd also made the fatal error of thinking that he could make a May-game out of Acton and his questions—much to the dismay of his mafia-father, who knew better.

And now—now, it seemed that the young man had outfoxed Acton—it couldn't be a coincidence, that he was here with Callie and smirking to beat the band. Callie had said he was the real estate representative who'd shown her new flat, and it was hard to believe this was all happenstance, instead of a nasty attempt to poke Acton in the eye.

But surely, Acton must have been aware? *Surely*, he'd been keeping track of Callie's new beau, the same way he kept track of everything? But Doyle duly noted that her husband didn't seem miscomfited—or whatever the word was—as he politely shook the young man's hand. "Rolph; how good it is to see you again."

Oh-oh, thought Doyle in acute alarm; Katy-bar-the-door.

"A small world," the young man agreed, with the smug air of the victor.

"Champagne?" Officer Shandera was serving drinks, and offered-up flutes to the new arrivals.

"Thanks—don't mind if I do," Rolph said, and took a healthy swig.

Doyle reluctantly remembered that she was supposed to be the hostess of this unfolding minefield, and so she offered, "Mary and I were just speakin' about how well the weddin' went."

"Congratulations, Mary," Callie offered with as much sincerity as the girl could muster, and she moved to give Mary a hug. "I'm very happy for you."

"Why weren't you invited?" asked Rolph.

But any awkward explanations were cut off by Savoie's approach to greet the newcomers. "Congratulations, Philippe," Callie said with a determined smile, and offered her hand.

Savoie bowed over it briefly, and then nodded to Rolph in his abrupt way. "Monsieur."

With an exaggerated air of familiarity, Rolph replied in a negligent tone, "Yes; so good to see you again."

With some surprise, Callie looked from one man to the other. "Oh—do you two know each other?"

Savoie offered, "Monsieur, he worked for me at my bakery."

"More like you worked for my uncle," Rolph corrected a bit pointedly.

Doyle braced for impact, but Savoie only smiled his thin smile, and bowed his head in acknowledgement. "D'accord."

Oh-oh, thought Doyle; Katy-bar-the-door, yet again.

It was something of a relief all around when Savoie ushered Mary over to join his brother and the solicitor, and when Acton moved to join that group, Doyle thought it best that she linger with Callie and Rolph; the girl had managed to greet Savoie with good grace, but it was probably best that she be separated from the happy couple as much as possible.

Pinning on a polite smile, Doyle asked Rolph, "D'you miss workin' at the bakery? I would have eaten-up all the profits."

The young man grimaced slightly. "It wasn't my cup of tea, frankly. The mornings were far too early."

"Your current schedule suits you better," Callie agreed with a smile. "Even though there are no free pastries."

"Definitely," Rolph agreed as he took another sip of champagne. "No need to roll out of bed before noon."

Doyle nodded in Mary's direction, and offered, "Mary will be managin' the bakery, when it re-opens."

Rolph raised his brows in amused surprise, and glanced over at the group by the windows. "She will? She doesn't look as though she could manage her way out of a paper bag."

"Rolph, you mustn't be rude," Callie protested, embarrassed.

"Blame it on the champagne—it is excellent," he replied, and then made an expansive gesture toward Doyle with his glass. "Sorry; sometimes I just speak my mind."

"I can relate; 'tis my own failin'," Doyle joked, trying to cheer him along for Callie's sake.

He laughed a little too loud. "I have to say it's amazing that you still have that accent. You'd have thought someone like him would have arranged for elucidation lessons or something."

"*Rolph*," Callie implored, mortified.

Steady, Doyle thought; he's trying to needle you into a reaction, and you mustn't give him the satisfaction—it's that "miscomfort" thing that Acton was talking about. Although I will say that it's interesting my husband has left me to fend for myself—he's not one to tolerate the wife of his bosom being insulted, left and right.

With a mighty effort, she managed to give a light reply. "My poor husband knows this accent is a hopeless case, my friend. As well be askin' the Cliffs of Moher t'melt into tha sea."

"I love your accent," Callie offered stoutly.

"If you say so," Rolph offered in an equivocal tone, and took another drink of his champagne, glancing about as though looking for someone more interesting to talk to.

In a bright tone—and making an effort to control her accent—Doyle offered, "I understand you met our Callie when you showed her flat; you must be an excellent salesman, and in more ways than one."

As could be expected, Rolph promptly returned his focus to Doyle so as to take this opportunity to preen. "Yes; my uncle owns the building, and I keep an eye on the comings and goings."

Just as Doyle was struggling to come up with another flattering topic, Gabriel interrupted to lean in, brandishing a bottle of champagne. "Allow me to top-off your glass, sir."

But as he poured into Rolph's flute, the young man scowled in disbelief. "What—what are *you* doing here?"

Gabriel straightened up. "I beg your pardon?"

"You're—you're Rory Flynn, from Sunshine Bakery."

CHAPTER 39

*G*abriel raised his dark brows. "You may be mistaken." Deftly, he shifted the bottle to offer his hand. "Vadik Gabriel, at your service."

But Rolph ignored his hand, and backed off a step. "No—no, I'm not mistaken." His eyes narrowed suspiciously. "Are you hiding out, or something?"

"Or something," Gabriel confirmed.

With an unpleasant scowl, Rolph lowered his voice. "What's your game? You'd better tell me—you wouldn't want me to blow the whistle."

"I am hoping to be introduced to your charming companion." Smoothly, Gabriel took Callie's hand in his own, and bowed over it. "A pleasure. Are you from the bride's side?"

Rolph couldn't resist replying with a touch of triumph, "No; she's Acton's half-sister."

Gabriel raised his brows with interest. "Is she? I wish I was."

With a smile, Callie confessed, "It's a bit of an adjustment."

"We'll switch, then. I don't fit in either, and maybe we'll both have better luck."

Rolph was clearly unhappy with this light exchange, and

warned in an ugly tone, "I don't know what your game is, Rory, but back off."

"You can switch with me instead, Gabriel," Doyle offered, desperately trying to lighten the atmosphere. "I'm the least-best fit of all of us."

"I think your husband would notice," Gabriel replied with regret. "Although I do think I could pull it off for a day or two."

Callie laughed, and Rolph promptly drew her away from them, his annoyance palpable.

"Well, he's a crackin' treat," Doyle observed in a sour tone. Catching herself, she immediately added, "Forget I said that."

"Not at all; remember that you're outspoken, and it is your failing."

"You mustn't eavesdrop," Doyle scolded. "Not to mention that it's a case of the pot and the kettle—you're the pattern-card for 'outspoken'."

"Ah, but I don't necessarily think it is a failing."

Doyle decided she was tired of being a polite hostess, and asked suspiciously, "What are you about?"

"Isn't it obvious? I am on my redemption tour," the young man replied, and wandered off to pour more champagne.

Doyle reviewed the room, and saw that Acton continued deep in conversation with the Savoie group, but that Callie and Rolph were standing apart, with Callie looking a bit stricken as she earnestly spoke to her beau in low tones. Since the young man was scowling unpleasantly, Doyle decided she'd best go smooth him over, for Callie's sake.

With a determined air, she moved to rejoin them. "I'm so glad you're here, Rolph; I think the newlyweds are tryin' to find a place on the outskirts of town—d'you have any advice? Everythin' seems so expensive, nowadays."

Rolph twisted his mouth in amusement. "That's hilarious, coming from you; my uncle says Acton's richer than anybody." With a smile, he drew Callie to his side, and bent to say to her, "You should ask him for a slice."

"I don't think he gives-out slices," said Callie, who was thoroughly embarrassed but trying to joke-away this unfortunate fact.

"Of course, he doesn't," Rolph conceded with a smirk. "You don't get to where he is by giving it away. They say he's tighter than a drum."

"Acton's very generous," Doyle defended, unable to completely control her temper. "St. Michael's and St. Brigid's would be the first to tell you so."

"What's that?" The young man asked, his interest keen.

Faith, lass; snabble it, Doyle reminded herself. The less said to this fellow, the better; don't let him goad you. "Oh—they're a couple of churches that we support," she explained vaguely.

The young man lifted his chin in a patronizing way and chuckled. "Another thing that's surprising—that someone like him would indulge you in stuff like that. You must be amazing in bed."

"*Rolph*," Callie beseeched, mortified.

Whilst Doyle tried to come up with a reply to this sally, they were thankfully interrupted by the solicitor, who leaned in to hand Callie her card. "We should meet-up and discuss your interview. Give me a call this week."

"Yes, ma'am," said Callie unhappily.

The solicitor then inquired after Rolph's uncle, who she knew through Sir Vikili, and whilst they were engaged in conversation, Doyle asked Callie in a low tone, "What's this?"

Callie replied, "Lady Madeline's investigators are coming in to speak to the staff at the Dower House next week, and they want to interview me, too."

Doyle blinked in surprise. "And Acton is aware of this?"

"Yes; he said we should be as honest and forthcoming as possible."

Now I *know* something's up, thought Doyle as she hid her alarm. That doesn't sound like my wedded husband *a'tall*. To encourage Callie, she offered, "Well, if Melinda's solicitor's protectin' you, you've nothin' to worry about; she's a fierce one."

"Yes," the girl readily agreed, and then lowered her voice, "She's a little scary."

"Terrifyin'," Doyle concurred. "I'd surrender to the coppers without even knowin' what I've done wrong."

Callie smiled, as Doyle had intended, and then they were startled when Rolph laughed a little too loudly at something the solicitor had said to him; rocking back on his heels and closing his eyes as he chortled. Callie glanced his way, worried, and Doyle wondered if mayhap he was a bit bosky; leave it to the young man to drink too much when he should be trying to mind himself, and make a good impression for Callie's sake.

With no small dismay, she was contemplating a potential future where Rolph might be a permanent fixture when Tim McGonigal came up to them—newly arrived—and Doyle greeted him warmly, happy to take her mind from such bleak thoughts.

"Dr. McGonigal," Callie said. "I keep meaning to come by for a visit."

Doyle remembered that Callie had harbored a girlhood crush on the good doctor, and wondered—with some desperation—if mayhap she could be dissuaded from her current course. "Faith, you two should get together for lunch, or somethin'," she offered in hearty encouragement. "Catch up on old times."

But before McGonigal could reply, Doyle found that her husband suddenly appeared at her elbow—better late than never, wretched man. "Tim," he said, and shook his old friend's hand. "So good to see you."

Whilst the two men were exchanging small-talk, Reynolds took the opportunity to sidle-up to Doyle, as distressed as he ever allowed himself to be. "Madam," he said, "If you have a moment—"

"What's afoot?" she asked, rather hopefully. "I don't think it's too late to cancel."

"I'm afraid Dr. McGonigal has not brought a guest, madam. We cannot sit thirteen at dinner."

Doyle blinked. "We can't?"

Acton turned to them, alerted by her tone. "What's this?"

Reynolds seemed reluctant to say, and so Doyle covered for him. "I'm worried that we can't have thirteen at dinner, Michael." Half-joking, she suggested, "So; either I take a tray downstairs with the boys, or we heave Rolph out the door."

Her husband contemplated this dilemma for a moment, and then—to Doyle's surprise—suggested to Reynolds, "Perhaps you could explain the situation to Miss Cherry, and ask if she would mind partnering McGonigal."

Whilst Doyle gave her husband a sharp look, Reynolds bowed his head in abject relief. "Very good, sir; I will send one of the servants to mind Master Edward and Master Tommy."

"No need," Shandera volunteered in a cheerful tone, as he walked by. "I'll go put them to bed—I've boys of my own."

Faith, Doyle thought, as she watched Shandera disappear down the stairway; it turns out that I'm merely a player in a play. A shame, it is, that no one bothered to give me my lines.

CHAPTER 40

hey sat down to dinner, Doyle doing her best to match Acton's unruffled air and entertaining the certain conviction that there was an operation underway that was just as war-gamed as any take-down operation at the Met.

She cast a reassuring smile at Mary's brother and his wife—who were equal to herself in being fish-out-of-water at an Earl's dinner-party—and noted rather regretfully that Reynolds had put Callie and Rolph directly across from the new-wedded couple, which may have been the correct protocol for the mysterious ways of dinner-party guest-rankings, but which was not necessarily conducive to dinner-party harmony.

And to make matters worse, it did seem that Rolph was a bit bosky, laughing too loudly at his own witticisms, and openly flirting with one of the servants from Trestles, who was doing her best to ignore him.

Undaunted, the young man turned his attention to Mary, seated across the table from him. "I hear you're to manage the—the bakery," he offered, leaning forward with his elbows on the table and smiling as though he was complimenting a precocious child. "Good for you; just don't expect the books to be in any kind of order." Pressing his lips together, he chuckled as though holding back a delightful secret.

"Thank you, I will do my best," said Mary sincerely, since she wasn't well-versed in recognizing barbed criticism when it was thrown her way.

Since Mary's new husband was very well-versed, Doyle hurriedly intervened to offer in a light tone, "Mary's expertise is in the bakin', Rolph—the books won't be her concern, I imagine."

"If you say so," Rolph offered indulgently. "Although you can't be much of a manager unless you keep the books, you know; a business is run on numbers."

Savoie smiled in amusement. "Your uncle, he knows the numbers. He used to run the numbers for Solonik."

"Well, isn't that nice?" Doyle intervened, a bit desperately.

But Rolph ignored her, as he angrily drew down his brows and stared at Savoie. "You—you don't know what you are *talking* about. Solonik was my uncle's *errand-boy*."

In response, Savoie made a patronizing, deferential gesture; his eyes gleaming.

Angrily, Rolph jumped to his feet, and then swayed a bit off-balance from the sudden movement. "Don't you give me that—that look; I will climb up on this table and—and piss on your *head*."

"I wouldn't advise it," Gabriel cautioned, as he hovered with a water pitcher.

Aghast, Callie pleaded, "*Please*, Rolph."

Doyle saw Acton signal to Reynolds, and the servant promptly came forward. "Perhaps you might like to lie down, sir," Reynolds suggested to the young man, in a discreet tone. "I will fetch coffee."

"No—no," Rolph protested loudly, as he jerked his arm from Reynolds' clasp. "I'm just telling this—this froggy—" He paused to blink, as though he'd lost his train of thought, and McGonigal rose to rather firmly take the young man by his arm. "Come along, now."

Thoroughly alarmed by his unfolding disaster, Doyle glanced over at Gabriel—who was supposed to be security, after all—but he appeared to have forgot his duties, as he stood and watched the others handle Rolph.

Between them, Reynolds and McGonigal took the recalcitrant guest in a firm grip, and steered him off toward the stairway. "Don't you *touch* me—" Rolph protested feebly. "Bugger—bugger off."

Into the silence, Callie rather reluctantly rose to her feet. "I should go with him."

"You should stay," Acton replied in a firm tone.

Seeing that Callie was inclined to bristle at this implied order, Doyle protested, "Let her go, Michael; we can't have thirteen at dinner, else Reynolds will leap out the window."

But to Doyle's surprise, Gabriel offered a solution, as he set down his water pitcher. "I'm with Reynolds—we can't tempt fate." He then said to Callie. "What say you and I go out and get a pint, instead?"

It seemed clear that Callie was equal parts surprised and tempted by this unexpected offer, as she glanced over toward the stairs. "Oh—I don't know; I think I should probably stay with Rolph."

For once, Gabriel's tone was dead serious. "He doesn't deserve another thought, embarrassing you like this in front of your family."

Callie held Gabriel's gaze for a long moment. "All right."

And—just like that—Gabriel was back to his joking self, as he took her elbow to steer her toward the door. "Are you old enough? I don't want to get cited for a 'contributing to the delinquency'."

Callie made a wry mouth. "Yes, I'm old enough."

"Let's get your coat then, since Reynolds is otherwise occupied."

Over her shoulder, Callie said to Doyle. "I'm so sorry, Kathleen."

"No worries. We'll handle Rolph."

And then, as the door closed behind them, Acton addressed one of the servants as though nothing untoward had gone forward. "If you would resume service, please."

Lizzie made to rise. "I'll help, until Reynolds returns."

"No, you won't," said Doyle firmly, as she rose herself. "I will, as long as everyone knows I'll do it from the wrong side, and such."

"I'll help, too," Mary offered.

"No—you're the bride, Mary. Everyone's just goin' to have to deal."

"I will carry the soup tureen for you," Acton offered, promptly coming to his wife's aid.

And—strange as it seemed—the atmosphere seemed to lighten considerably as Lord and Lady Acton went around the table, serving-up the soup course.

After this was accomplished, Doyle took-up Gabriel's abandoned water pitcher to replenish the goblets, with Mary laughing because the ice from the pitcher dislodged all in a clump —as it was wont to do—and made a watery mess on the damask tablecloth.

"If you pour from the side of the pitcher, Lady Acton—" Lizzie suggested.

"Faith, it's not as though I've never poured water," Doyle protested, and deftly lifted one of Savoie's spoons to hold the remaining ice in place, as she continued around the table.

"What is the next course?" Acton asked, as he returned the soup tureen to the side-table.

Understandably a bit flustered, the Trestles servant replied, "The fish course, sir."

"You must be mistaken; my wife cannot abide fish."

"Whist, Michael," Doyle called out. "The fish are welcome, just not on my plate."

"Nothing like a good fried cod," Mary's brother pronounced hopefully.

"I am afraid it is poached salmon," Acton advised, as he lifted the silver lid from the serving tray. He then asked Reynolds, who was returning up the stairway, "Have we any fried cod, Reynolds?"

"I regret to say that we do not, sir," said Reynolds, who hadn't turned a hair upon viewing this bizarre scene. "My deepest apologies."

"No worries," said the brother with forgiving smile. "I'll give this a try."

Doyle had come 'round to the end of the table, where Lestrade was leaning back with one hand resting rather casually on Lizzie's chair-back, next to him. He leaned forward to place a hand on her belly. "This *bébé*, when does it come?"

"My due date is in two weeks," Lizzie replied politely.

Doyle saw Williams' brows draw down, bristling at the other man's familiarity, and so she offered in a light tone, "A little boy— so excitin', and he has a big brother at home."

The Frenchman made a sound of regret, as he moved his hand slightly on Lizzie's belly. "As for me, I always thought it would be my brother, who would give you *les bébés*."

"*What?*" demanded Williams, utterly shocked.

Lestrade chuckled, as his gaze slid to Lizzie. "Ah. He does not know, your husband."

"Doesn't know *what?*" Williams demanded of Lizzie. "What's he *talking* about?"

Lizzie, who'd turned a bit pink, said quietly, "Nothing, Thomas."

Withdrawing his hand, Lestrade apologized to her, his thin smile remarkably similar to Savoie's. "I should not have said. Forgive me, *ma petite*."

"*What's he talking about?*" Williams repeated, in angry disbelief.

"It was nothing," Lizzie replied. "Mr. Savoie was shot at Wexton Prison, and I tended to him."

Amused, Lestrade raised his brows in a manner that insinuated there was much more to this story.

Seeing that William's own brow suddenly looked like a

thundercloud, Doyle desperately interjected, "Our Lizzie was very brave. Truly."

But Lizzie's husband was not going to be distracted, and he angrily demanded of his wife, "Was there something between you and *Savoie*?"

"Thomas," Lizzie replied in a firm tone. "Stop."

But Williams was like a dog with a bone, and turned to demand of Lestrade, "What do *you* know about this?"

"I do not say," the other man replied with a shrug. "You must ask my brother."

"Thomas," Doyle begged. "No more brawlin'—I'm havin' flashbacks to the docks."

In his insinuating way, Lestrade said to Lizzie, "I am sorry to have blundered, *ma petite*. I did not know it was a secret."

Williams leapt to his feet, his hands curled into fists as he bit out furiously, "You will *stop* calling my wife that."

With an effort, Lizzie struggled to her feet. "Get my coat, Thomas; if you can't behave yourself, we should go." She suddenly paused, and then abruptly sat down again, her face pale.

"Are you all right? Doyle asked, setting down the pitcher.

"I think my water broke."

Mother a' Mercy, thought Doyle; it's all a massive disaster, back and edge. "Go fetch Dr. McGonigal," she advised Lestrade. "And then stay with Rolph—you've stirred up enough trouble."

"*Oui, madame*," the Frenchman replied in amusement, and then moved toward the stairs.

"Should you lie down, Liz?" Williams asked, worried.

"I think we should go to hospital," Lizzie replied in her level voice. "Once the water breaks, there's no going back."

Acton offered, "I will call for the driving service to come around to the front."

Lizzie, ever practical, asked Doyle for her phone. "Let me call the agency about Connor—they'll have to send someone to relieve the babysitter."

"You'll do no such thing," Mary insisted immediately. "We'll take Connor—it will be no problem at all."

But Doyle read Williams' expression aright, and quickly insisted, "Let us fetch Connor, Mary. You're a newlywed, and we've got staff coming out our ears."

"Thanks," said Williams, who then solicitously took his wife's hand. "Are you all right, Lizzie?"

With a small smile, she readily replied, "I've never been better."

CHAPTER 41

*L*ater that same night, Doyle found herself propped-up on a nest of pillows in a luxurious bed at The Grenoble Hotel, sitting beside her husband and watching the fire in the fancy fireplace. Acton had determined that the best way to conclude the evening was to show up unannounced and demand the best suite at the hotel—which of course they scurried to give to him.

"You are a strange and wonderful man," Doyle remarked.

He made no reply, as he continued to finger her hand, resting in his lap. He was a little tired, after such a tumultuous turn of events, and not inclined to speak much.

"Throwin' Gabriel like a fishin' lure in front of our Callie, and movin' people about like so many chess pieces. I suppose you can take the nob out of the Middle Ages, but you can't take the Middle Ages out of the nob."

"We shall see," he replied.

Indeed, we will, she thought—and my hat's off to him, because it was masterfully done; if we'd offered any private strictures on Rolph's unsuitability, no doubt we'd have been met with stubborn rebellion by Callie. Far better to simply expose the young man's faults for the girl to plainly see, and have a worthy alternative immediately at hand.

Not to mention the secondary plot, to remind Williams that his wife was a rare prize who must be jealously guarded. Truly, the whole thing had been better than a raree-show at the Dublin docks —the quality of the pasties notwithstanding.

She decided she may as well say, "I know it all went accordin' to plan, husband, but you truly shouldn't try to manipulate people the same way you manipulate evidence. People are mighty unpredictable."

"I would disagree," he replied, as he continued to finger her hand. "People are of all things predictable."

She made a wry mouth. "Now, there's a fair point; I suppose I meant to say that love is unpredictable."

"Yes," he agreed, and lifted her hand to kiss its back.

With a small smile, she added, "Rolph said I must be amazin' in bed, to cajole you into humorin' me."

His hand stilled. "Good *God*."

She giggled. "I'm that glad you weren't present, my friend."

"I suppose I cannot be offended; he makes a valid point."

Laughing, she turned to kiss him in appreciation, and then nestle into his chest. "Promise me he'll be out of our hair, soon."

"I do so promise," he replied, his hand idly stroking her back.

Belatedly, she was reminded that perhaps she shouldn't express such a wish for fear she'd be taken literally, and so she cautioned, "Not that I'd want him to meet with an unexplained accident, or anythin'."

"No. I will confess that I feel a bit sorry for Denisovich."

"Aye. Imagine if that was our Edward—you love him, even as you wring your hands in despair."

"He's young."

Doyle made a face. "Not an excuse; he's a crackin' knocker—has no idea when he should button his lip, and mind himself." She glanced up at him. "D'you think that whole romance was a plot by Denisovich, tryin' to roil-up some trouble for you?"

"No," he replied, and it was the truth. "I think Rolph saw an opportunity, and took it. Denisovich knows better."

She eyed him. "What do you have on our Mr. Denisovich?"

"It is rather a long story."

Laying her head on his chest so as to watch the fire, she sighed. "Keep your secrets, then. No one can hold a candle to you, in the secrets-keepin'."

He made a small sound of regret, as his hand continued to stroke her back. "Not this time; I am sorry to have caused you so much distress."

"Whist; I truly can't blame you for tryin' to keep a lid on this mess, Michael—it was a shameful episode, all around." She lifted her face and told him sincerely, "And well-done, for takin' up your sword and buckler, and comin' to their rescue—it couldn't have been easy for you to go meet wretched Corso for tea, and have to make nice."

"A small sacrifice, all things considered."

She laid her head back down and smiled. "Not to mention havin' Lestrade throw Savoie in Williams' face—the man's like a bull with a red flag, on that subject."

"A very predictable reaction," he agreed.

"And a lesson well-learned—for Williams and for Lizzie, too."

"We can hope."

Idly, she pulled at the hair on his chest. "Will Williams ever find out about her foolishness?"

"No."

"I suppose that's for the best," she agreed. "It's so hard to believe, that someone like our Lizzie would go off the rails like she did. Although I suppose I shouldn't sit in judgment; I'd be sunk in misery if you didn't love me madly."

"I, too."

She rewarded this pronouncement with another lingering kiss, and then settled-in to gaze at the fire again. "It just goes to show that superstition is a powerful thing, Michael; it's so very temptin', to think that we might be able to control things so as to suit ourselves."

He didn't reply—no doubt because sorting-out things so as to suit himself was his usual mode of operation—and so she insisted, "'Tis a failin', Michael, and 'tis a lesson I've had to learn, myself. We can't think we're so righteous that we always know best. It's the same with admonishin' the sinners; we're supposed to wade-in and sort-out the sinners, but we can't do it unless we acknowledge that we're all pullin' in the same boat. Everyone has to pull together, and hold each other up."

She thought about this for a moment, watching the crackling fire. "There's where the true magic is—the holdin' each other up. It makes you lift your head from your tunnel-vision, and instead take a long, grateful look at what binds everyone together."

"Very wise words," he replied quietly.

"Well, I'm somethin' of a prophetess," she teased. "Don't forget that the Santero was terrified of me."

"No; I'll not soon forget."

They lay in contented silence for a space of time, and then she said, "Am I gabblin' too much? D'you want me to let you sleep?"

"No," he said, his eyes closed. "I like to listen to you."

This was the truth, and so she continued, "I suppose Mallory's Flynn's death is not even goin' to be a cold case—it's goin' to be a nothin'-case."

"Yes. I am inclined to let the matter rest."

With a sigh, she admitted, "I can't blame you, and we're almost lucky that no one can figure out a cause-of-death. There can't be an investigation, if there isn't even a case."

"I would agree that it is very providential."

She lifted her head to eye him. "Does 'providential' mean 'lucky'?"

"More or less."

"Then why don't you just say 'lucky', Mr. Fancy-speak?"

"Because I am told it is superstitious to believe in luck."

She laughed. "Touché, in plentitudes. What's goin' to happen to the sex-tape people?"

His chest rose and fell. "Private reprimands, mostly. I imagine a few people will be asked to resign—it depends upon what is revealed."

"Well, just don't work your wiles on Yandra, my friend. I know it's a potent weapon in your arsenal, but please keep your poor wife to mind."

"Always," he replied.

Doyle added, "I wouldn't be surprised if she wasn't told much about the rig in the first place. She's a weak link—a bit like me. We have the same taste in men, too."

"Yes," he agreed, after a pause—his hand had stilled, and he was not really paying attention.

She smiled, and crawled her way up to kiss him gently. "I'm goin' to call for room service—I didn't get to eat much, this fine night. Go to sleep."

But he wasn't quite asleep, as he murmured, "Only put a robe on, before you open the door."

"No point; there's no repairin' our reputations, here."

But she was to receive no reply, as his head turned into the pillow, and he began breathing deeply.

"Good night, Michael," she whispered, as she pulled the coverlet over him. "I'll watch over you, for a change."

EPILOGUE

*H*e stood on the bridge and watched the water flow beneath him, coursing and silvery in the early-morning light.

His heart was heavy; it grieved him, that it had come to this. But The Husband was asking many questions, and if he became aware of The Remnant, he would destroy them all. Such a chance could not be taken; far better to allow him to believe that the secrets of The Red-Haired Policewoman lay safe within his keeping.

Lifting his bag of bottles, he shuffled off to find someone with a phone, so as to report the girl's death.

Printed in Great Britain
by Amazon

22853341R00148